I0603560

TWISTED LITTLE TRUTHS

SAINT VIEW HIGH #3

ELLE THORPE

WWW.ELLETHORPE.COM

Copyright © 2020 by Elle Thorpe

All rights reserved.

No part of this book may be reproduced in any form or by any electronic or mechanical means, including information storage and retrieval systems, without written permission from the author, except for the use of brief quotations in a book review.

V:3

For Jolie Vines.
I couldn't do this without you. Thank you for all the years of critiques, the getting me unstuck, the marketing advice, and most of all, your friendship.

1

LACEY

"Lacey, no," Selina screamed. "You can't shoot. She's your mother!"

The gun slipped from my fingers and clattered to the floor. It barely slid an inch along the tiles before the man picked it up and aimed it at me.

A great ball of hysterical laughter bubbled up my throat and let itself loose into the room. The three of them—Selina, my aunt who'd raised me and loved me like her own. The man, who was still unidentified. And the woman who was apparently my mother—all stared at me with wide eyes.

Tears welled and blurred my vision, but that didn't lessen the turmoil swirling inside me, building itself up in my head until I was sure I'd crack.

I walked right over and pressed my forehead to the gun.

Selina and my mother both gasped. The barrel dug into my forehead, but I relished the bruising pain. I pushed harder, aching for it. Anything to distract from the realer pain that this woman, standing across the island counter with a gun trained on my aunt, was the mother I'd lost when I was just a child.

Hardly the fairy-tale reunion I'd once dreamed of.

"Go on," I hissed to the man. "Do it."

"No," Selina screamed. "April, stop this!"

April.

The name sent a shock wave through me. That was her name. I'd all but forgotten.

Around the gun barrel, I eyed the man. His gaze was hard, full of irritation. "Pissed you off, didn't I?" I laughed. "Such a big, burly guy. And yet I had you. It took a bomb drop like my long-lost mother returning, for you to get the upper hand. What kind of thug for hire are you, anyway?"

"You've got a smart mouth, girly," he gritted out. "Watch it."

I raised an eyebrow. "Yeah? Or what? You gonna shoot me?"

Selina's squeak of terror reminded me I was poking a bear.

His patience snapped. He took a step forward, forcing me back.

The crack of a gunshot echoed through the deathly silent room.

Drywall exploded to my right. I flinched away, ducking and covering my head on instinct, little pieces of plaster flying across the kitchen as the bullet entered the wall. Selina's screams filled my ears, almost as loud as the bullet leaving the gun.

"What the hell?" the man yelled, recovering quicker than I did. "You crazy bitch! That nearly hit me."

April's voice was low and calm. "Next time, I won't miss. Get that gun off my daughter."

I glanced between the two of them and laughed again. *Fuck.* I was seriously cracking up. This was all too much. "It's fake," I choked out. I pointed to the gun now hanging limply in the man's hand. "Movie prop. So good luck shooting anyone with it."

He trained it on me again. "Let's test the theory, shall we?"

I rolled my eyes and focused on April. "Where did you find this one? He's not big on the smarts, is he?"

I could have sworn the corner of her lip turned up. Whatever. I wasn't doing this for her entertainment.

I was pushing my luck. I knew it. The gun might have been fake, but this was still a full-grown man. He could hurt me in other ways. Hell, we were in a kitchen, and Angelique's favorite set of knives was displayed on the countertop behind Selina. It would take only moments for this guy to waltz around the island counter and pluck one from the holder. Or for him to storm across the room and hurl me into a wall. He probably had a hundred pounds on me.

But I couldn't seem to stop. I had no control, and I was desperate to take some of it back.

"Lower the gun, George," April said.

I snorted. "George? Shouldn't you be working at a bank or something with that sort of name?"

George glanced over at April, and then tossed the gun onto the floor with a grunt of annoyance. "What now then? We just gonna stand here all day?"

"Georgie Porgie has a point," I said to April. I was struggling to think of her as my mother. I didn't recognize her. If Selina hadn't identified her, I would have never guessed. I really couldn't remember much of anything from the years before I lived with Selina and Uncle Lawson. All I had were feelings, rather than true pictures of what my life had been.

Feelings of love. Hugs. Kindness.

This woman holding a gun didn't fit.

"What do you want?" I asked.

April bit her lip. "Not this," she admitted.

"Well, you're the one who seems to be in control right now, so fix it. Make your demands. Take whatever you want and go back to wherever you've been for the last thirteen years."

She flinched, her eyes hardening again when she looked at Selina. "What have you been filling her head with?"

"Hey," I yelled. "She's loved and cared for me when you abandoned me. Don't go accusing her of filling my head with anything. You're the one who left."

April shook her head. "You don't know what you're talking about."

"Don't I?"

April's mouth pulled down. "Give me your keys."

"You're stealing my car now? Could have done that ages ago, without the gun show." Bitter anger rolled through me. Was that why she was really here? To steal from us? I hated that something buried deep inside me was affected by that. I dug through my purse, finding the keys easily, and threw them hard across the room.

She caught them with her free hand, wincing a little as the jagged metal hit her palm.

Good. I hoped it hurt.

I hoped it hurt even a quarter as much as I was.

"I'm not stealing it. We're all getting in it."

She jerked the gun, as if remembering she still had it trained on Selina. "Walk."

I stubbornly dug my heels in.

"Lacey, please. Don't make me be the bad guy here. I didn't plan for you to see any of this. This isn't how it was supposed to go."

"Oh, so you didn't pre-think breaking and entering, holding two women hostage, then kidnapping them? Geez,

Mom." The sarcasm dripped from my voice. "What the hell did you plan, then?"

"Just walk, smart-ass." George moved forward, arm outstretched as if to grab me, but then he seemed to think better of it. His eyes darted to the bullet hole in the wall beside us.

"Guess we know who wears the pants around here, huh, G-Man?" But I didn't want him touching me, and I was smart enough to know that he would if I didn't do as I was told. Plus, I wasn't leaving Selina with these nutcases. I scuttled to her side and grabbed her hand. A sob broke free from her mouth and I squeezed her fingers, trying to reassure her. Something instinctual told me April wasn't going to shoot me. But I honestly wasn't so sure about Selina. The hate April radiated in my aunt's direction was palpable.

Outside, I scanned the darkened driveway, praying Rafe's car would be there. But the only vehicles to be seen were mine and April's rust-red Explorer. The boys and Jagger were going to Colt's place to talk to his mom and sister, but then we were all going to meet back here. I was supposed to be calling our lawyer. Colt was being held by the police right now, and he needed someone on his side.

"Get in the back," April directed.

The sarcastic comments hovered on the tip of my tongue, but they were only delaying the inevitable. So I got in, sliding to the far side. Selina followed, forced into the middle seat, with April next to her. She tossed George the keys, who got in behind the wheel, grumbling as his long legs hit the steering column. He fumbled at the side of the seat, pulling at the adjustment levers. The back of the seat jerked forward.

I didn't bother trying to hide my laugh. "Wrong one." I

wished the interior of the car were light enough that I could have seen his expression.

He eventually got the seat shoved back so far my knees just about touched it, and got the car started. "Where are we taking them?"

"Well, that confirms that kidnapping wasn't in your master plan," I quipped.

April sighed, ignoring me. "To the house."

George seemed to know which house April was referring to without asking further questions. We drove out of the driveway, and April lowered the gun to her lap, though it still pointed in Selina's direction.

Beside me, Selina trembled. It occurred to me that I should be scared, too, and later, I probably would be. If we both got out of this alive, I'd probably break down into a boneless heap and cry for a week. But there was no room for that right now. I was just numb. And that was better. Easier.

I stared out the windows as we left Providence, the turns George made familiar. I'd driven them every day for months.

We were going back to Saint View.

2

LACEY

George parked the car outside a house in the crummiest part of Saint View. I'd been here just days before. Stood right there on the sidewalk with Colt, looking up at my childhood home and wondering what it had been like when I'd lived there.

"What is this place?" Selina asked, wrinkling her nose. She peered up at the house, but there was no hint of recognition on her face.

"It was mine," April said quietly. Then glanced over at me. "Ours."

I pressed my lips together, not interested in this little trip down memory lane. Especially since I had almost no recollection of ever living in that house. "We just going to sit here?"

"No. Get out." April pulled the door handle.

George grabbed his, too, but April stopped him before he could get out. "You stay here with Selina."

I gripped my aunt's fingers tighter. "I'm not going anywhere without her."

April scraped her fingers through her hair. It was dark

like mine. Slightly wavy and tied back into a messy bun. The finger raking didn't help any.

"Nothing will happen to her, I promise. I just want to talk to you. Alone."

"In an abandoned house?"

April didn't say anything, just waited.

"Go," Selina whispered to me. "I'll be fine." There was a touch of resignation in her words.

I hated it. "No."

"Just hear what she has to say. Then maybe she'll let us go."

Frustrated, I threw my hands up. "Or maybe she'll shoot us both in the head!"

"I don't want to shoot anyone," April said softly.

I glared at her.

She stared back. Her expression was hard, but she wasn't angry like I was. She rolled her eyes. "Your father was stubborn. Guess you got that from him."

"I didn't get anything from either of you. Except my DNA. You've been out of my life almost twice as long as you were in it. Anything I am is because of Selina and Lawson."

She nodded, resigned. "You're probably right."

She opened the cylinder and emptied the bullets into her palm, tucking them into her pocket. Then she dropped the gun to the floor. "Ten minutes of your time, Lacey. That's all I'm asking for."

Selina nudged me, and I huffed my way out of the car and into the cold night air. The interior of the car had been warm, pressed shoulder to shoulder with Selina, the body heat of four people filling the small space and making it cozy.

The cold, dark streets of Saint View sent me crashing back down to earth. Most of the houses in this street were abandoned, just like the one we stood in front of now. Dull light glowed in the windows of a handful of other houses farther down the street, but no one looked our way. An abandoned car sat idle, opposite the house Colt had grown up in, the one right next door to mine.

Colt.

Fuck. I needed to get to him. Get him help. The quicker I got through April's bullshit, the better. I stormed around the car and headed for the front door of the house. "You coming?" I snapped in her direction.

She hustled to keep up with me.

At the door, I waited, assuming it would be locked. But April grasped the knob, and it turned easily in her hand. She looked as surprised as I was. "Guess someone broke the lock."

Yanking up on the handle while pushing forward with her shoulder, she got the door to swing open with a protesting creak from the old wood. "You could never open it yourself," April said. "It always stuck like that. And you were too short to get the lift you needed to get it open." She stared at me for a long moment then shook her head slowly. "You aren't that little girl anymore."

"Haven't been for a long time." I moved past her and strode inside the darkened room. I wrinkled my nose at the unpleasant mustiness that permeated the air. Then I fished out my phone. The notifications on the screen informed me I had a missed call from Rafe. I bit my lip, tempted to press the call button.

But something stopped me.

The tiniest part of me wanted to know what we were doing here and what April would say. She'd mentioned my dad a minute ago, and a horrible thought struck me. "Is George even that guy's real name?" My father's name had been Tony. But that was pretty much all I knew of him. "Please tell me he's not my father?"

April shook her head. "You really don't remember at all, do you?"

"I was barely five years old. And my psychologist says I suffered a significant trauma when you left. So you tell me whose fault it is I can't remember?"

She lowered her gaze. "That's fair. No, George isn't your father. Your father died in a hit-and-run accident."

Pain burst over my chest, but I clamped down on it. It was stupid. I didn't even remember the man. Why should his passing even affect me one iota?

But it did.

I didn't want it to. So I schooled my features into something hard and angry. "When?"

"You'd just turned five."

Surprise jolted through my system. "What? I was still living with you then."

"You've obviously blocked that out, too."

Maybe so, but something didn't add up. "Lawson said the two of you disappeared. He never mentioned my father had died. Why would he say that?"

April finally lifted her gaze to me, her expression expectant, like I should know the answer to my own question. That grated. Did she think I was stupid? I was rapidly losing the smidgen of patience I had left. What did it even matter after all this time? I wasn't going to suddenly start begging. I thumbed out of Rafe's missed call to turn on the flashlight function, but the house was no more attractive in the beam of light I cast around the space. Yellowed wallpaper peeled from the walls. The hardwood floors were so badly scuffed they'd give you splinters if you walked on them barefoot. A layer of dirt and leaves and strewn about trash littered the floor.

I strode to the stairs, testing my weight on the bottom one first before climbing them, uncaring whether April followed or not. Just a week ago, I'd wondered which bedroom had been mine, and now, some sixth sense urged me to go upstairs and find out.

On the landing, I turned right down the hall and stopped in front of the first bedroom. The door was closed. It had maybe once been white, but now it was covered in a multitude of colored spray paint and unintelligible words and symbols.

"That one was yours."

I'd known without her even saying it. I twisted the handle and opened the door.

The air was clearer up here, the musty, moldy odor disappearing the minute I stepped through the doorway. A quick flash of the light from my phone told me why. I moved across the small room to the smashed window letting in fresh air and gazed down at my car parked on the street outside. From this angle, all I could see was the roof. But there were no signs of a commotion from within, so I presumed Selina was safe.

A large, jagged piece of glass from the broken window caught my attention, and I coughed to cover the sound as I picked it up. When I turned to face April, who was hovering in the doorway, I tucked it behind my back.

She might not have been holding her gun anymore, but that didn't mean she was unarmed. For all I knew, she had another gun inside her jacket. Or a switchblade in her pocket. I wouldn't be vulnerable. I'd been that girl once before. I wouldn't be her again.

But April didn't look like she was about to reach for a

weapon. Her face went soft in the glow from my light, and she gazed around the room with eyes that shone in the darkness. The walls were a faded pink, but there was no furniture. No toys. No books. Nothing but a feeling and April's word to tell me this room had once belonged to me.

"Your bed was over there." April pointed to the left side of the room. "A freestanding wooden wardrobe for your clothes opposite. It was an antique, with a brass lock and skeleton key. Your dad found it at a yard sale, the month before you were born. We didn't have a car, but he borrowed a cart from a neighbor and hauled it three blocks, back here by himself. He spent a week sanding it back by hand and painting it—"

"Yellow," I said suddenly. I turned to stare at the spot the wardrobe had sat in. "It was sunshine yellow with stickers...."

"Stickers of rainbows. You were our rainbow baby. You know what that means?"

I shook my head, still staring at the spot the drawers had been and wondering where the memory had come from. I could suddenly see them, as clear as if they were really right in front of me, my messy, little girl clothes spilling out.

"We lost a baby before you. Late-term miscarriage. We were devastated. But you were our rainbow at the end of a dark period."

I shook my head. "Guess you're the sort of people who can walk right by a rainbow without even stopping to notice it's beauty then, huh?"

A tear spilled down her cheek.

It should have had an effect on me. Should have broken through the walls I'd erected around myself, not just tonight, but over the past thirteen years. But those walls were impenetrable. Held together by her rejection, and that constant feeling of missing someone, even though I couldn't remember her face. Her tears now meant nothing to me.

"You sound just like him," she whispered. "Hard. Harsh. Critical."

"Who? My father? I told you, I'm nothing like either of you."

She shook her head. "No, not your father. He was a stubborn old goat, for sure. But he was a good man. Kind. Loving. He would have moved mountains for you. No. You sound just like Lawson." Her face hardened at the mention of her brother's name.

Irritation prickled at me. "Lawson wasn't hard or harsh."

Her laughter was laced with scorn. "Oh, sweetheart. You have no idea."

Irritation turned to anger again. "Don't call me that. And how dare you? Lawson and Selina are good people. They took me in when you cast me aside like a piece of trash. I'd be nothing without them. I'd just be some other abandoned kid, lost to the foster system, along with the millions of other kids who were unlucky enough to be born to shitty parents."

My rant brought Banjo to mind, but I couldn't dwell on him now.

April's mouth dropped open. "That's not how it was. That isn't how it was at all! They've filled your head with lies."

I scoffed, "Even if they had, *April*." I slung her name at her like an insult. I wasn't going to call her Mom. Selina was my mom. "They were the only ones here to do it. Where were you? Off doing your own thing, too selfish to even take me with you."

"He made me!" She bit her lip like she'd said too much.

"What? From beyond the grave? So my father was a

controlling prick, as well as good and kind and all that other bullshit you just spouted?" I gripped the piece of glass so hard it pierced my skin. Like with the gun to my head, I welcomed the sting. It gave me something to concentrate on. Blood dripped through my fingers.

April's gaze flickered to the glass and the blood spilling to the floor, then slowly stepped aside. "I wanted this to help. I thought if you were here, you would understand... You should go."

I blinked. Wow. I was being dismissed again. Just like when she'd left the first time. But this time, it was fine by me. This woman wasn't my family. My family was Selina out in that car, and my boys who needed me. I wasn't going to hang around, playing April's games. I shoved past her and ran down the stairs, dropping the glass amongst the overgrown weeds that had probably once been a lawn. I went straight to the driver's side door and yanked it open. "Get out."

George looked up from his phone. "Huh?"

"Do as she says, George," April called from the porch.

I glared at him.

He peered at April, shrugged, and got out of the car. I practically dove behind the wheel and slammed the door shut, hitting the central locking button and sending all the locks down simultaneously.

Selina let out a yelp from the back seat as I gunned the engine.

"What happened in there?" she asked.

I shook my head and put my foot down on the gas. The last thing I saw was April's face in the rearview mirror, her cheeks stained with tears.

When I put my hand to my face, I found mine were, too.

3

APRIL

George stared helplessly at me, weeds as tall as his knees growing from the ground I had once kept neatly trimmed. I'd been so proud to have a house of our own, even it was government owned and subsidized. I still remembered the day Tony and I had moved in. The memory warmed its way through my body. We'd gotten hitched at the courthouse, him in blue jeans, me in a cheap pale-pink sundress I'd bought at a thrift shop. We'd had to pull someone in off the street to be our witness, since neither of us had any family—at least none we spoke to—to attend. But it hadn't mattered. I'd loved that man to the very depths of my soul and had giggled hysterically when later, after we'd said our I do's, he'd carried me across the threshold of the crappiest house in the crappiest area of Saint View.

This house had been ours. And that was all that mattered. That, and the tiny baby growing inside me.

George clicked a finger in front of my face, snapping me back to the present. "April. Wake up. What the hell are we supposed to do now?"

I blinked around at the dark street. Lacey had driven off, tires screeching in her haste to get away from me. My heart squeezed. I'd gone about this whole thing wrong. I didn't even know why I'd brought the gun. I'd just been so desperate to see my daughter. I didn't know Selina. I had no idea what sort of resistance she'd put up. But I truly hadn't meant for things to escalate the way they had. "Call your brother. Tell him to drive here then take you to pick up our car."

"What if they have the police waiting for us?"

I grimaced. "Just be alert. If there's cops, forget it."

George grumbled, but as always, he did what I asked. He seemed to have already forgiven me for the shot I'd fired in his direction earlier. He was a good man. Simple, perhaps. But he'd been decent to me. Treated me with kindness and respect. It didn't matter that we didn't share the same soul-consuming love I'd had with Tony. No person could be lucky enough to have that twice in one lifetime.

George's brother pulled up a few minutes later, and George moved for the passenger side door. "You coming?"

"No. Get the car and meet me back here."

He didn't seem happy about that, but I went to his side and pressed a chaste kiss on his cheek. "Please."

He sighed and wrapped his arm around my shoulders. "One day you're going to tell me exactly what's going on with all of this."

We both knew I wouldn't. He'd asked a million times about my past. More often after I'd heard Lawson's name on the news and declared that I needed to go back to Saint View. But I'd never told George the full story. I'd never voiced a word of it to anyone.

Lacey was the only one who needed the full truth. It was

her story. Hers and mine and Lawson's. With Lawson dead, I could finally come back. Finally tell her everything.

That's what I'd wanted to do tonight. I hadn't counted on her anger and aggression. I hadn't counted on her walking in while I held a gun on the woman who had raised her. It had all gone to shit, and when I'd watched her push that glass into her skin, I knew I had to let her go. I couldn't stand to watch her hurt herself.

I'd already hurt her enough.

George released me and got in the car without saying goodbye. I watched the taillights disappear around the corner, and then I swiveled on my heel, and wandered back up the garden path, and inside the house I'd never really left. At least not in my heart.

Thirteen years earlier...

Two blurs of dark hair and skinny legs ran around the coffee table, chasing each other and squealing at the top of their lungs. For the tiniest moment they eased my constant worries, and I took the time to smile at my daughter and the boy from next door who had become her shadow. "Lacey. Colt. Go play outside. You're being too noisy."

Colt charged for the back door, and Lacey ran after him with a quick wave over her shoulder at me.

"They were okay," Tony said weakly from the couch. "They were just having fun."

The frown that permanently marked my forehead returned, and I tucked a blanket around him more tightly, despite the warm weather. He was always cold lately. He'd lost so much weight; it was hardly surprising. He was little more than skin and bones. As if to prove my point, his body shivered violently.

"You're getting worse," I accused. It was something I hadn't said out loud when he'd become too weak to even make it up the stairs to our bed. But I'd watched him get sicker and sicker. Lacey seemed mostly oblivious, too young to notice the black circles beneath her father's eyes, or the sunken hollows of his cheeks that had once been full and pink with good health.

"I'm fine."

That was what he'd been saying for the past month. But day by day, he'd grown worse. Until he'd had so much time off work, they told him not to come back. With only my waitress salary to buy food and pay the rent, we had not a single spare penny to our names.

"We need to go back to the clinic. This isn't just going to go away like they said it would. You need tests. Medication. There's something seriously wrong here."

Tony let out a hacking cough, and I grimaced at the pain it caused him. This was why I'd done it. This morning, from my bed, I'd listened to him cough until he'd vomited, and realized the love of my life was slipping away. And I was letting it happen.

Tony shook his head. "You heard the doctor last time. It's a virus. I'll be all right soon."

"It's not a virus!"

"They'll just tell us to go to the hospital if we go back."

"Then that's what we'll do."

He gave me a tired, defeated look. "We can't afford it, baby. You know that. You think I haven't noticed that you're only eating one meal a day?"

My empty stomach didn't matter. I voiced my deepest fear, the one that had been curdling my stomach for weeks as I watched Tony waste away from some unknown disease. "I can't afford for you to die either."

He didn't react. I suspected the statement wasn't all that shocking to him. But what I said next would be. "I called my brother. He should be here any minute."

"No." Weak as he was, Tony's eyes blazed with pride. "I won't take charity."

"You don't have to. I will. I'm going to ask him for a loan. To pay your hospital bills. And for any medication you need. We'll be able to pay for your treatment up-front."

"And yet, we'll owe him."

I bit my lip. "I know. But what other option do we have?"

Tony fell silent, his head flopping back against the pillow again.

I sank down onto the couch by his feet, fingering the satin edge of the blanket. "I hate this as much as you do."

Tony stretched out a hand, and I took it, threading my fingers through his.

"I know you do, baby. I just hate that he thinks he's so much better than us. He grew up here, too. Right here on the streets of Saint View. And now he looks down at us like we're trash. He's never even met Lacey. She's nearly five years old, for fuck's sake, and he's never even come around to visit."

Nothing he was saying was a lie. I knew it all. My brother had always dreamed of getting out of Saint View, and I couldn't fault him for that. He'd worked hard. And found a woman with money and connections, who he honestly seemed to love, judging by the one time we'd seen them on the beach. But in the process of bettering himself, he'd shut the door on where he came from. I was a blip in his otherwise polished armor. A flea he wanted to flick off as fast as he could, so he could pretend it had never bitten him.

For years now, I'd let him do that. I'd let him live his new life. Let him be free of the so-called chains that tried to drag him down. Those chains being me, and my little family.

I was an embarrassment to my brother. I knew that.

I'd let him erase me.

But I couldn't be invisible any longer.

When the purr of a well-tuned engine filtered through the open windows, I squeezed Tony's fingers and went to open the door.

Lawson, older than me by two years, got out of a sleek black machine, the sun glinting off the polished paintwork. It was all smooth lines and reeked of money I couldn't even dream of. He picked his way along our garden path, as if he were worried about getting Saint View dirt on his perfectly polished loafers.

A prickle of irritation rolled up the back of my neck. I'd spent hours yesterday, after working the graveyard shift at the diner, pulling up weeds and making sure the grass was neat and tidy. My yard might not be pretty since I couldn't afford to buy flowers to plant. But I did the best I could with what I had. I was proud of it.

Lawson stopped in front of me, running his gaze over my clothes, face, and hair critically. "It's been a long time."

I nodded, reminding myself I needed my brother's help. So I buried any irritation and tried to give him a smile. We'd been friends as kids. Before either of us had really realized the sort of poverty we lived in. Before Lawson's dreams outgrew my own.

But there was no sign of that little boy inside the man who stood before me now.

"Thank you for coming," I said politely. "Will you come inside?"

He didn't even try to hide the way his nose wrinkled, but he followed me up the steps without voicing his opinion on where I lived. With my heart thumping behind my ribcage, I showed him through to the living room.

Tony struggled to sit up, but a bout of coughing overcame him.

I rushed to his side. "No, don't sit up. Just rest."

He couldn't answer me to protest. The coughs kept coming; sharp and painful sounding, and my heart ached to see Tony's pain. To Lawson's credit, he strode into our small kitchen, and there was a moment of cupboard doors opening and closing, before he located a drinking glass and filled it from the faucet. When he returned, he placed it quietly on the coffee table, then stepped away to lean against one wall, arms folded across his chest while he watched on silently.

I grabbed the glass and held it to Tony's parched lips. He spluttered on the first few sips, but soon the coughing died down, and his eyes fluttered closed as he fell asleep, exhausted from the effort of being so ill.

I straightened and turned to Lawson with pleading eyes.

"He's bad," Lawson said before I could even say anything.

I nodded. "There's nothing more the free clinic can do for him. I need to take him to hospital. Get proper tests done and get him some medication for whatever this is."

"What's that got to do with me?"

I blew out a breath and let my pride go with it. "I need a loan. The money to pay his admission and for medications. They won't give him the care he needs without money or insurance."

"You don't have insurance?"

I blinked like he'd just spoken another language. Was he really that naïve? Did he really think I would have called him if I'd had a viable alternative? "Tony lost his job," I said by way of explanation. Not that his job at a worksite had offered health insurance anyway.

Lawson tutted but didn't speak, and I realized he was going to make me beg.

Fine. So be it. I'd grovel if I had to.

"I need money, Lawson. Please. I'll work triple shifts to pay you back."

Lacey's squeal of laughter from outside caught his attention, and instead of answering me, he wandered to the back door, looking out through the small window beside it. He spun back to me, dark eyebrows raised in surprise. "You have children?"

I nodded. "The boy isn't mine. But the girl is your niece."

His eyes widened, and he turned back to watch her through the window. "What's her name?"

"Lacey."

"How old is she?"

"Nearly five."

He stared out at the kids playing for a long moment, while I studied him curiously. His gaze tracked Lacey as she ran around the yard.

"You can meet her, if you like?"

He nodded.

I cracked open the window to yell through it. "Lacey? Come here a second, please."

She ran to the door, pigtails bobbing, and twisted the knob, letting herself back in. She stopped dead in her tracks when she noticed Lawson and gave him a wary glance before looking to me for reassurance.

I plastered a bright smile on my face and nodded enthusiastically at her, letting her know it was okay. "Lacey, this is your uncle, Lawson."

He knelt so he was eye height with her and held out a hand for her to shake.

She tilted her head to one side, studying him, but then took his hand, her little fingers engulfed by his, and jerked her hand up and down, shaking with a strength that belied her small amount of years. "Nice to meet you, sir."

Pride poured through me. She was a gutsy one, my girl. And I was more proud of her than anything in this world.

Lawson chuckled at her formal choice of words, which

sounded adorable in her childish voice. "Nice to meet you, too, Miss Lacey. I don't want to hold you up from your game. I can see your friend is waiting for you."

I glanced out through the glass door at Colt scowling in Lawson's direction. I had to stifle a smile. That boy was fiercely protective of my daughter, even at the young age of five. He was adorable.

Lawson patted Lacey's hand. "Would it be okay if I came back another day to see you? One day when you aren't so busy playing? Maybe I could bring you a present? What do you like, dolls?"

His words surprised me, but Lacey's brown eyes lit up with excitement at the prospect of a present. We did our best on her birthdays and Christmas, but she didn't ever receive gifts for no reason. "Colt says dolls are stupid. But I like dolls with brown hair, the same as mine."

Lawson smiled softly at that. "Then that's what I'll bring."

He straightened to his full height, and Lacey ran back outside to Colt, telling him loudly that she had an uncle and he was going to bring her a present.

I swallowed thickly. "I wish you hadn't done that. You can't make promises you won't keep to a four-year-old. It's not fair."

He frowned at that. "Who says I won't keep it?"

I somehow doubted that, but I didn't question him any further. He still hadn't said anything about the money I'd asked him for. We wandered back to the living room, where Tony was sleeping. It wasn't a peaceful sleep. His chest heaved with the effort to breathe. Tears pricked at my eyes.

"I can't give you a large sum of money like that. Selina would notice it missing from our account."

All the hope I'd had rushed out of me. "Oh. I under-stand." I didn't really. I knew I was asking for a lot. Tony's hospital bills would probably not be cheap. But the car

Lawson had driven up in probably cost a hundred thousand dollars.

He pulled his wallet from his pocket and plucked a card from the holder. He placed it on the coffee table.

I peered at it over his shoulder. It was an insurance card.

"I won't report that stolen," he said quietly, with a glance out the back door again. "Do you remember my date of birth? You'll need it."

Air whooshed out of me, and I blinked at him in shock. Was he seriously suggesting what I thought he was suggesting? "Lawson, that's insurance fraud. I can't."

Lawson looked over at Tony's wasting body. I followed his line of sight, seeing exactly what Lawson saw. Tony wouldn't make it without medical intervention.

Lawson sighed sadly. "Take the card, April. What choice do you have? That little girl needs a father."

4

———

LACEY

I drove to the border where Saint View met Providence before I steered the car to the side of the road. Fingers trembling, I sat there, staring out the windshield at nothing in particular while my heart hammered.

Selina fit her petite figure between the two backrests, climbing over the center console to sit in the passenger seat. She took one look at my blotchy, wet face and broke into tears of her own. We launched ourselves at each other and held tight, while we both cried out the terror and fear and shock.

It was Selina who pulled away first. "Are you okay?" Her gaze ran over me frantically, checking for injuries.

I shrugged. I had no idea what I was. "Are you?"

She didn't answer. "What did she say?"

My head was a swirling mass of confusion, made worse but the constant thud of adrenaline. "I don't even know. My father is dead."

Selina gasped, then squeezed my good hand tight. "Sweetheart, I'm so sorry."

The sincerity in her voice and her gaze made me pause. "You didn't know?"

Selina's eyebrows furrowed together. "No? How could I have?"

"She said he died before I came to live with you and Lawson."

"That's horrible."

It was. "She said Lawson knew."

"Sweetheart, I don't think that's true. Your uncle and your mother had a falling out before you were even born. He had nothing to do with them. I only met her once when we ran into her and your father at the beach. They didn't even come to our wedding, though I insisted on inviting them."

I sniffed. Sounded about right. "So she was a cold-hearted bitch even then."

With concerned eyes, Selina gave a gentle sigh. That was so typical of her. She was too good and kind even now, to hear me talk badly of someone else. A part of me hated that I wasn't like her. But I couldn't bring myself to find that sort of forgiveness within myself. I might have blocked out my life with April, but I remembered the aftermath. I remembered the random bouts of tears and loneliness I couldn't explain. And how I'd wondered about her over the years, convincing myself that something had to have happened to her to force us apart. Those emotions had run so deep, until time had faded them. But here she was, back in Saint View, completely intact and unharmed, bringing them all back to the surface. She hadn't wanted me and had dumped me when I was no longer interesting to her.

Selina didn't comment on my lack of empathy. She just handed me my phone, which I'd dropped on the front seat.

"The boys have been calling you. You should call them back."

I blinked at her. "They have?" I hadn't even heard my phone ringing. I'd just been hell-bent on getting out of Saint View and away from my batshit-crazy mother. And whoever the fuck George was. Creeper.

I fumbled with my phone, trying to make sense of the notifications on the screen. Selina was right. There'd been multiple missed calls while I'd been driving. A combination of Banjo, Jagger, and Rafe.

I closed my eyes, trying to sort out what was most important. "Colt's been arrested."

"What? Who's Colt?"

I bit my lip. I wasn't sure this was the time to tell Selina what Colt meant to me. But hell, I had to make her understand why getting him a lawyer was so important. "He's the one who saved me from the beach that night I was attacked. We're..." I shrugged. "You know."

"Together?" Selina asked, eyes going wide. "What about Banjo and Rafe? The three of you are so sweet...."

"It's not like that. I love Banjo and Rafe." I blinked at that, realizing I'd just told Selina I loved Rafe before I'd even told him. But it was true, and I'd need to rectify that ASAP. How had my life become so insane that telling a boy I loved him was something that would have to wait until there were less pressing matters to deal with? "Colt and I are different. The boys understand. They all understand. I never meant for this to happen but..."

"But here it is." Selina shook her head. "I'm not going to pretend I understand any of this. But all I need to know is, do these boys make you happy?"

I nodded hard. "They do. They complete me, Sel. It's like

the four of us are a jigsaw puzzle. We just fit together, none of us quite whole without the others."

She nodded slowly. "I can get on board with that. You know I already care for Rafe and Banjo. And if this Colt is now part of that, then you'd better tell me more about his arrest."

"First, we need to go to the police and report April and George."

Selina slumped back in her chair. "I've been thinking about that, while you were in the house, and while you drove. I don't think we should go to the police."

"What?" The woman was insane. "Did you forget that lunatic held a gun on you? Not to mention the fact she kidnapped us."

Selina rubbed a hand across her sternum. She was haggard, and not just because of the late hour. Her hair was a mess, her skin mottled from crying. Exhaustion tainted her movements with a slow and sluggish brush. "I didn't forget. But, sweetheart, she's your mother."

"You're my mother."

She smiled softly at that. "I know. And I love you. But aren't you the least bit curious why she's back?"

"No," I bit out stubbornly.

"You think I don't know when you're lying?"

I huffed a breath.

I knew Selina saw through my fake bravado. But she didn't comment on it. "That's why I can't go to the police. What happened tonight is a serious crime. What if they catch her and charge her? She could go to jail, and then how would you get the answers to your questions?"

"I'm not going to get those answers anyway. Because I'm not going to see her again. She and George have probably already slunk back into whatever dark hole they slithered out of. And good. I hope I never see either of them again."

"If that's truly what you want, then I'll support it. But I won't be the one who takes away the opportunity to get to know her. Maybe not as mother and daughter, but you could be something else. If you wanted to be."

I looked away. The feelings that brought up were too hard to deal with tonight. I gave up convincing her and changed the subject. "We need to get Colt a lawyer."

Selina took my phone from my hand and punched the call app. "I never thought there'd be a day where calling a lawyer at one in the morning was the least concerning part of my evening."

I turned the car back on and put it in gear, slightly more in control of myself than I had been. I managed to drive back to our place, while Selina apologized profusely to Liam Banks, our family lawyer, and sent him down to the police station to help Colt.

I pulled into the driveway right as she said goodbye. Rafe's car sat in the exact same spot April and George's Explorer had been parked earlier. We both just stared at it, but then Rafe and Banjo were rushing through the front door to my side. When I got out, it was with slow, stiff movements, like I'd aged in just the few hours we'd been apart. Maybe it was the time of night, or the culmination of everything, but I suddenly felt a hundred years old.

Rafe swept me into a hug, Banjo crowding in behind, sandwiching me between them. They were warm, strong, and immediately eliminated some of the tension. Rafe moved back, sweeping his hands down the sides of my face to cup my cheeks. "Where were you? We've been calling and calling. Are you okay?"

I tucked my fingers over my injured palm so he wouldn't

see. For the first time since it had happened, it gave a throb of pain. "I'm okay. We can talk about it later. What happened at Colt's place?"

Selina motioned silently that she was going inside, and I gave her a curt nod before forming a little circle with the boys.

Banjo shoved his hands in his pockets. "Willa and Aria were hysterical. The police hadn't even gone there to inform them that Colt had been arrested."

"He's eighteen, they don't have to."

"Which meant we were the ones to break it to them." Banjo grimaced.

It obviously hadn't gone well. "Shit. Where are they now?"

"Coach was going to drive them down to the police station to find out what was going on. But we wanted to come here and check on you. Did you manage to get the lawyer?"

"Selina called him just a few minutes ago. He's on his way."

The urgency went out of both boys in a rush. Rafe slumped against the side of my car. Banjo pulled me into his arms and kissed my forehead. "Thank you."

I leaned against him, drawing comfort from his bigger frame and the solid beat of his heart beneath my ear. "I don't know how much good it will do, though. What if they charge him with murder?"

It was the one thing none of us had dared to voice. But none of us had an answer for it either.

5

COLT

The police station bustled. There was a rapid movement of people in and out the main doors, some in handcuffs, escorted by officers. Others were frantic family members. Plus, a single homeless-looking guy, who seemed intent on getting arrested just so he had somewhere warm to sleep. I watched it all through a tiny window in an interview room. A woman had taken my phone and keys, bagged them in plastic and stuck on a hastily filled out label before tucking them away in storage. My fingerprints had been scanned, and now I was waiting for whatever came next. A mug shot? An interrogation? Unlike a lot of the guys who grew up in Saint View, I'd made it to eighteen without getting arrested. So I had no idea of the protocol.

A numbness washed over me. It was like I wasn't even inside my own body. I went through the motions, not protesting, not offering any resistance, knowing there was nothing I could do to stop this nightmare from unfolding.

I was probably going to be charged with murder. I knew that. It was what the cops had said, as they'd slapped cuffs on me, and then hauled me away from the dance. From my friends.

From Lacey.

My heart squeezed painfully at the thought of her. She'd held my gaze for as long as she could, until the very last second, and that was what I held on to now. If I closed my eyes, I could still smell her perfume. Still feel the slinky material of her dress. Still feel the warmth of her body, pressed against mine while we danced beneath a thousand fairy lights in the crummy Saint View High gymnasium.

Fuck. This had all gone so wrong. But I couldn't bring myself to regret going to Providence School for Girls that night I'd saved her from the fire. If I hadn't been there, I would have lost Lacey forever. The thought of her perishing in the flames, alongside her uncle, was unthinkable.

A familiar logo on the front of a baseball cap caught my eye. SVHF. Saint View High Football. Beneath the brim, Coach's shrewd blue eyes scanned the waiting room. My mom and sister were close behind, the three of them rushing toward the information desk.

I stepped away from the window. I didn't want to see them. Or more accurately, I didn't want them to see me. Not like this. As a kid, my mom had done everything in her power to keep Aria and me away from the grittier side of Saint View. In our neighborhood, you were more likely to join a gang, and be shot by the time you were eighteen, than graduate high school. She'd fought tooth and nail for Aria to get that scholarship to Providence School for Girls. And she'd been so ecstatic when she'd won. We'd celebrated with store-bought chocolate cake and ice cream, Mom still in her nurses' scrubs, the three of us squished around our tiny kitchen table. The memory should have made me smile. Except that day was the catalyst for every day after. The horror Aria had endured. And now I was probably going to go to jail for it, too.

The door opened, and two people slipped inside. A woman in plain clothes—a detective, I noted, without even needing to see her credentials. Cops and detectives were a dime a dozen in Saint View. You learned to spot them pretty quick. They never fit in as well as they thought they did. The man who entered second towered over her. He was a big, heavyset guy, a pudgy gut straining at the buttons of his uniform.

Bushy eyebrows drew together and he frowned in my direction. "Sit down."

"I'm good."

Apparently, that was the wrong answer.

"Sit down before I make you."

The detective let out a sigh of frustration and took one seat at the table. That left only one other seat, the one opposite her. The guy leaned back on the door, blocking the small square window.

I eyed him carefully, not moving at first. But when he didn't budge, I grudgingly pulled out the metal seat, letting it drag over the concrete floor with an obnoxious scrape.

The big man narrowed his eyes.

"You're Waller's dad, aren't you?" I realized with a start. Owen had the same beady eyes as his father. And while Owen might not have had the beer gut or the sagging jowls, there was no mistaking their family resemblance.

The detective glanced between the chief and me, confusion in her expression.

He gave her a hard look. "Start the interview."

She blinked. "His lawyer isn't here yet."

"He didn't ask for one."

The detective didn't seem happy about that.

I folded my arms across my chest. I'd been fully prepared to talk. To explain exactly what had happened that night, and my part in it. I was innocent and had nothing to hide.

But I wouldn't say a word to this guy. This was the same man who'd dismissed my sister's claims when we'd reported the attack. The same man who'd raised a son capable of beating and attempting to rape someone he'd called a friend.

"Changed my mind. I want a lawyer."

"Smart move," the detective muttered. She stood and faced Chief Waller. "I'll come back when the public defender arrives."

Any relief I might have felt was short-lived. Waller's lips pressed into a thin line. "Don't go anywhere. I'll be back."

He opened the door. The heads of everyone in the waiting room swiveled in my direction. My gaze met Aria's, and she yelped when she recognized me and grabbed at Mom's arm. The door banged shut before Mom could look up from the paperwork she was filling out.

"Fuck," I muttered.

"Hey." The detective's voice caught my attention. She pushed a card toward me.

I picked it up, turning the small white rectangle over and reading her name off it. "Detective Simone Jones." The name rang bells in the back of my head. It suddenly dawned on me. "You worked on my sister's case, didn't you?"

Detective Jones nodded. "When I saw your name come through on some paperwork, I got myself assigned to the case. You're in a lot of trouble, kid." The detective's voice was low. "Word of advice?"

I cocked an eyebrow in her direction and waited.

"Zip your mouth."

My stomach twisted. "I didn't do anything wrong."

The frown between her eyebrows deepened, and she shot a glance at the door behind her before turning back to me. "I think we both know that doesn't mean shit around here."

I dug my fingers into the cold, hard metal of the chair. The unsaid, "You're screwed," hung in the air between us. I tucked her card into the pocket of my pants.

The door opened again, and a harried man came in, barely keeping hold of a folder of papers and a beat-up briefcase, Waller close behind him. I didn't look past them to the waiting room, where my family was. I couldn't bear it.

"You the lawyer?" the detective asked.

The new guy peeked at the chief. "Apparently. But I don't know anything about this case, so if you could just give me a minute to catch up."

"Sure." The detective gave me a 'hang in there' smile. I couldn't help but like her. Even if they had completely failed my sister. But I remembered the woman's kindness. She'd come to our home a few times to speak to Aria. She'd always been polite, never acting like we were scum.

"Were you the one in the car the other day?" I asked her. "The one who chased us?"

She frowned at that. "Excuse me?"

I shrugged. "Guess not then."

"Enough chitchat. Start the interview," Waller grumbled.

The lawyer dropped the folder of papers on the floor, and I groaned internally. They might as well throw the key away now. This guy looked barely old enough to have even finished college. And the chief was obviously trying to make things worse by preventing him from preparing.

None of that was good for me.

A phone mounted to the wall by the door rang shrilly. Waller seemed intent on ignoring it, but the ringing didn't cease, and eventually, Detective Jones eyed it. "Are you going to answer that, Chief? I can't record an interview with that in the background."

I'd swear I could hear the chief's molars grinding from across the room. His arm shot out and grabbed the phone. "What," he barked down the line. He listened for a moment and then spun to peer out the little window in the door behind him. "You're fucking kidding me?"

Apparently, whoever it was on the other end wasn't kidding at all. Without any sort of goodbye, Waller slammed the phone back down and opened the door.

On the other side, a smiling man in an impeccable, very expensive suit stood in the doorway. His dark-blond hair was slicked smoothly to one side, and despite the fact it was probably two a.m., he seemed as fresh as a motherfucking daisy. He flashed a blinding white smile at Chief Waller and pushed past him into the room.

The detective's lips turned up in a tiny smile.

"Junior," the man said to my public defender, who was frantically trying to gather the papers he'd dropped. "You're fired."

The defender's mouth dropped open. "What?" He glanced at me.

I shrugged. I had no idea what was going on either.

The new guy tilted his head like he was a puppy, confused by my reaction. Then stuck his hand out in my direction. "Liam Banks. Knight family lawyer. They said you might require my services?"

My eyes widened. "Lacey called you?"

"Her aunt, Selina, actually."

I cringed, knowing my public defender was useless, but that didn't change the fact I didn't have a cent to my name. "I can't afford you."

"You can't afford free?"

I eyed the expensive watch, glinting at his wrist. There was no way in hell this guy did pro bono jobs. Which meant Lacey, or rather, Lacey's aunt, was paying for his time. I hated the idea of owing them money. But then I remembered the fresh meat public defender I'd been given and pulled my head out of my ass.

Lacey was trying to help me, and I wasn't about to throw that in her face on account of my stupid, Saint View pride. I nudged the public defender with my elbow. "Sorry. You're fired."

The poor guy actually seemed relieved. He scurried from the room quicker than a mouse with a cat on its tail.

Liam Banks silently eyed both the detective and Chief Waller. "This better be good," he finally said. "Because I don't really like getting out of bed at two a.m. on the weekend. I had this stunning blonde tucked up beside me, so if we could get this show on the road, so I can get back there, that would be great." He held his hand up to me for a high five.

Completely bewildered, I slapped my palm against his.

Then he turned to the detective. "Please tell me you have something more than the CCTV footage of this kid jumping a fence."

Pink blushed her cheeks. She shot a glance in Chief Waller's direction, who looked ready to blow a fuse, before she admitted, "Actually, we don't have much more than that."

"That video puts him at the scene of a murder," Waller demanded. "He's the only suspect."

"Lacey Knight was also there, and you didn't arrest her in front of a school full of students, drag her out in cuffs, and publicly humiliate her. Why is that, Chief? Could it possibly have something to do with the fact you have a personal vendetta against my client? I've been told there's some bad blood between him and your son? Does that have anything to do with this?"

"Of course not!"

"Then at best, you have trespassing on a private property. You want to investigate him for the murder of Lawson Knight? Go at it. But we both know this charge isn't going to hold up to a stiff breeze, let alone a murder trial."

He pushed to his feet. Then eyed me and jerked his head, indicating I should do the same. Slowly, I followed suit.

If Waller had been pissed off before, he was doubly so now. For a second, I didn't think he'd let us leave. But then he slowly stepped aside.

Liam smiled. "My client and I will return at the much more sensible hour of nine Monday morning, and will answer any questions you might have about what he saw at the school on the night of the fire and Lawson Knight's murder. I'm sure he'll be most pleased to help you with your inquiries, right, Cole?"

"Colt," I corrected.

Liam flapped a hand around like it really didn't matter. "After you."

And just like that, I somehow walked out of the police station a free man.

Aria, my mom, and Coach all swarmed me the minute

we got outside. Tears streamed down Mom's face, and she hugged me so tight I thought I'd crack a bone.

"What happened?" She shot a glance at Liam and then remembered her manners. She stuck her hand out to him. "Willa McCaffrey. Colt's mom. Are you his public defender?"

Liam coughed at the term, like it was a slur. "I've been hired as his lawyer, yes."

"And the charges have been dropped? They said he was being charged with murder? How is he just walking free?"

Liam shook his head. "They don't have the evidence for that." He turned to me. "But that doesn't mean you're off the hook. They were unprepared for me tonight. They pull this sort of shit all the time with the public defenders. Those poor bastards are so bombarded with cases; they can't defend any of them effectively. Waller knows that and uses it to his advantage on the regular."

Coach looked ready to punch someone. But instead, he rested his hand on my shoulder and squeezed. Despite the fact I wasn't big on people touching me, it was nice to know he had my back. After Aria herself had accused me of murdering Lawson, I'd confessed everything to them. How I'd gone to the school to confront Lawson about what he'd done to Aria. And how I'd found the place on fire, dragged Lacey's barely conscious body outside, then taken off the minute I'd heard the ambulance and fire trucks pulling in. I knew they believed me. But I had no idea if Liam Banks would. Or more importantly, a jury, if it came down to that.

Away from the interrogation room, Liam was a different guy. Gone were the dazzling smiles and fake merriment. Out here, he pinned me with a hard gaze. "We've got a lot of work to do before we go back there on Monday. We need to make sure your story is solid. And you need to do exactly what I tell you."

I bristled at that idea. I'd never been one to take the demands of others easily. "I didn't do anything wrong."

"That's what they all say. You want to go to jail?"

I bit my lip. "Fine. I'll do whatever you tell me."

"Good. Then the number one thing you're going to do is stay the hell away from Lacey Knight."

6

LACEY

I woke to morning sunshine streaming through the windows of the pool house. And for the longest moment, I just basked in the golden glow, warm and safe with Banjo's sleeping face just an inch from mine, and the warmth of Rafe's body tucked to my back.

Then everything that had happened last night came crashing back in, hitting me in the stomach like someone had kicked me. A whimper fell from my lips.

The guys were awake instantly. Rafe tightened his arm around my waist, burying his face into my halo of hair. Banjo's eyes blinked open and immediately filled with concern.

"Is it Colt?" He grabbed his phone from the nightstand, scanning it for a message.

I took the phone out of his hand. "No, it's not that."

We'd barely had a chance to talk last night. All I'd felt capable of doing after we knew Colt was safe and had been released into the custody of Liam Banks—at least for the time being— was falling into bed. None of us had even gotten changed.

"My mom is back in town."

Rafe sat up behind me, and I flopped onto my back so I could see them both.

"Why didn't you tell us?" Rafe asked.

I shook my head. "Because there was a lot going on. And it isn't easy to say that my biological mother held a gun on us."

"What!" they yelled in unison.

I cringed at the noise and pulled them back down into the warmth of our bed. "Yeah, you didn't notice the bullet hole in the wall of the kitchen?"

Banjo's jaw hung open in shock. "I don't think we even went in there."

"A nice reminder of our reunion, don't you think?" A laugh bubbled up out of me, but it held no trace of humor. Both guys stared at me, their worry etched into their expressions. I filled them in on the details of our run-in with April and George, and watched as their eyes grew wider with every passing comment.

When I was finally done, Rafe swore low. "Fuck. I was so worried about Colt, and thinking about what happened with my dad, I didn't even... I would have never..."

At his tortured expression, I reached up, stroking my fingers down the side of his stubbled face. "How could you have known? And it doesn't matter now, anyway. I'm fine. And she's gone."

"Thank God for that. Crazy bitch. She could have shot you!"

But Banjo's voice was quieter. "I don't know. Sounds like she was desperate. People do crazy things when their back is against the wall."

I had a feeling he wasn't just talking about April. Banjo

was empathetic by nature, but he'd almost let his brother force him into prostituting himself not that long ago. He knew all about being desperate enough to do something rash.

I squeezed his hand. "What you did and what she did aren't the same."

He didn't acknowledge that. I couldn't blame him. I hated thinking about it, so I could only imagine he didn't like being reminded of it either.

He eyed me carefully instead. "How do you feel about her returning?"

"Nothing," I said too quickly. "I feel nothing. I don't care."

Banjo looked doubtful, but I didn't want to see that expression on his face. I couldn't bear it. Banjo had always been able to see past the defenses I put up. Our childhoods had been similar, both of us losing our biological parents at an early age, and sometimes that made him more perceptive to my feelings. I knew he was thinking about how he'd feel if his biological parents had suddenly reappeared.

But he and I weren't the same people.

His heart was big. Pure. Honest.

Mine was harder. Darker. And had no room for mothers suddenly reappearing after thirteen long years.

Whatever we could have had was gone. Disintegrated in the years of missed piano recitals, school assignments, friends, and boys. My life was full. And I had no need for anyone who wanted to disrupt that.

In fact, I wouldn't mind forgetting she'd ever come back. And I had two very good ways of doing that right here beside me.

I slid my fingers to Banjo's shirt, now rumpled and

untucked after sleeping in it. His tousled hair fell over his eyes, but he watched me with interest from beneath, while I made quick work of the buttons. I pushed the material off his shoulders, exposing his tanned, toned biceps and chest. I placed a kiss right over his heart, loving how honest it was, even if mine was the complete opposite.

Rafe caught my mood, placed a kiss on my neck, and slid my dress away from my collarbone. He trailed his lips across the bare skin there, while Banjo exposed my breasts. My nipples hardened instantly, and I lifted so I could shimmy the dress down over my hips.

Neither of them asked if this was what I really wanted to be doing right now, the morning after all our lives had blown up. That unspoken connection between the three of us always made me feel grounded. Safe. Whole. It was exactly what I needed. Their stability while the rest of the world crumbled around us.

I twisted my head to claim Rafe's lips and let his warm tongue slide into my mouth. He unbuttoned his own shirt in a matter of seconds, shedding it to the growing pile of clothes at the end of our bed. Banjo's head lowered, and he sucked my nipple into his mouth, running his tongue over the stiff peak, just the way he knew I loved. I pressed one hand to the back of his head, encouraging him. The other I snaked up to the back of Rafe's neck and pulled him closer. Our kiss deepened, and I fell into it, drinking in everything he gave. I let his kiss and Banjo's mouth on my breasts drive out any unpleasantness that lingered from last night.

"Get naked already," I murmured against Rafe's lips, but the words were meant as much for Banjo. And for myself. I wanted nothing between us. I hooked my fingers in the elastic of my panties and wriggled out of them, before helping the guys, shoving their pants off in haste.

Banjo was quicker. Released from his underwear, his cock stiffened, and I helped it along by wrapping my fingers around the base and stroking him from root to tip. On instinct, his hips rocked forward into my grasp.

I knew Rafe had succeeded in getting his gear off, too, when his hot, hard length brushed over my ass. I reached behind with one hand, so I could stroke them both simultaneously. A thrill ran through me at the position of power they let me have over them. It was a heady feeling, lying sandwiched between the two of them, controlling their pleasure, their actions, their desires.

Lying, beaten on that beach after Owen's attack, I'd promised I'd be their princess no longer.

I'd sworn I'd be their queen.

It had come true.

These two guys worshipped my body. Rafe's fingers trailed down my spine and over the curve of my ass, palming it and sending a dirty thrill through me at the promise of his touch back there. I hadn't forgotten how that felt, or how much I'd liked it the last time he'd done that.

Banjo, ever able to read my mind, or perhaps the way I was grinding back against Rafe's touch, twisted, and reached for the bedside drawer. He produced a little purple tube of lubricant. My breath fluttered in my chest because I knew exactly why he would have bought that.

He cracked open the top, squirted a small dollop onto his fingers, then reached beneath the blankets. To my surprise, he nudged my hand away from his erection and then smoothed the gel over himself. Before I even had a chance to take him in my hand again, he slid his dick between my legs.

His hardness glanced straight over my clit, spreading the lube between my lower lips. His dick didn't nudge at my entrance, the angle wasn't right, but the glide over my clit was delicious. I clamped my thighs tighter together, giving Banjo more friction to work through. He groaned.

I giggled at that. "The one time I'm glad I don't have a thigh gap."

"Your thighs are fucking perfect. Just like every other inch of you." He closed his eyes, continuing his slow thrusts.

The click of the lubricant opening again caught my attention. Rafe copied Banjo's actions, pushing my hand away and covering his dick with the slick gel. I held my breath as he wriggled behind me, and then his dick was moving between my ass cheeks.

I froze for a second, knowing I couldn't take him there, not yet. "Rafe."

But his dick slid right past my back entrance, merely skimming it, turning me on, but not pressing inside at all. He was mirroring Banjo's actions, the two of them lubing me up and driving me mad. I wondered if their dicks touched between my legs. I suspected they did, and damn if that wasn't a huge turn-on. I loved watching the two of them explore their physical connection.

But this morning, they seemed to be concentrating on me. Banjo went for my nipples again, tweaking them hard, sending pulses of sparks right through my body.

It wasn't enough. I kissed him roughly, pushing my tongue inside his mouth and loving the way he tasted. Even first thing in the morning, he was so completely Banjo, and I couldn't get enough of him. "I want you," I whispered.

He reached for the bedside drawer, but I grabbed his hand, stopping him. Then twisted so I could see Rafe, too.

"I slept with Colt bare," I confessed. "Just for a second. We got carried away."

Banjo looked a little surprised, but all he said was, "That doesn't mean we have to. What you do with one of us doesn't mean an auto pass for the others. It's up to you."

But I wanted to. God, I so wanted to feel them bare inside me.

"You want to," Rafe husked out, reading me right. "Fuckin' hell. That's hot. And I can't believe I'm gonna say this, but I care about you too much not to. We can't. Not until we've all been tested. And we get you some birth control."

He was right. We all knew it. But ugh. "My libido hates when you're sensible."

"I can make it up to you." Rafe's voice was that low, deep, possessive growl and my lady parts hummed with pleasure. He ripped a condom open and rolled it over his length.

I watched, distracted by the sight of his fingers touching his dick. "Oh yeah?"

In response, he pulled me on top of him. On instinct, I parted my legs, so my knees sank into the mattress, taking some of my weight.

But that also left me open to him, his thick cock pulsing at my entrance, just begging to find home.

His gaze bored into mine. "Gonna have you screaming 'oh yeah' in a minute." He grabbed the back of my neck and pulled my mouth down to meet his.

God, I loved kissing him. And when his dick glided up inside me, hot and slick, I moaned into his mouth. He stretched me deliciously, giving me no time to adjust to his size, but I was so turned on there was no need to wait. He slid out easily, then in again, lifting his hips and bracing his abs to thrust into me. I broke our kiss, sitting up to ride him, my tits bouncing while he palmed my thighs. I glanced over at Banjo and grinned at him. He got to his knees, too, so we were similar heights, and claimed my lips.

There was nothing like the feeling of both my guys inside me. Rafe filling my core, Banjo's tongue inside my mouth. I knew I wasn't fully ready to take them both at once, but soon. I wanted that. Wanted them.

I braced myself with one hand on Rafe's chest, while I used the other to wrap around Banjo's cock. He groaned while I pumped him, and I worked both guys in the same rhythm.

For a moment, I was a sex goddess, completely owning this threesome.

That all came unraveled when Banjo trailed his fingers from my hip, across my ass cheeks and between. His fingers slid through the lube there, still slick from Rafe's earlier attentions, and pressed against the puckered star of my ass.

Pleasure built so quickly between my legs it took me by surprise. I gasped, breaking away from his kiss and flopping forward shamelessly to give him better access. He chuckled at my response, but when I glanced up at him, there was nothing but heat in his eyes. He moved behind me as I lost my rhythm completely.

But Rafe took over, cupping the side of my face, and forced me to look at him. "Ride me, Lacey. Nice and slow and easy. He's gonna make this so good for you, but only if you do what you're told."

I wanted to come, right then and there. I'd seen glimpses of Rafe's dominant side before and was desperate to bring more of that out of him. So I did as I was told. I braced myself on the bed, my hands either side of Rafe's head, and rolled my hips slowly.

Rafe nodded his approval. "Keep going."

That pressure grew between my legs, aching to burst free, but the slow rhythm Rafe set wouldn't let me topple over the edge. I needed him hard and fast, but he wouldn't let me take it, instead driving me higher with his sudden display of dominance.

Fuck, that was hot. I reached for my clit, but he batted my hand away, taking over himself. I paused, with Banjo's finger against my ass, wanting more.

"Keep moving, Lacey," Rafe directed. "Concentrate on me."

I slid up and down his dick and gasped when Banjo leaned over me, pressing his fingertip just inside.

"Good?" he whispered into my ear.

It was more than good. It was fucking amazing. I was riding the edge of an orgasm that I desperately wanted to fall into. I dropped my head back onto Banjo's shoulder, panting with need. My gaze locked with him, giving him all the permission he needed.

Rafe pinched my clit at the same time Banjo's thick finger moved all the way inside. A shout ripped from my chest, a moan of ecstasy and I toppled over the edge I'd been so desperate to find. My body squeezed and pulsed, but neither of them stopped. Rafe took over the rhythm, pumping into me from below, his finger hard and fast on my clit, while Banjo worked me from behind. The sensation of something foreign was there, but completely obliterated by the mind-numbing sensations it produced. I'd never come so hard, pleasure roaring through me like a wildfire.

Slowly, I came down off cloud nine, gradually floating back down to earth with the realization that I wanted Banjo and Rafe to feel as good as I did.

I took back the control.

I sat up, Rafe's dick still sheathed inside me and spun, so I was riding him in reverse, my face pointed to his feet...my face pointed at Banjo's dick. I grinned up at him, while I ground against Rafe, his groans echoing around the room at the new angle.

I leaned forward, gripping Banjo's base and slipping his cockhead inside my mouth.

His hands immediately speared into my hair, gathering it up and scraping it away from my face, giving him a better view of me sucking him. He held himself desperately still, not moving at all, letting me control the depth and speed I took him at.

That wasn't what I wanted. I wanted him to lose control, just like I had.

I let his dick pop free and raised my gaze to meet his. "Stop holding back."

He hissed. "You want me to fuck your mouth, Lacey? That what you asking?"

Yes.

His fingers fisted tighter in my hair, and I relished the sharp stinging of my scalp. When his dick pushed past my lips, I hummed, the sound full of my pleasure at having him inside me again. He started slower than I would have liked, shallowly thrusting the head of his thick dick over my tongue. His gaze never left mine, always checking to see if I was all right. But I was more than all right. I moaned my encouragement, not wanting to take my mouth off him to voice what I wanted. What I needed.

He knew.

He always knew.

His next thrust filled my mouth completely. And the one after that hit the back of my throat. I worked at relaxing my muscles there, and he went no further, but his eyes rolled back, so I knew this was deep enough. And I loved the feel of it. His quick, sharp thrusts, his dick spearing into my mouth, my tongue working his ridged underside.

Rafe gripped my hips while I concentrated on sucking Banjo. His fingers guided me in time with his thrusts, keeping us moving together, until his groans became louder and he tensed beneath me.

"Fuck! Lacey!" he yelled. His fingers stilled my movements as he spilled himself inside me, my body still giving off mild pulses from the mind-blowing orgasm I'd experienced just minutes ago.

A fire lit up in Banjo's eyes, watching his best friend come inside his girl. I gripped his balls, and with a shout, he found his own release. His hot cum filled the back of my throat, and I swallowed it down quickly, wanting to make him feel as good as he made me. His grip on my hair loosened, and eventually, he pulled from my mouth, completely spent. But ever the gentleman, he dipped his head and kissed me, no doubt tasting himself on my tongue.

Completely spent, I flopped back on Rafe, my back to his chest, while we both tried to catch our breath. Through my blissed-out haze, Banjo gave a laugh and added himself to the top of our pile.

"Oof, Banjo. You weigh a ton," Rafe grunted from the bottom. Without any prompting from the other, Rafe and I simultaneously slapped Banjo on his naked ass, and he and I both fell to the bed, in a happy, if sticky and sweaty, mess. He kissed my nose sweetly. "I love you."

"Love you, too," I whispered back. Then turned to Rafe, remembering my realization from last night.

But when my gaze met his, he shook his head slightly.

The words I wanted to say died on my lips as he kissed me softly and then headed for the bathroom.

I watched him go, then focused on Banjo. "Is he okay?"

Banjo blinked open an eye. He was still basking in post-orgasm bliss. "Huh? Rafe? He's fine."

I suddenly wasn't so sure.

7

LACEY

*R*afe seemed his normal self again after he emerged from the shower, but when he and Banjo decided to go down to the football field to kick the ball around, I declined their invitation to join them. If something was bothering Rafe, then I wanted to give him a chance to talk to Banjo. I was well aware that the three of us didn't need to live in each other's pockets, and that the two of them still needed time alone, just like I craved individual time with each of them.

So even though they both pouted, I shoved them out the door, promising I'd see them later tonight. I needed to go talk to Colt anyway. And I wanted to do it alone.

I drove back into Saint View and made a beeline for Colt's place. I had to pass the old house I'd once lived in but steadfastly refused to turn my head in its direction. I pushed out all thoughts of April, and where she might be now, refusing to let myself wonder.

She wasn't worth my time.

I'd keep telling myself that until I believed it.

I parked outside Colt's place, and a sudden swarm of

butterflies took hold of my stomach. I stared up at the window of his bedroom in the attic, but it was empty of his handsome face. I was so distracted looking for him; I didn't even notice his front door open, until his sister was storming across the lawn, with an expression like thunder.

"Shit," I murmured, opening my door. "Aria. Hi."

"Sit your ass right back down," she yelled.

Here we went again. Aria and I had been there, done this, before. Though last time, I'd at least made it to the front door. Seemed this time, Aria wasn't even willing to let me get a toe past the sidewalk.

I held my hands up in a sign of defeat, hoping that would pacify her long enough to have a conversation. "Please. Can we just talk? Your brother—"

I'd been going to say her brother was important to me, and that we needed to work out our differences. Sister or not, what I'd found with Colt was too important to let go of. She didn't like me and thought I was a stuck-up snob, like most of the others from Providence. I got that. I'd made it worse by not recognizing her from the time we'd been at school together. But we'd been in different grades, and it was a big school. Couldn't she forgive that I might not have remembered her? Truthfully, I thought she was being a bit dramatic with all the hate she kept slinging my way.

"My brother is nothing to you," she hissed. She rounded my car and got right up in my face, so we were nose-to-nose.

"This isn't what I wanted," I tried to explain. But I didn't back down. If I had to fight for Colt, I would. I would never in a million years have thought I'd be fighting his sister, though. Gillian? Yep. Even now, I wasn't one-hundred-percent sure she wasn't about to pop out of the woodwork and try to stake her claim on him again.

But not Aria.

"Colt said we were friends once, you and him and me. Do you remember that?"

She paused for a moment, and I thought I might have found a chink in her armor. So I prodded a little harder. "We were neighbors, right? Colt said your mom was always trying to push us together because we were both girls."

She ran her tongue over her lips, but then pressed them together stubbornly.

"You do remember, don't you?"

"We weren't friends. Not really. It was always you and Colt. And I was the annoying kid sister."

I dared a tiny smile, hoping it would encourage her to keep talking.

"I don't remember a lot. I was only tiny. But I did follow you around."

"Little girls tend to worship their big brothers, I guess?" My smile grew, both at the thought that Colt and I had been inseparable, but also at the vision of his dark-haired sister following. It jostled loose a memory that took me by surprise. "You fell one time." I looked down at her knees, as if they'd still be covered with the scrapes. "Colt told you to stop crying...."

"But you were nice to me. You brushed away my tears, and took me by the hand, and found my mom. When she got down a box of Band-Aids, you insisted on putting them on for me."

I remembered. I remembered all of that, suddenly so clearly it was like the scene was playing out behind my eyes.

But then Aria's expression hardened. "I never worshipped Colt. It was you I loved like a sister. Even when I was just tagging along and annoying Colt, you never made me feel like that."

"And then I left." Colt had said something similar. I

knew how me leaving their lives so abruptly had hurt them. But... "Aria, that was out of my control."

That was met with stunned silence. I'd obviously said the wrong thing, again, though I didn't know how.

The fire that blazed behind her black eyes practically made them glow. "You think I don't know that? You think I blame you for leaving back then? You were five years old, Lacey. What the hell were you supposed to do? No, I don't blame you for that. But you aren't one of us anymore. You're one of them."

"Who?"

"The Providence crowd. I watched you every day. I tried smiling and waving at first, but you ignored me. Just like the rest of those stuck-up bitches. All any of you ever do is take. You just take whatever the hell you want and damn the consequences. Not that there are any, right? Consequences? What are those? There are never any repercussions for your actions. Not when you have the money to cover your sins."

My mouth dropped open, but slowly, bits and pieces of things Colt had said came back to me. "Something happened to you at Providence, didn't it?" I asked her quietly, my stomach churning with rising dread.

Moisture built in her eyes, and one tear dripped down her face. "I thought the other girls were bad. I'd had such high hopes when I won that scholarship. It was supposed to be my ticket out of this hellhole. You know Mom tried coaching me, before I even started? Told me to try to make friends with the other girls. She told me to smile and ask about their interests, and I listened, because I so badly wanted to fit in. But none of them cared. I was just the charity case from Saint View."

"But you stayed..."

She nodded. "I stayed. Because I worked hard for that

scholarship. And even if I wasn't making any friends, at least I was receiving a good education."

"Then why did you leave?"

I just waited, a lump forming in my throat.

Cheat. Liar. Rapist.

They'd been the words on the photos that had been shoved into my locker by Gillian. She'd sworn she just found them in her backpack and had taken the opportunity to publicly shame me.

Aria had access to Gillian's backpack. Gillian had practically lived with Colt when they'd been dating. It would have been nothing for Aria to slip those photos inside her bag.

The blood drained from my face as all the pieces fit together.

But I still needed her to say it. My eyes locked with hers.

"Your uncle raped me."

The world spun around me. "No."

Her laugh was bitter and harsh. "You know it's true."

I shook my head, eyes wide. "How would I have known that?"

"You think I was the only one?"

Horror washed over me. I didn't want to hear it. Couldn't. The thought was unimaginable. But when I stared into this girl's eyes, there was a burning honesty there that stripped me raw.

She was telling the truth.

But I was too frozen, too broken, to say anything at all.

Aria sniffed in my direction. "You really didn't know?"

"I swear it. I didn't."

She ground her teeth together. "Then think yourself lucky. Think yourself lucky he kept his hands to himself when you were around. Think yourself lucky that you don't have to live with the memory of what he did, every day of your whole miserable life."

Her words were like a knife, slicing through my chest, my gut, cutting off limbs and stabbing me right through my heart. I couldn't have been more broken by her words than if she'd taken a baseball bat to my body.

"Why didn't you go to the police?"

"I did. But what power does a girl from Saint View have against an upstanding member of the Providence community like Lawson Knight? Graduated with honors, principal of the most prestigious school in a hundred-mile radius, doting husband and father..."

"I'm sorry," I whispered. They were useless words. I knew that. But it was all I had.

She didn't respond. It was as if I hadn't said a thing.

"You can't be here," she said finally. "And not just because I can't stand to look at you. Colt's lawyer said he needs to stay away from you."

"What?" I choked out. This was too much. She'd already rocked my world and now she was ripping the carpet out from beneath my feet.

"Just go, Lacey. Whatever game you were playing here in Saint View, it's over."

8

LACEY

My confrontation with Aria left me shaken to the core. With trembling fingers, I drove away from her place, but I couldn't go back to Providence. When I did, I'd have to work out what the hell I was supposed to do. Or say. I'd have to repeat the words, "Lawson raped Aria McCaffrey," to Banjo and Rafe, and worse, to Selina.

I couldn't be the one who broke her heart like that. I just couldn't. I needed a breather. A break. Some time to sort through the jumble of thoughts and feelings in my head.

So I found myself driving with a new purpose, to the other side of Saint View, where Jagger lived.

Jagger's mom took one look at me, tears streaming down my cheeks, and stepped aside. "They're in her room."

I nodded, mumbling my thanks, and moved silently through their little house, to Jagger's bedroom in the back. It was only as I put my hand on the doorknob that I realized Jagger's mom had said "they" were in her room. So instead of just waltzing in like I normally did, I knocked. I definitely didn't want to walk in and see Aaron's junk or something.

But when she yelled out to come in, it was Meredith lounging on Jagger's bed, scrolling through her phone. They both froze when they saw me. I barely had the door closed before I burst into a fresh round of heartbroken tears.

I'd never seen either of them move so fast. Within seconds, I was in the middle of a three-way hug, being squeezed so tight my ribs should have cracked.

Neither of them asked what was wrong. Neither of them made any demands from me. They just held me while I cried.

When I finally dashed away the tears and untangled myself from their embrace, I faked a smile. "Hanging without me?"

Meredith led me over to Jagger's bed, while Jagger ran out to the kitchen and returned with a chair. She spun it backwards, straddled it, and rested her chin on the backrest. "We sent you a message not long ago."

I looked down at my phone, clutched between my fingers. There was a little number one in a circle by the message icon. "Sorry. I was too busy dodging the bombs Colt's sister was throwing at me."

Jagger's purple-coated lips pressed into an unhappy frown. "What's up with that chick, anyway? She has an unhealthy attachment to her brother."

I buried my face in my hands. "It wasn't about Colt. Not entirely." I lifted watery eyes to my two best friends—one I'd known half my life. The other I'd known a handful of months. But that didn't matter. Jagger had proven her best friend status over and over again. I trusted both of them with my life. With my secrets. "Lawson raped her."

"What!"

Meredith's yell was so loud Jagger and I jumped.

But if Meredith noticed that she'd scared us half to

death with her volume, she didn't show it. "That's bullshit." She pushed to her feet, pacing across the small section of threadbare carpet that covered Jagger's bedroom floor. "She's a liar."

It was only then that Meredith noticed Jagger and I staring at her with huge eyes.

She lowered her voice a little. "Sorry, but that is complete garbage."

Jagger bit her lip and shot me an apologetic glance. "I hope it's not true, for your sake, Lace." She turned to Meredith. "But I'm really uncomfortable just flat-out calling Aria a liar. Why would you lie about something like that? That's a huge accusation to make."

My stomach was a lead ball, heavy and draining. "I don't want to believe it. Truly, I don't. But I don't think she was lying. I could see it in her eyes."

Meredith stared at us like we'd suddenly sprouted extra heads. "Why would she lie? Why *wouldn't* she lie? Do you know how easy it would be for a girl like that to accuse a wealthy man in a position of power? What easier way is there to extort a man for money?"

"A girl like that? What does that mean?" Jagger bristled. "You mean, a girl from Saint View? Don't forget where you're standing right now."

Uncomfortable tension swept into the room like a chilly blast. "I'm sure Meredith didn't mean it like that, right, Mer?" I asked, hoping like hell I was right. Because that comment really had been out of line.

Meredith's cheeks went pink, and she came back to sit beside me on the bed. "Sorry," she said to Jagger. "I really didn't mean it to be insulting. I just meant that there's a motivation there, for her to lie. A financial motivation."

I shook my head. "That doesn't make sense. If she were

going to try to extort money, wouldn't she have just done that quietly? She told her mom. And Colt. That's why Colt was at the school that night to save me from the fire. He was trying to talk to my uncle. Who wouldn't take his meetings. If Lawson had nothing to hide, why avoid Colt and Willa?"

"This all sounds completely legit to me," Jagger declared. She had a stubborn glint in her eye, and I knew, that after everything Meredith had said, she was putting herself in Aria's shoes. "Something terrible happened, and Aria had the guts to confide in her family. Of course they're going to go up to that school and try to talk to the man who attacked her. What's suspicious is that Lawson wouldn't talk to them."

Meredith's huge hoop earrings swung, bouncing off her cheeks when she shook her head hard. "Why didn't they go to the police? Why go to Lawson?"

"She said they did go to the police and the police dismissed her."

Meredith lifted a shoulder. "Well, there you go. If the police didn't believe her, then why are you?"

Irritation pricked the back of my neck. "How can you say that, after everything that happened with me and Owen? You think they wouldn't have just dismissed me, too?"

Meredith's eyes flashed. "That's completely different."

"Is it? How? Because I'm from a different zip code?"

Meredith threw her hands up. "I think the real question is, how are you willing to believe the word of this girl you barely know, over the uncle who loved and raised you for most of your life? A man who is no longer here to defend himself. Do you really think Lawson was capable of something like that?"

Guilt flooded my system. She was right. I didn't think him capable.

But I hadn't thought Owen capable either.

"You know what?" Jagger said. "I think we all just need to take a deep breath for a second here."

She was right. The tension between her and Meredith was palpable. I'd caused that. They'd been hanging out as friends, exactly as I'd wanted them to, before I'd waltzed in and blew everything up. "I agree. I appreciate your opinions." I looked to Jagger and then Meredith. "Truly I do. But I don't want this to cause a rift between us. You two are the easiest part of my life right now. And I just really need it to stay that way. I need something to be easy."

A little of the fight went out of Meredith, and she squeezed my hand. "We got you."

Jagger reached out a hand to me, too. "What she said."

"Okay, so all of that aside, what the hell do I do now?"

"Talk to Colt," Meredith and Jagger said in unison.

I sighed. "You say it like it's so easy. I tried that this morning. His sister is like a savage pit bull guarding a bone. She said his lawyer warned him to stay away from me."

Jagger frowned. "Why?"

"I don't know."

"All the more reason to talk to him then." She picked up my phone from Jagger's bed and handed it to me. "Call him."

He and I weren't big on phone calls. His one-syllable style of answering questions didn't translate well when I couldn't see his face to determine what he truly meant. But I wanted to hear his voice. Needed to reassure myself, and maybe him, too, that even though there were forces trying to keep us apart, I was willing to fight. What I'd felt with him last night, dancing beneath the fairy lights, had been special. The kind of special that didn't come along every day. There were words I'd wanted to say. My leg bounced uncontrollably while I scrolled through my contacts, looking for Colt's name. Butterflies took off in my stomach as I pressed down on the call button. "What if he doesn't answer?" I hissed to the girls.

"Then you call back later," Meredith whispered back. Though I had no idea why we'd both dropped our voices.

The call connected, but the hello that came down the line wasn't the one I'd been expecting. I glanced at the screen, making sure I'd called the right number, but it was definitely the number I'd save for Colt.

"Lacey? It's Willa. Colt's mom."

My eyes widened. "Oh. Hi. How are you? Is uh, Colt home?"

His mom, I mouthed to Jagger and Meredith. Meredith grimaced.

I turned away and faced a wall, not wanting to be distracted by either of them anymore.

Willa sighed. "I know Aria told you he can't see you right now."

"Yeah, but I thought..."

"Whatever you thought isn't going to happen. I'm sorry, Lacey. Truly, I am. But I have to think of my son first. And if his lawyer says to stay away from you, then that's what he has to do."

My heart sank. She wasn't being a bitch, like Aria had been. Her words were soft and apologetic. But firm and no-nonsense, too. She'd been kind to me once. Probably a lot more than once, actually. I had a feeling there were years of kindness that I couldn't remember. But now she was putting her family first.

I couldn't blame her.

Maybe I needed to do the same.

"I understand," I said slowly. "Willa?"

"Mmm?"

"Thank you. Again. For everything."

She didn't reply. I gently ended the call.

"What. The. Fuck. Was. That?"

Meredith had her hands on her hips. When I glanced over at Jagger, she was just as scowly.

"What?"

Jagger tilted her head to one side, like a dog trying to work me out. "That's it? You're just going to give up and stay away from him?"

"What else am I supposed to do? Everyone has warned me away, and it's not like he's reached out to me."

Jagger stood and stormed to her closet. She riffled through it, yanking out a pair of jeans, a hoodie, and a bandana. Everything was black.

"What are you doing?"

She whirled on me. "I watched you two last night. You're in love with him." It was an accusation more than an observation.

My mouth gaped open. But apparently Jagger wasn't done.

"And he's in love with you. I'm not doing this Romeo and Juliet bullshit. Because we all know how the fuck that ended. I've never had a best friend and I'd prefer you don't end up a Shakespearian tragedy."

She gave Meredith and me a hard look. "At dark, we're gonna get you to your man."

9

BANJO

I lined the laces on the pigskin up with my fingers, like I'd been taught in the peewees, and passed it across the field. Right into Rafe's waiting hands. The ball came down beautifully, cradled in his arms. And then it was on. With a huge grin, he jogged toward me.

I bounced lightly on my feet, starting up a slow jog of my own, trying to read his body language to determine which way he was going to feint, in order to get around me.

We'd been playing together for years, but Rafe was good, giving nothing away.

"Whatcha got, Banjo?" he taunted, faking left.

I went with him. "More than you," I yelled back. I blocked his run, and he changed direction. "And I'm not just talking about on the football field."

He snorted on a laugh and put on a burst of speed, heading for the makeshift touchdown line we'd marked out. But I was quicker. I barreled into him, stopping him from scoring but sending us both to the ground in the process. We hit the dirt with a bone-jarring thud.

Rafe groaned from below me. "You're a savage. No pads, remember?"

I laughed and moved off him, pulling him to his feet. "You all right?"

Rafe shoved me, sending me sidestepping a few feet. "Yeah, fine." But then he winced as he put his weight on his left foot.

"Fuck, no you're not. Lean on me. We'll go sit for a minute. Shit, Coach will kill us if you're injured."

Rafe rolled his eyes, but he did let me take some of his weight. "I'm not injured. I barely even twisted it. It'll be fine tomorrow."

"Or it'll be twice as bad."

Rafe shrugged. "How about we just sit and you stop being a pussy about it?"

I led him over to a park bench, and we both sank down onto the painted wood.

"Man, the parks are nice around here," Rafe commented. "This seat doesn't even give you splinters."

"There was no broken glass in the playground either."

"No shit? We ain't in Saint View anymore."

"Yeah. How's the ankle now?"

Rafe lifted his foot and rolled it experimentally. "It'll be fine."

"Good."

A chilly wind meant we had the park to ourselves, families smart enough to keep their kids home. Snow might be a rarity, but Mother Nature was eager to let us know that winter was here. The sweat we'd worked up was rapidly cooling, and Rafe shifted closer to me, radiating a pleasant warmth, even through his clothes. It was nice. I liked being close to him. Touching him. I had no idea if I was allowed to in this sort of setting, but I wanted to push my luck. Push us.

But only if he was ready. Slowly, as if he might turn around and snap at me like a dog who'd had its tail pulled, I snaked an arm around his shoulder.

He didn't shift away. But still, I had to be sure I wasn't making him uncomfortable.

"You good?" I asked quietly.

"What do you mean?"

"Well, we haven't really talked about the two of us. I don't know where I stand with you. It's fine when it's just you, me, and Lacey, and we're behind closed doors. I know where the boundaries are then. But here," I gestured between the two of us, "I don't know what this is. Am I allowed to put my arm around you like this?"

"I wouldn't still be sitting here if you weren't."

I chuckled. "Fine. But there's no one here right now, is there? How would you feel if there were? Would this still be okay? And this is a tame-as-fuck public display of affection. If I kissed you right now, are we still good? Or will you punch me in the face?"

His voice dropped an octave, and he swiveled on the seat so we faced each other. "Try it and find out."

I leaned in until my lips hovered just over his. "You fucking punch me now and I'll never kiss you again. Just sayin'.'"

Rafe smiled against my lips, then closed the gap between us. I tightened my hold on his shoulders, while lifting my free hand to cup his face. He hadn't shaved this morning, and his stubble scraped along my palm. He slanted his head, deepening the kiss, our tongues meeting and gliding together until a rush of need coursed through me. We'd only just had sex that morning, but suddenly I was pulling at his shirt, drawing him closer, wishing there weren't so many barriers between us, the least of those, the fact we were in a very public place.

"I don't want to be on the down-low with you," he whispered.

My heart stuttered. "I don't want that either. I don't know how the fuck we're going to explain any of this—the dynamic between you and me, and you, me, and Lacey. And hell, Colt, too—but I don't care." I glanced down, fiddling with the button on his shirt. "I just know I don't want to lose you."

He leaned his forehead to mine. "You won't."

Our kiss this time was harder, possessive. We grabbed at each other until he groaned and pulled away. "Shit, stop. We can't do this here. And if we keep going...."

"If we keep going, what?"

His gaze bored into mine. "If we keep going, I'm going to want to do more than kiss you, Banjo. A lot more. You get what I'm saying?"

Heat swept through my body, and I groaned as my dick kicked to life, wanting to get in on the action.

Rafe's gaze strayed to my lap, and when his eyes lifted again, there was fire there. "I want more than just kissing and blow jobs."

"Fuck," I muttered.

"I just want to make sure we're on the same page."

I grinned. "How 'bout we go home and I show you exactly what page we're on?"

He froze, his fingers clenching into the fabric of his pants. "So just to be one-hundred-percent clear. That's a yes? To fucking?"

I rolled my eyes. "Jesus Christ. Do you seriously need me to say it?"

"Yeah, I think I do."

"I want to fuck you, Rafe. I want you to fuck me. Can we stop fucking talking about fucking and just go do it already?"

He snorted on a laugh. "Ah. Such subtle romance."

Sore ankle forgotten, we grabbed our stuff and got the hell out of there.

We left the park right as another couple were entering. The man looked down at mine and Rafe's joined fingers, and I braced myself for backlash, or at the very least, a disapproving glare, but when he met my gaze, his smile was wide and friendly.

I stopped, something about him familiar. "Hey, I know you, don't I?"

"Banjo, right?" the man asked. "Yeah, we met on the beach awhile back. I wasn't sure if you'd remember."

"That's right. You were out jogging. We talked about my surf comps. Sorry, I don't recall your name?"

"Don't think I gave it to you. I'm George." He pointed to his partner. "And this is April."

The woman held a hand out to me, and I took it with a smile. It faltered a little when I noticed that her fingers trembled. "Nice to meet you. This is Rafe."

I dropped Rafe's hand so he could take April's.

She smiled softly at him. And then back at me. "It's really lovely to meet you both."

"You, too. Enjoy the park. It's really quiet today."

Rafe and I walked away, but April's voice called after us. "Wait."

We both stopped and looked over our shoulders.

The woman wrung her mitten-covered hands, the

tremble from her fingers now visible across her entire body. "I'm Lacey's mom."

Rafe and I froze in unison.

He recovered quicker than I did. He spun around, yanking my arm so I had no choice but to turn with him or have it snapped off. Rafe's furious gaze darted between George and April. George had tensed, as if he were expecting one of us to start throwing punches. But April's body language spoke of nothing but defeat. Her shoulders slumped, and she clasped her hands nervously. George edged closer to her.

A low growly noise vibrated from Rafe, so I squeezed his hand a little harder and stepped slightly in front of him. I knew he'd never hurt a woman, but these people had held Lacey captive. And Rafe loved Lacey as much as I did. He might not have admitted it yet, but I knew he felt it. Rafe was fiercely protective of the people he loved. I'd seen that time and time again in the way he carried himself around Colt, Jagger, and me.

"You've got a lot of nerve showing up here," he spat in April's direction. "You should be in jail."

She nodded. "I don't know why I'm not."

I knew why. "That's because you don't know your own daughter. You have no idea how good and kind she is."

"Something she obviously didn't get from you," Rafe snarled.

April took the insult without trying to sling one back.

"What is this?" I asked. And then I turned to George. "Why were you on the beach that day?"

"We've been following you," April admitted. "All of you."

"What?" Rafe yelled. "When? Where?"

The big man rubbed the back of his neck awkwardly. Pink flushed his cheeks. "We followed her and Colt in a car.

And I saw you and Lacey at her house one night, during a storm. I swear, it was only for a second, and when I saw that you were, uh, occupied, I got the hell out of there. For what it's worth, I'm really sorry. I never meant to see anything like that."

Rafe's voice was a roar of anger. "Then maybe you shouldn't have been creeping around in the dark, peeping through windows! Are you for real right now?"

I tightened my grip on him, though I wanted to take a swing at George myself. But my curiosity won out over my irritation that this guy had completely invaded Rafe and Lacey's privacy. And there was one question that yelled louder than all the rest. "Why?"

April raised a shoulder. "I just want to know my daughter. I want to know the people in her life."

Rafe let out a harsh laugh. "You've got a funny way of showing it. Most people would have turned up with flowers. You stalk us, then show up with a gun. You could have fucking killed her."

April eyes became pleading. "I swear, she was never in any danger. I know we went about it the wrong way, but I was angry and desperate."

A tiny twinge of sympathy dislodged itself inside me. I knew what desperate felt like. I didn't want to have anything in common with this woman, who'd so recklessly endangered Lacey's and Selina's lives, but I couldn't help it. "What do you want from us? Lacey isn't here. Which I'm guessing you already knew, since you've been following us."

"I just want a chance to explain. To know her. I was hoping..." April tugged at her ear.

I recognized the mannerism instantly.

Rafe did, too. "Fuck," he swore beneath his breath. "Lacey does that."

"I know," I murmured.

Rafe yanked his hand from mine. "I can't listen to this anymore." He stalked back toward the road, not waiting for me.

I shot one last look at April. A tear spilled over and down her cheek, and my stomach clenched. The longer I stood here, the more I saw Lacey. It wasn't just the ear tugging. It was the brown of her eyes, and the way her eyebrows pulled down when she cried. They were such similar builds, that from a distance, I could have easily mistaken this woman for her daughter. Is this what Lacey would have wanted? For me to stand here and do nothing while her mother cried for a second chance?

"Please talk to her, Banjo. There's so much she doesn't know about me. About her dad, and why I left. Her uncle isn't who she thinks he was."

I squinted at her, trying to get a read on just how honest she was being. I obviously took too long, trying to work out whether this woman could be trusted, and she saw it as a sign of hope.

She shoved her hand into the pocket of her pants and pulled out a rumpled business card. "Would you give her this? Please? It's my number. Tell her I'm sorry. And I should have let her come to me, in her own time. But when I heard he'd died, I finally saw my chance..."

I held up my hand. "It's not me you need to say this to."

She nodded quickly and stepped back. "You're right."

April's eyes went big when I held my hand out for the card. "I'm not promising anything. Even if I give her this, there's a ninety-nine percent chance she'd going to rip it to shreds."

A determination that looked all too much like Lacey crossed April's face. "I know. And if that happens, I'll just keep trying. Until she tells me herself that she never wants to see me again, I'm not giving up."

I didn't have the heart to tell her that overcoming the stubborn gene she'd passed to her daughter might be the bigger challenge.

10

APRIL

Thirteen years earlier...

*L*acey's little fingers stroked sleepily through the dark hair at the back of Tony's neck as he carried her up the stairs to her pink bedroom. "Gotta read me a story, Daddy," she mumbled into his shoulder.

He chuckled. "Always with the stories, huh, baby girl?"

Lacey didn't answer. She was already asleep when he placed her tiny body down on the bed that still looked too big for her. He fondly smoothed her hair from her forehead and dropped a kiss there. "Sleep well, my Lacey. I love you."

The tender scene caused a lump in my throat. And when Tony left our daughter's side and wrapped his arms around me, we both just watched her sleep for the longest time. As we stood there, I counted my blessings. Not just my beautiful, smart, funny daughter. But for the man beside me. Just a few months ago, I'd been worried he wouldn't see Lacey's fifth birthday. And now here we were, with a five-year-old, her daddy in good health and continuing to improve every day. Even still, I clutched him a little tighter.

Like he so often did, Tony could read my mood. "I'm fine, baby. You heard the doctor. I'll be fighting fit in no time."

Thanks to the medication. That was what had made all the difference. He'd been touch and go when we'd finally taken him to the hospital, booking him in under Lawson's health insurance. The doctors had warned me over and over that he wouldn't make it. But my man was a fighter. And he'd fought every day since to keep himself here. For me, and for Lacey. But as it so often did, guilt trickled in. That medication cost hundreds of dollars a month. Lawson's insurance card was the only thing keeping Tony alive.

We'd committed a crime in getting Tony the help he needed. And while our backs had been against the wall, the guilt ate at my conscience.

I buried my face in Tony's chest and breathed in his familiar scent. Then I pulled myself together and smiled brightly at him. I didn't want to dwell on what we were doing. It sucked me into a bad place, where my head yelled accusations about the decisions I'd made. I didn't want to hear it. There'd been no alternative, I knew that, but the voices threatened to drag me down anyway.

Tony held me tight for a moment, but when I didn't voice my worries, he kissed my forehead, too. "Going to put the trash out. The collectors come tomorrow morning."

I moved away. "I'll just tuck Lacey in, and then I'll be down."

He swatted me on the behind, lightening my mood a little, and went down the stairs. There was a rustle from the kitchen, and his footsteps scratched along the wooden floors, headed for the front door.

I went to Lacey's side, kneeling by her bed, and tugged the covers up to her shoulders, tucking her in firmly so she wouldn't get cold during the night. I found the switch for the lamp on her bedside table and turned it off before pushing to my feet.

There was a screech of tires outside, and then the crash of a trash can hitting the ground, empty cans jangling across the potholed pavement. I glanced out the window, shaking my head at the disappearing taillights of a yellow sports car, fishtailing around the far corner of the road.

Trash covered asphalt, the can that had been hit on its side, spewing apple cores and beer bottles.

Amongst the mess, a dark shape lay motionless.

A tiny cry escaped my lips.

And then I was running for the stairs, thundering down them, tripping in my haste to get outside. I didn't feel the pain as I fell. I scrambled back to my feet and bolted out the door, across the lawn, and onto the street.

A blood-curdling scream echoed through my ears, and for a moment, I didn't realize it came from me. I dropped to my knees, the asphalt taking off the top layer of skin, but I didn't feel it.

Tony's body was completely lifeless, his eyes wide open, a trickle of blood falling from the corner of his mouth.

One by one, people came out of their houses. Their touches on my shoulder didn't register through the screams of panic and pain that engulfed my body. I couldn't make sense of anything. Somebody pulled me away, and I fought them off, struggling to get back to the man I loved.

Willa from next door, Colt's mom, came running across her lawn, already in her pajamas, her feet bare. Through the blood rushing in my ears, I registered her presence. She was my friend. We had coffee together sometimes, while we watched the kids play. I knew she was a nurse.

"Willa, please," I yelled. "Please!"

I couldn't say more than that. I wanted to plead for her to help him. Beg for her to keep him alive. Do that thing doctors and nurses did, where they pounded on his chest and breathed into his mouth until he jerked upright, and we'd all relax in relief and maybe even smile because he was okay.

But Willa looked up at me with grief-stricken eyes. She grabbed my hand.

All I could think was that her hands were cold. So cold. Or maybe it was mine. I didn't know.

"April, stop. He's gone."

I didn't know what she meant. Stop what? Gone where?

Lacey's cry of fear cut through all the rest.

Instinct to protect my child reared its head, and I jerked, spinning around until I spotted her.

My sweet girl stood in the doorway, watching it all with tears streaming down her face, Colt's little arm protectively wrapped around her shoulders.

11

COLT

The mattress beneath my back bounced as I tossed the football toward the sloped ceiling of my bedroom, idly watching it fall back to land in my hands with a thud.

I threw it again.

And again.

I caught it easily each time, little skill required to keep it from bouncing to the floor and rolling across my room. But I liked the repetitive movement. It gave me time to think.

Though all I thought about was Lacey.

But that was a million times better than thinking about the alternatives. My lawyer was taking me to the police station tomorrow, to give a full statement about my involvement in the Providence School for Girls fire.

I didn't imagine it going well. Even if my lawyer managed to keep me out of jail, how long would it be before Waller found something that did stick? It was clear they had it in for me. When were the police ever on the side of a poor kid from the slums? They lined their pockets with dirty cash and didn't think twice about it. I'd scored a lucky break in having Liam Banks on my side. He'd seemed certain they didn't have enough to form a case against me. He'd coached me on what to say, and what not to say, but I wasn't good at that stuff. I was no actor. I'd done what I'd done. I wouldn't regret it. I wouldn't lie, and I wouldn't fudge the truth. I'd been there to talk to Lawson Knight. And in the process, I'd saved his niece.

Then fallen in love with her.

Fuck.

I paused at a knock on the door downstairs, and for the tiniest second, hoped it was Lacey. But I'd heard every word of her argument with Aria. She wouldn't want to know me now that she knew what Aria had accused her uncle of.

I loved Lacey, but I knew my sister. She was just like me. Neither of us were liars. Lacey hadn't heard Aria crying in the bedroom below mine. She hadn't seen her change from the bubbly, outgoing girl who had big dreams for her future, to the girl she was now, who'd distanced herself from all her friends and rarely left the house.

Lawson Knight was a rapist.

There was no doubt in my mind.

But Lacey wouldn't see that. How could she? She'd loved the man like a father. So I went back to throwing the ball in the near darkness of my bedroom, only a single low-watt lamp casting a vaguely orange glow in the darkness.

"We're selling home security, ma'am," a feminine voice floated up the stairs.

I snorted, grateful I wasn't the one who'd had the unfortunate luck of dealing with a door-to-door salesman. I waited for Aria to slam the door in the woman's face, but when that didn't come, I determined my mom had been the unlucky fool. She could never say no to these people. She always had to politely listen to their spiel, then she'd try to kindly inform them we didn't need any of whatever they were selling, and then they'd take advantage of her kind nature and keep her talking with inane questions because she was too nice to just shut the door on their faces.

I was an asshole, so it was usually me who saved her.

But not tonight. I didn't have it in me to move from my spot on this bed.

Something scratched along the outside wall, like a tree branch, scraping in the wind. Except I'd pruned back the big old tree in our front yard not that long ago. I knew for a fact that unless the wind had snapped a branch right off the tree and sent it hurtling through the air, it had no chance of touching the house.

It wasn't even windy.

But when the noise came again, curiosity got the better of me. I placed the ball down on my bed and sat up, peering outside the window. It wasn't a big window, and it was slightly higher than my current eye level, so all I could see was the night sky.

Downstairs, the woman still blathered on about home safety. A dark shape moved across my eyeline, right as the woman launched into the top ten reasons to have locks on your upstairs windows. Muscles tightening, I sprang to my feet, not entirely sure what to do when there was someone outside your third-story bedroom. Did I push them off the roof? Shit, that could end in me facing a second murder charge. That wasn't a short fall, and I somehow doubted Liam would be excited if I called and told him I was responsible for the person lying in a mangled heap on my lawn.

Maybe I could wait for them to come inside and then beat the shit out of them? That seemed a better option. I moved into the darkest corner of my room and waited. Silently, I balled my fingers into fists, adrenaline spiking through my body. The window was unlocked. As usual. It was on the third fucking story, why the hell would I lock it? If people around here wanted to rob you, they weren't particularly stealthy about it. They'd just watch the house until no one was home and then break a window on the ground floor. Or they'd storm the house with a gun and rely on you being scared shitless of retaliation, to prevent you from calling the cops afterward.

They didn't climb buildings like the Spiderman outside.

The window cracked open. Downstairs, Mom chatted on. I couldn't call out or I'd give away any element of surprise I had.

I dropped into a fighter's stance, irritation rolling through me, fueling the fire inside. Fuck this guy. Thinking he could just enter my house like this.

"Jagger! Shit. Hold it steady," a voice whisper-shouted from outside.

The fight went straight out of me like a fizzled balloon, and I rushed to the window.

Lacey's head jerked, her big brown eyes blinking at me in the darkness. She clutched at the top of the ladder she was perched on. "Uh, hi?"

I just stared at her, trying to work out what the fuck was going on. And then I peered past her to Jagger, who stood at the base of the ladder. "What the hell are you two doing?" I hissed. "You're going to get yourself killed. Or arrested." I grabbed Lacey's arm, suddenly terrified she'd topple off the ladder. With my free hand, I shoved the window all the way up and dragged her inside.

On the ground, Jagger did a silent victory dance, fist pumping the air before pulling the ladder away from the window. Another figure appeared from the direction of our front door, and I knew instantly by the golden curls shining in the streetlight, it was Lacey's friend, Meredith. She wasn't decked out like Jagger and Lacey in all black. Was she wearing a business suit? But she ran to pick up the other end of the ladder, and she and Jagger disappeared into the night.

I whirled on Lacey.

She tugged off a black beanie, her long dark hair falling down her back. "Surprise?"

"Surprise? I was just standing there, contemplating pushing you off the roof or kicking your ass!"

She grimaced. "That wouldn't have been great."

"You don't say!"

She frowned. "Don't be mad. I just wanted to see you."

All my anger, completely fueled by shock and worry, went out of me. And I remembered exactly why she'd had to go to such lengths to get my attention. I'd handed my phone to Mom when Lacey had called earlier. Let her do my dirty work for me. But now Lacey was forcing me to be the one who ended this.

I didn't want to. This was exactly why I'd been avoiding her all day. "You can't be here."

"So I've been told. And yet, here I am." She moved to my bed and perched on the edge of it.

I leaned back against the wall, folding my arms over my chest, a tiny smile pulling at my lips. But then I remembered what Aria had told her today, and the smile disappeared.

"You know the full story now. About Aria. So why are you here?"

"Because we need to talk. About that. About your arrest. About what happens now."

She was right. We did. But she wasn't going to like what I had to say. And neither did I. It was easier to just let my gaze drift to her sexy-as-fuck mouth and remember what it had felt like pressed to mine.

Pink flushed her cheeks. "Stop it."

"What?"

"You're staring at my mouth like you want to kiss me."

"I do."

She sucked in a breath. "Then kiss me."

I shook my head. "Can't."

"Because of your lawyer?"

"And because of my sister. And because you're with Banjo and Rafe, and how the fuck do I fit into that?"

She threw her hands up in the air. "You were okay with it last night."

She was right. It was a lame excuse. I'd spent half my day thinking up half-baked excuses why we shouldn't be together. Truth was, I was still okay with it. If they made Lacey happy in ways I didn't, then I was good with that. I wanted Lacey in whatever capacity she'd have me. But I'd promised my mom and Aria that I'd stay away from her, at least until my lawyer sorted out any charges that were going to be brought against me. "Maybe it's better if we just end this now."

"No."

I raised an eyebrow. "No?"

"You heard me."

I couldn't help it. I strode across the room to stand in front of her. She looked up at me with those huge eyes that somehow seemed to reach right into my soul. They always had. Goddamn her. I tucked a stray piece of hair behind her ear, and she closed her eyes, leaning into the tiny touch.

I pulled my hand away. "I'm trying to make this easier for you. For both of us."

She pushed to her feet, her eyes full of fire. "And what if

I don't want easy? Not from you. I knew what I was getting into. And yeah, Colt. You make my life one complicated mess. But you aren't the only one. That doesn't stop me from loving them. And it doesn't stop me from loving you."

The words hit me so hard I couldn't breathe. "Take it back."

"No."

I scraped a hand through my hair. "Lacey, take it back."

She inched forward so her breasts grazed my chest. Her gaze locked with mine, and I saw her steely determination. It was just one of the things I loved about her.

"Colt. I love you. Deal with it."

I snorted on a laugh.

A smile curved her lips, and when I shook my head, gave in, and grasped the back of her neck, her smile grew wider.

"Least romantic 'I love you' in the history of forever," I whispered against her lips before I claimed them with my own.

She fisted her fingers in my shirt, dragging me closer, drawing me in with her intoxicating scent. I loved this girl. There was no doubt in my mind about that. I had no idea what to do with it, or even how to say it. Gillian and I had never been big on I love yous. It wasn't in either of our natures.

But I could show Lacey. I gripped her hips and hoisted her into my arms. Her legs wrapped around my waist, her arms around my neck. I slanted my head, deepening the kiss. Our tongues slid together, and I walked her to the wall, pressing her into it so I felt every inch of her body pressed tight to mine.

But then she dropped her legs, standing up on her own again, and pushed me away. She gave me the cheekiest grin. "And this is where you say, and repeat after me, because I know you prefer to communicate in grunts, single syllables, and kisses that make me want to rip your clothes off. But sometimes a girl likes to hear things, too. So say, Lacey…"

She was something else. A little firecracker with a whip-smart sense of humor. And she could read me like an open book. "Lacey," I repeated, trying to hold back my laughter.

She frowned and batted my chest with the back of her hand. "Quit laughing! This is serious business."

I raised one eyebrow. "Get on with it then, because I'd rather get back to the idea of ripping clothes off."

"Say, Lacey, I love you, too."

Her voice faltered on the last word, telling me that while she came off as tough and confident that I felt the same way about her, she really wasn't one-hundred-percent sure. And fuck. Suddenly, that got to me.

"I'm not saying that."

Her gaze filled with disappointment and dropped to the floor. "Oh."

I put my finger beneath her chin and tipped it up. She had her eyes squeezed closed.

"Lacey. Look at me."

She shook her head.

I rolled my eyes. "Can you quit being stubborn for two seconds while I tell you in my own fucking words how much I love you?"

To my surprise, she didn't open her eyes. "Lace?"

She shook her head. "I can't. I'll cry."

"Fine. That's all you're getting then."

She opened her eyes and laughed. "Now who's being unromantic?"

I shrugged. But then I leaned down and stole another kiss, because maybe we didn't do words well, but we got an A+ in chemistry.

I pushed her up against the wall again, caging her in, my hands either side of her head. "This can only be behind closed doors."

She pouted.

I thumbed her bottom lip. "For now. I've got to go give a statement to the police. Then we'll see what happens."

"Liam will handle it. You don't need to worry."

"He thinks they'll charge me with trespassing. And maybe breaking and entering."

Her mouth dropped open. "Are you serious? You broke in to save me from a fire! Can't I testify on your behalf or something?"

"Let's hope it doesn't get that far. Trespassing might just be a fine. Or maybe community service... And technically, I was trespassing."

She huffed out an angry sigh. "Chief Waller needs a good throat punch."

"If we go back to training, I could teach you." I grinned at her. "Man, I'd love to watch that. He'd never even see it coming from you."

She grinned. "I want to train again."

I cocked my head to one side, then put my lips closer to her ear. "You remembering what happened last time we trained?"

"When you pulled a gun on me?"

I chuckled. "I was talking more about how close I was to getting those little gym shorts off you and taking you right there on those mats."

A shiver ran through her at the memory.

"We can meet there, after hours. No one needs to know."

She nodded, but then she bit her lip. "It's Thanksgiving next weekend."

"Yeah, so? You gonna be too full of turkey to train with me?"

She shook her head. "It's just...Banjo lives with me now, so I know he'll be there. And after everything that happened last night with Rafe's dad, I don't know that he's going home either. I was thinking I could make Thanksgiving dinner. For all of us."

I frowned. "I don't know how I could swing that. Even if Liam gets my charges dropped or downgraded to a fine, I should probably spend the day with Mom and Aria...."

"What if they came, too? Coach as well?"

"Have you told your aunt about what her husband did to my sister?" I tried to keep any accusation out of my voice. I didn't want this to be a thing between us. What her uncle had done wasn't her fault.

"No," she admitted. "It's not that I don't believe Aria. But I just can't say those words to Selina. How could I? It would destroy her."

I nodded. "I understand."

"You do?"

"Yeah, but I think it's better I stay away. It's your prerogative not to tell her. But it would be too hard for me to sit at the table of the man who'd done that to my sister. And I couldn't ask my mom or Aria to do it either."

"I wasn't thinking. I'm sorry."

I pressed a kiss to her forehead. "How the hell did this all get so complicated?"

She wrapped her arms around my waist and laid her head on my chest. "I don't know. All I know is I love you."

"I love you, too," I murmured.

But even as I said the words, I wondered if they'd be our downfall.

12

LACEY

Rafe still hadn't gone home when Monday morning rolled around. But he and Banjo had left our little pool house love nest at some ungodly hour, citing early football practice. I'd just buried my head beneath the pillow; grateful I wasn't a jock.

I'd found Selina sipping her morning coffee in the kitchen and pulled up the stool next to her when she patted it. Angelique put a steaming mug in front of me, and I thanked her profusely before taking a sip.

"Excited about the long weekend?" Selina asked.

I shifted so I was facing her. "Actually, I wanted to talk to you about that. Thanksgiving in particular."

"First one without Lawson," she said quietly.

It punched me hard in the gut that I hadn't even really considered that. Or how she might feel about our first holiday without him. Guilt swamped me. I'd been replaying Aria's accusations for the last twenty-four hours; trying to reconcile the man she claimed my uncle was, with the gentle, kind soul who'd taught me how to ride a bike. I just couldn't comprehend how he was capable of such evil.

Yet, I hadn't doubted Aria. If anything, I doubted myself and my poor judgment of character. I'd overlooked the evil in Owen, too. I was obviously good at only seeing what I wanted to see.

"I was thinking about making a big Thanksgiving dinner. We have Banjo here now, and he has no family to go to. I wanted to make it special for him."

Selina put her cup down so hastily milky-brown liquid sloshed over the sides and onto the white marble counter-top. "Yes! I think that's a great idea. We'll give Angelique the day off, and I'll help you cook. We can make all the traditional sides."

I found myself nodding at her excitement, though neither of us were a whiz in the kitchen, spoiled by Angelique's mouthwatering meals. Instantly, I imagined smoke pouring from the oven in black plumes, and pumpkin pie with soggy crust. But I loved the idea of the two of us spending the entire day together making a feast for the people we loved.

She pulled a notepad from the junk drawer, and a pen, and turned to a clean fresh page. "Right, so there'll be you, me, and Banjo, of course. I'll invite Pamela. If that's okay with you?"

"Of course." I'd always found my aunt's best friend a little hard to relate to, but she and Selina were tight, and the woman's husband was never home, always away on some sort of business trip, so she probably wouldn't have plans.

For the same reason, Meredith came to mind. "I'll bet Meredith's parents will be out of town. So she'll come, too."

"Rafe? I noticed he stayed here again last night."

I cringed. "Do you mind?"

"No, but he's probably going to have to face whatever is going on at home sooner or later, don't you think?"

"He'll be hard pressed to avoid it when his problem is the ruler of our school."

Selina's wrinkled her nose. "Can't blame him for avoiding his father. That man is a painful leech."

That was putting it nicely. I steered the conversation back to Thanksgiving. "I'll ask him. Maybe Jagger and her family, too?"

"I'd love to meet them," Selina agreed, jotting their names down on the list. "Colt?"

I shook my head quickly. Probably too quickly, if Selina's raised eyebrows were anything to go by.

"I thought he was part of your posse now?"

I smiled at that. "They aren't my posse."

"Oh really? What do you call three men following you around like lovesick fools then?"

"My squad?"

We both laughed at that. I could only imagine the look of disgust Colt would grace me with if I ever called him part of my squad. "He'll be doing something with his family. They're very close."

Selina eyed me as she took a sip of her coffee. "Family is important. There's someone noticeably absent from this list. Her name starts with an A."

A prickle of irritation rubbed at me. "You are not seriously suggesting I invite April to Thanksgiving?"

She lifted one shoulder. "It was just an idea."

"A stupid one!"

Selina raised one eyebrow, and I dropped my gaze to my hands. "Sorry for yelling."

"I should think so." She leaned over and kissed my cheek before pushing her stool away from the countertop. "I need to go get ready. I have a feast to shop and prepare for. This is going to be great."

From the minute I got to school, my body kicked into autopilot. I parked my car. Went to my first class, then my second. Sat at my usual desks and watched the teachers without actually taking in anything they were saying.

My phone, bulging from the pocket of my jeans, was obnoxiously still. I'd switched it to silent but kept expecting it to buzz with a text or voicemail message from Colt. I couldn't stop thinking about him. He was supposed to be making his official statement to the police. I was half terrified they'd have found, or doctored, enough evidence to keep him this time. I had faith in Liam Banks. Lord knows his ginormous fees practically guaranteed a good result, but I wouldn't breathe easy until I saw Colt for myself.

By lunchtime, Colt still hadn't called, and I was officially worried. He should have been here by now. He'd promised last night that he'd see me at school. Banjo, Rafe, and I had been texting amongst ourselves all morning, and I knew neither of them had heard from him. I just prayed I'd walk into the cafeteria and see his cocky stare gazing back at me. I was scared to think about the alternative.

Ahead, among the crush of students, something caught my attention. I strained my neck, trying to peer around the shoulders of the boys in front of me and caught another glimpse. Flowers. A huge bouquet of assorted roses, carnations, and greenery, the display so extravagant, it could only be for a celebration.

My heart skipped a beat. I pushed past the guys in front of me and struggled to get through the mob around the administration office. Excitement bubbled up inside me, something drawing me forward, instinctively knowing it was Colt, and that those flowers were for me.

My instincts sucked.

I stopped in front of the bouquet, but when it lowered to reveal the holder's face, it wasn't Colt's beautiful dark eyes I stared into.

"Well, fancy seeing you here in the slums."

Owen's sly voice was like nails down a chalkboard. Except it screeched down my spine, ripping and tearing at my flesh, opening old wounds that had barely even healed. Every muscle in my body locked up.

Other kids still moved around us, but it was like the entire world had switched to a slow-motion blur. All I could focus on was the fact Owen, the boy who'd once been my friend, the boy who'd attacked and betrayed me, now stood in front of me in a place I should have been safe from him.

How bizarre that Saint View High, with its metal detectors, armed security guards, and near daily brawls on the campus quad, had become a place I felt safe.

"What are you doing here?" I choked out.

"Brought you flowers. Isn't that obvious?"

I stared at him, fighting down the bile that rose from my stomach at the very sight of him. Everything about him brought back that night on the beach. Him forcing himself on me. Him ripping at my clothes, while I scratched and fought and bit him.

He burst into overdone, faked laughter. "Oh, sweetie, look at your face." Then he leaned in, so it was only me who'd hear. "As if I'd waste my money on a gutter whore like you. Your pussy has been pounded so many times by the riffraff I'm scared of even standing this close to you, for fear of an STD. You finally found your people, didn't you? You fit right in here, with the rest of the trash."

I narrowed my eyes, but where Owen's voice had been quiet and deadly, mine was loud and proud. "Say what you like, Owen. I chose these people. Over you. Maybe that says more about you than about me."

A snort of laughter came from someone passing us. I couldn't tell who, and maybe it wasn't even directed at us. It could have been part of another conversation entirely. Owen glanced sharply in the direction the sound had come from. But then his anger smoothed over into a bright smile, his attention directed over my shoulder, but somehow, I knew the fake display was still for my benefit.

"Look who it is. The one ray of sunshine in this fucking shithole of despair," Owen said loudly.

Gillian stopped at my side, her silky blonde hair falling over her shoulders in waves. She glanced at me quickly, then turned away. I frowned. There was something different about her today. But before I could ponder that further, Owen thrust the flowers into her arms and gathered her to his side, wrapping an arm around her petite shoulders.

"No thank-you?" he asked, fake smile still plastered on his face, but a hint of irritation in his tone.

She gazed down at the flowers instead of at his face. "Thank you."

He seemed satisfied by that, not seeming to notice, or maybe he just didn't care that Gillian's thank-you sounded about as enthusiastic as if she were being led to slaughter. I stared at her hard, but she wouldn't meet my gaze.

"Are you coming to my masquerade party?" Owen asked, drawing my attention away from Gillian.

With a start, I realized he was asking me.

"Will there be lobotomies performed there? Because I'd rather get one than go anywhere you'll be."

He shrugged. "Just thought you could visit your dear dead uncle while you were there."

"What?"

Gillian was the one who got in first to explain. "He's—we're—throwing a party at the cemetery. Weekend after the recital."

I gawked at Gillian, but when she wouldn't meet my gaze, I turned back to Owen. "You can't have a party at the cemetery!"

"Who says I can't? It's the perfect place. Lots of open area in the middle of nowhere so we can have the music as loud as we want. Lots of dark corners to make out in. We all know you get off on public sex. I bet the graveyard really gets you going, doesn't it?"

He was such a cocky son of a bitch. "You're truly disgusting. I suppose it's too much to hope that you'd have any respect for the dead, considering you have none for the living. You do realize throwing a party there is illegal."

He leaned in closer to me, close enough his warm breath misted over my cheek. "Not so much a problem for me, is it?"

My blood boiled because he'd proven time and time again that he was above the law.

Fuck, I was sick of that.

But Owen wasn't done. He had to twist the knife. "I'm just going to be dancing all over sweet Uncle Lawson's grave. Seriously, Lacey. I'll put you and your thugs on the invite list. I'm sure your uncle will be watching over you, while you let them plow you three ways. What a show!" He pulled a dollar bill from his pocket and held it my direction. "Wouldn't mind watching myself. Here's my cover charge."

I let the dollar bill float to the floor.

My gaze locked with Owen's. Anger and frustration

burned behind his gaze. I knew all he saw in mine was steely determination. I'd stand there all day if meant I wasn't the first to back down.

In the end, Owen didn't back down either. It was Principal Simmons who bustled out of the administration offices and straight over to me. "Lacey, have you seen Rafe?"

I didn't answer.

"Lacey," he snapped.

I jerked my head in his direction. "What?"

He bristled at my tone. "Rafe. Where is he?"

I just stared at Rafe's dad. I had no loyalty to this man. If he couldn't find Rafe, it was because Rafe didn't want to be found. I wasn't about to help him.

I turned back to deal with Owen, but he and Gillian had disappeared. The lingering scent of fresh flowers and the disgust that coated my skin was the only evidence he'd even been there.

13

RAFE

With my shoulders pressed to the sun-warmed bricks at the back of the gymnasium, I took a long drag on my blunt, letting the swirl of toxins fill my chest. I closed my eyes, basking in the warmth of the winter sun, and for a moment, I could pretend I didn't have a care in the world.

"Wanna give me a drag of that?"

I blinked an eye open, then did a double take when I realized it was Colt. "Guess this means you managed not to get arrested again?"

He plucked the blunt from my hand and took a drag, blowing smoke circles into the afternoon air. "Did get charged with two counts of criminal trespassing, though. Gotta go to court. Lawyer said it'll probably just be a fine."

"How big?"

He grimaced. "Up to four G's. For each count."

"Fuck." That might as well be a million dollars to a kid from Saint View.

"Yeah."

I eyed him. "That all that happened?"

"Yeah. That's it."

But when he didn't meet my gaze, I suspected he wasn't telling me the whole truth. There was no point in pushing him, though. Years of friendship had taught me Colt wouldn't talk before he was ready. Nothing I said now would convince him otherwise, and would only push him further into his own head.

So I chose to look on the bright side and hoped my instincts were wrong. "Better than a jail cell. You tell Lacey yet? She's stressing."

"Not yet. Needed a minute to chill out."

"And you figured you'd find a sure thing back here?"

Colt sniggered and produced an unlit joint from his pocket. "Brought my own. The fact you're already here is just a bonus."

I watched while he lit his joint, and we both leaned back on the wall again, smoking side by side. A crackle from the outdoor PA system had Colt peering at the speaker above our heads. It spat out something practically unintelligible, and Colt blew a smoke ring in its direction. "Did they just call your name?"

I shrugged. "Probably." That was what had drawn me out here in the first place. "My dad has been summoning me to his office all day."

"Avoiding him?"

"Wouldn't you?"

Colt side-eyed me. "Probably. But what are you gonna do? Just pretend you didn't accuse him of a murder in front of the entire dance on Saturday night?"

"More like I'm afraid *he'll* pretend it didn't happen."

Colt's gaze turned sympathetic. "Yeah, that'd suck. You really think he did it?"

"He didn't deny it. He knew Lawson. He's got a history of

snapping and resorting to violence. He wanted his job. His life. Fuck, I dunno." I pushed off the wall, pacing back and forth in front of Colt. "It's just easier to avoid him than to actually face it. You know what the biggest thing is?"

Colt didn't answer, but his shrewd black gaze focused on me intently.

"If he did this. If he's found guilty. That's it."

Colt sighed. "He'll go to jail. I know your dad is an asshole, but that would still be hard for you to watch."

"No, that's not it. He's a violent man. Hell, if he went to jail, I'd be happy. Because it would mean he was away from my mom. She could actually have some sort of life again, you know? The one she's too scared to have now. The one he won't let her have, because he's such a controlling prick."

I stopped pacing and stared up at the clear blue sky. If my mood could have changed the weather, a storm would have rolled right on in, full of dark-gray clouds and lightning. "If he did it, that's the end of me and Lacey."

He stretched out a leg and nudged me with his foot. "Nah, man. She loves you. You aren't your father."

"You don't know that. What if I end up exactly like him?"

"You won't."

Deep in my heart, I knew he was right. I wasn't like my dad. I despised the way he thought nothing of backhanding my mother. Or throwing punches at me. I tried to imagine myself doing that to Lacey, or a child we might have someday, and the thought made me want to heave.

Colt slung an arm around my shoulders. "You aren't like him. You never have been."

I squeezed my eyes shut tight and finally voiced my real concern. "What if he did it, and that's all she can see every time she looks at me? What if all I do is remind her of someone who hurt her?"

"Did she tell you that her uncle raped Aria?"

I jerked and took a step away in shock. "Are you joking?"

He didn't need to answer that. It wasn't the sort of thing you joked about. And everything in his expression told me he was deadly serious.

"That's how I know she'll still love you, even if your dad did do it. Because I still love her, even though her uncle was a monster." Colt shrugged. "Who we come from doesn't define us. They can only take our happiness if we let them."

Colt stubbed out the butt of his joint, squashing it beneath the toe of his sneaker. "I need to go tell our girl I love her. You gonna be okay?"

I gave him a quick jerk of my head. "I'll catch up with you later. I need to go talk to my dad."

I ignored the flapping about of my father's secretary and strode down the hall to let myself into his office without knocking.

His head jerked up in surprise, but when he saw it was me, his expression darkened. "Where the hell have you been?"

I opened my mouth to answer, but then a skinny pair of arms wrapped around my middle, squeezing me tight. "Mom?"

She buried her face in my shirt, her shoulders shaking.

My father sneered at her, like her emotion revolted him. "Oh, for God's sake, Rose. Cut it out."

I shot my father a disgusted glare and wrapped my arms around my mother. I dropped a kiss on the top of her head and whispered, "I'm sorry. I should have called you."

"Damn right you should have called." My father spat the

words at me like I was scum. "You think you can just cause a scene like you did on Saturday night and then not show up for two days? Where the hell have you been?"

I glared at him. "I was at Lacey's. We both know you could have come to find me if you'd really wanted to."

"I'm not going to chase you all around town."

I fought back the urge to roll my eyes and instead concentrated on my mother. I hugged her tight, and eventually, she stepped back, raising her eyes to mine.

One was swollen, covered by makeup, but I'd bet anything it was completely black beneath the goo she'd caked on top to hide my father's sins. Guilt swamped me. He'd taken his anger at me out on her. That black eye was my fault.

"How could you?" I seethed. I wanted to launch myself across his scuffed wooden desk and wrap my fingers around his throat.

"Rafe, I ran into a cupbo—"

"Bullshit!" I yelled at her, hating the way she flinched, but fuck me, it needed to be said. I put my hands to her shoulders and guided her to a chair. But what I really wanted to do was shake her. Not hard enough to hurt her, I'd never do that. But fuck, I needed to make her listen to me. "How long are you going to let him keep doing this to you? I'm out. I'm done. I won't come back. Come with me. We'll get a place. Just you and me. Somewhere he can't keep doing this."

Mom's hand fluttered around her mouth, her eyes wide with confusion. Her gaze flicked to my father's.

But he was fully concentrated on me. "Get your hands off your mother."

"Oh, that's rich. You can beat the shit out of her, but I can't touch her? Shut up, old man. Why am I even here? So you can flaunt what you did to her? Are you trying to make me feel worse than I already do?"

His blue eyes, so like mine, were as sharp and glittering as diamonds. Without looking at it, he picked up a manila folder from his desk and threw it at me. It opened before I could catch it, sending receipts fluttering to the floor.

I made no attempt to catch them. "What's this?"

"Proof I wasn't anywhere near Providence School for Girls when Lawson Knight was killed. Receipts from everywhere I went that night."

I rolled my eyes. "You could have given your credit card to someone else. I suspect even you're smart enough to create an alibi to cover up a murder."

He lifted the phone on his desk, his finger hovering over the keypad. "You want CCTV footage? I'll get that, too." He raised one eyebrow in challenge.

I sat myself in the chair, crossing my arms over my chest, raising an identical eyebrow, accepting his challenge. "I got all the time in the world, Dad. Pretty sure you can give me a late pass to algebra, right?"

If steam could have physically come out his ears in that moment, it would have. The irritation in his expression was almost comical. But I was more than willing to call his bluff.

He stabbed some numbers into the phone, then looked at me, presumably while waiting for someone to answer his call. I didn't believe him for a second.

He rested his elbows on the desktop. "What makes you so sure it was me, anyway?"

"You mean, apart from the fact your temper is short and you have no qualms taking it out on people?"

He ground his molars so hard I expected his dentist wouldn't be happy the next time he went in for a checkup.

I leaned forward. "Because you haven't once denied it.

You haven't once said, 'I didn't kill Lawson Knight.' You were his best friend in college. He dumped your loser ass, didn't he?"

Dad smiled, but there was nothing friendly about it. "We drifted apart."

"Liar."

He tucked the phone beneath his chin and narrowed his eyes at me. "Fine. You want to know the truth? He stole my life. I met Selina first. Did you know that? We were at a bar, he and I. I saw her walk in with her best friend. All high tits and blinding white smile. Fucking beautiful."

Anger built in my gut. "Nice of you to say something like that in front of your wife."

"I already know," Mom said quietly from her chair beside me. "He's never made a secret of the fact I was his second choice."

God. How had he beat this woman down so much she stayed with him, even knowing that? I glared at him. "Selina doesn't even remember you," I accused.

"Because I never saw her again after that night. Not until years later, when Lawson and I found ourselves attending the same inter-school functions. He introduced her to me like we'd never met before. And then it made sense, why he'd completely ghosted me after that night. Anything he had was because of her. She had all the connections. All the money. Lawson wouldn't have even graduated if it hadn't been for me letting him cheat off my notes."

Someone must have answered the phone because he suddenly sat a little straighter. "Anton. Todd Simmons again. That CCTV footage we discussed? I will need it after all." He paused for a moment, then replied, "Rafe dot Simmons at gmail dot com."

A split second later, my phone binged.

Dad hung up the phone without thanking whoever it was he'd been speaking to. "Go ahead." He motioned. "Check out my alibi."

With a mixed feelings, I pulled my phone from the pocket of my jacket and brought up my email. There was a single message in my inbox, without a subject, but the sender was *Anton@dollhouse.com*.

I stabbed at the email to open it and found an attached video. I glanced up at my father.

"Press 'play'. I'm looking forward to watching you eat your words."

He was entirely too gleeful for this to have been a setup. I knew before I even hit 'play' that I'd been wrong. But I pressed it anyway, not sure whether I was stubbornly hoping I was right, or whether I was relieved the man who I shared DNA with actually wasn't a murderer.

The grainy CCTV footage was the inside of a strip club. A girl in a bikini and towering heels worked a pole, while a few lone drinkers sat around her, throwing dollar bills onto the stage. My father was in the center of the frame, clear as day, looking drunk off his ass. I checked the timestamp at the bottom right of the screen. It checked out.

He sat back smugly, crossing his arms over his chest. "I'll take that apology now."

"I'd rather eat dog shit."

"Child."

Maybe so. Maybe it was childish not to admit when I'd been wrong. But damned if this man deserved anything from me. He might not have murdered Lawson Knight, but he'd been slowly killing my mother, and me, for the past eighteen years.

But all of that was over. At least, for me.

I turned to my mother and grabbed her hands, pulling

them onto my lap. "Please. Think about what I said. I can help. You can start over."

My father cleared his throat.

In that one sound, I knew what she'd say. That was all he needed to do to remind her that he owned her.

I put her hands down gently. "Lacey is making Thanksgiving dinner on Thursday. I'd love it if you'd come."

I walked out before she could voice the no I knew was coming.

14

LACEY

I woke up at the crack of dawn on Thanksgiving morning and slipped out of bed as silently as possible in order to let the boys sleep. The last few days had been rough. The three of us had skipped school on Tuesday morning to go to Rafe's place and pack his things. He'd sent his mom a text message saying when we were coming so we didn't startle her, but she hadn't been home for the entire two hours we'd stayed there, loading Rafe's possessions into my car.

I'd seen the hurt in his eyes as he'd realized she was deliberately avoiding him, and my heart broke in two. Selina had watched us bring his things into the pool house and then engulfed him in a motherly hug of her own. I'd mouthed the words "Thank you" at her, over his shoulder. She hadn't even blinked when I'd asked if he could stay with us as well. I knew I was asking a lot of her, but her mothering instinct was strong. It always had been. And I think she maybe secretly liked having the boys there to fuss over. She'd never had a son, or even a nephew. And now, in the space of weeks, she'd found two.

Selina seemed to have a similar idea to me, because when I made my way inside the main house, she was already bustling around the kitchen in an apron, tendrils of hair escaping a messy bun that sat atop her head. She grinned as I came in and tossed a pinch of flour in my direction. "Go get dressed. We have a lot to do today."

"I agree, but it's six a.m. How long have you been at this for?"

She shrugged. "I couldn't sleep, so I thought I'd make an early start."

I frowned at the bags beneath her eyes. "Did you get any sleep at all?"

She busied herself with the dough she was kneading. "For a little bit. Nightmare woke me up, and then it was all over. I was just staring at the ceiling for hours. But hey, insomnia means we already have a pumpkin pie in the oven!"

I gave it a cursory glance, because Selina making anything from scratch, and before ten a.m., was definitely something to make a big deal over, but I was more worried about the nightmare she'd had. "Was it about Lawson? Your nightmare?"

She turned away. "I guess it was to be expected. First Thanksgiving without him and all. Brings up a lot of memories."

It did for me, too. Like how we'd spent last year eating Chinese takeout and watching movies instead of the game, because Lawson wasn't really into sports other than golf. This year would be different. Football was life to Banjo and Rafe, and I was actually grateful for it. I didn't want it to be the same as when Lawson was here. We needed to move on and make our own traditions. I was stuck in some weird place when it came to memories of him. Half of me missed him desperately and hated the sadness his absence brought with it. But I was still struggling with what he'd done to Aria. In my head, he'd morphed into two different people. One, a good, kind man who'd loved me dearly. The other a monster.

I had no idea how to think of them as a whole. And so I kept my mind on other things. It was just easier if I didn't think about him at all.

Brushing those thoughts aside, I ran upstairs to shower and dress, and when I came back, Selina handed me the list she'd made. "There's more on the back."

My eyes bulged at the sheer amount of food she'd planned to make. "This is crazy. It's just the four of us, Meredith, and Pamela, isn't it?" Jagger and her family had plans to see relatives, so they'd turned down my invitation.

Selina pulled open the refrigerator door and buried her head inside, looking for something so her voice was muffled. "Pamela is bringing a friend. There might be a couple of others, too, I'm not sure yet."

"People from tennis? It's a bit rude they haven't given you an official answer."

Selina's smile from behind a pile of fresh vegetables was flippant. "Look how much food we have. If one or two extra people show up, we'll still be eating leftovers for a month."

I eyed the biggest turkey I'd ever seen. It was practically ostrich-sized. "Is that even going to fit in the oven?"

We both tilted our heads and squinted at it.

Selina grimaced. "There's a very real chance deconstructed turkey could be on the menu tonight."

We both giggled at that, and I put on an apron to get to work.

The guys got up late and wandered up from the pool house with Rafe's arm slung over Banjo's shoulders. I smiled at their easy familiarity with each other, and grinned when they made a beeline for me, sandwiching me between them.

"It smells amazing in here," Rafe said into my hair, while Banjo claimed my lips.

His kiss was brief, respectful of the fact Selina was in the room, and when he moved back, he snatched a green bean from a bowl on the countertop. I batted at his hand but then Rafe was stealing my attention, drawing me into his arms and pressing me tight to his chest like he was scared I was going to run away.

"You okay?" I whispered.

He nodded. He'd been doing this a lot for the last two days, I'd noticed. If he and I were in the same room, he'd head straight to my side and pull me onto his lap at any opportunity. Even with Banjo, he'd become more touchy-feely than he normally was. I didn't know about Banjo, but I was loving this new affectionate side of him. Not that he'd ever really been standoffish, but until the last few days, a lot of the physical connection between us had been charged with sexual chemistry. While I still wanted to rip his clothes off constantly, I liked that he seemed content to just hold me.

There was love in his actions. That was the difference. Yet neither of us had voiced it. I needed that to change. I knew he was still hurting from his parents' rejection. I needed him to know I loved him. But the right moment hadn't come up again. We'd had no time together, just him and me. And saying I love you to someone for the first time was something that shouldn't be said with an audience.

It was midafternoon before the feast was ready, and we all got changed for lunch. The guys helped me set the huge table in the formal dining room that we never used when it was just the four of us here at home. The stools at the counter in the kitchen were so much cozier and inviting, but a special meal called for the big guns. We set the table with linen napkins, shining silver cutlery Angelique had polished the day before, and a gorgeous flower centerpiece Selina had ordered especially for the occasion.

The guys had dressed nicely, Rafe in black slacks and a white button-down. Banjo in a similar pair of pants I suspected he might have borrowed from Rafe, his shirt ocean blue. He'd scraped his hair back into a ponytail, the short lengths just barely staying within the elastic band at the nape of his neck. While I loved when his hair flopped in his face, this version of him was distinctly more grown-up and somehow even sexier than his usual beach boy vibe.

A knock at the door interrupted my ogling.

"That'll be Pamela," Selina called from the kitchen. "Can someone let her in while the others come help me start bringing out all this food? This turkey weighs a ton."

I grimaced at the guys and headed for the door. "Sounds like she needs your muscle."

Banjo flexed playfully as he walked backward out of the room, Rafe trailing after him. My gaze focused on the pop of Banjo's biceps beneath his shirt, and I drooled over the way the material strained over his muscles.

The knock at the door came again, and I pulled it open with a big smile. I hadn't seen much of my aunt's best friend lately. Selina had not so subtly started going out a lot more, giving the guys and me the run of the house. But while

Pamela was a more vapid version of Selina, a complete trophy wife whose husband paid her money instead of attention, I still liked the woman. I'd missed her the last few weeks. I was happy she'd be spending Thanksgiving with us.

Until I saw her 'friend.'

"Hey, princess."

My stomach dropped.

Banjo's brother had his arm slung around Pamela's neck, her body turned into his, her face lifted to him like she was worshipping some god.

Augie Mitchell was anything but. Sure, the porch light glinted off his closely cropped golden hair, the exact same shade as Banjo's. Sure, he had the broad shoulders, the chiseled abs, and year-round bronze skin of some Adonis. But everything beautiful about Augie was on the outside.

On the inside, he was mean. Cold. Cruel. This was the man who had tried to push Banjo into prostituting himself because money meant more than happiness. This was the man who had nearly destroyed the boy I loved.

"What are you doing here?" I bit out.

Pam frowned. "What? Selina invited me."

Augie chuckled. "She doesn't mean you, sugar. Lacey and I go way back."

Pamela's mouth dropped open. "You don't mean..." Her gaze darted frantically between Augie and me.

I scrunched up my face in disgust. "Ugh, Pamela. No. I wouldn't touch him with a ten-foot pole. I need a hazmat suit just being this close to him."

"Lacey! Don't be so rude." She stepped a little closer to him, as if it were Augie who needed protection. He clenched his arm around her more tightly.

I could have gagged. What the hell was this? Was he her boyfriend? That wasn't wholly surprising. She was married but only in name. Everybody knew she and her husband lived completely separate lives. Or had she paid him to be here? My head spun.

Selina appeared at the door behind me, completely oblivious to the tension between Pamela and me, and no clue as to who Augie was. She squealed and pushed past me, throwing her arms around Pamela like they hadn't just seen each other two days ago at their personal trainer's. She pulled her friend inside, and there was nothing I could do but step aside while Pamela introduced Augie to my aunt.

Watching the situation rapidly spiral out of control, there was only one thing left for me to do. I left the others standing in the doorway, hanging up their coats, and high-tailed it to the kitchen.

"Hey, babe? Where do you want the beans?" Banjo asked, picking up a glass bowl full of vegetables. "Do these go on the table now or—"

"Banjo, I—"

He looked up from the dish, his gaze meeting mine only briefly before sliding past me.

The bowl slipped from his grasp, smashing onto the kitchen tiles and shattering into a zillion sparkling pieces.

"Oh no." Selina rushed forward but stopped when she took in Banjo's horrified expression. "Hey, sweetie, it's okay. Nobody really likes green beans anyway."

She was completely oblivious to the silent nightmare playing out behind her.

"Pam?" Banjo choked out.

I gawked at him. That was not what I'd expected him to say. "What? You know her?"

But it was like Banjo hadn't even heard me. His gaze darted between Pamela and his brother.

Augie's delighted laughter filling the room. "Well, isn't this quite the reunion?"

I glared at him. Pamela elbowed him and shot a panicked glance at Selina, who still seemed completely oblivious, distracted by getting out the Hoover to clean up the mess.

"Get out," Banjo growled.

That finally got Selina's attention. She jerked around and stared at him like he'd grown another head. I couldn't blame her. She only knew him as the easygoing sweetheart he was. She wasn't used to him speaking in that tone.

"Banjo?" she questioned carefully, like he was a time bomb about to go off.

"Augie is his brother," I explained.

"And Pam pays him for sex," Banjo said coldly. He turned to me. "She was the one, that night when I finally left and came here. She was supposed to be my first client."

My mouth fell open at the exact same time Selina's did.

She whirled on her best friend. "Is that true?"

Pamela bristled, but her cheeks were pink. "Augie and I have a...physical agreement, yes."

"What about Banjo? Fuck, Pamela! He's barely eighteen." Protective anger laced Selina's tone this time. I wasn't even shocked that she'd casually dropped an F-bomb.

"I thought his name was Jordan! That's what he told me. I didn't know he knew Lacey. Or that he was eighteen."

Augie snorted. "Yeah, you did. You liked how young he is."

Pamela shot him a dirty look. "He's of legal age."

"There is no legal age for prostitution!" Selina spun on Augie. "What are you acting so smug about? You preyed on your brother. You think that makes you the big man?"

Augie lost all trace of humor. His eyes darkened. "Watch yourself, bitch."

That was the wrong thing to say.

The tether that had been keeping Banjo in place snapped in the face of a direct threat to Selina. He launched himself across the space, swinging punches at his brother. Selina and Pamela both yelped and scuttled to the far side of the kitchen, away from flying fists.

Banjo's body crashed into Augie's, sending them both back into the drywall that protested with a crack.

"Banjo! Stop," I screamed, helpless to do anything to stop the two brothers from pummeling each other. My screams brought Rafe running from the dining room. He took one look at the commotion and threw himself right into the middle of it.

"Stop," I screamed again. In the back of my mind, I was on the beach again, completely helpless while Colt pounded the shit out of Owen, until he was so beaten and bloody I thought he was dead. My stomach rolled at the sound of flesh against flesh.

Something cracked, and then there was a howl of pain, though I had no idea who it came from. Blood spattered against the white walls as the three of them tussled. Pamela and my aunt stood clutching at each other, eyes wide, but doing nothing to stop them.

I glanced around the room, searching for something I could use to break them up, but all I could see was oven mitts and dishwasher detergent and the world's biggest turkey, baked to perfection and currently getting cold. I doubted a drumstick was going to be of any use with the three of them determined to kill each other. With nothing better to use, I yanked the fire extinguisher from one of the kitchen cupboards, popped the released ring, and pointed it at the three men. "I said, stop!"

Gusting bouts of white powder sprayed out, covering the three of them.

But it had the desired effect. All three stopped at stared at me, bewildered expressions on their faces.

"Get out, Augie." I seethed, pushing my way between him and my guys. "Before I call the cops. Don't ever come back here." And then I spun on Pamela. "You, too. I can't even look at you right now."

She shot a dismayed glance at Selina.

Selina just nodded. "We'll talk about it later. Just go. Your date appears to need medical attention anyway."

Blood dripped onto Augie's lips, his nose noticeably out of place and already swelling. Something inside me was oddly satisfied by that. Banjo shook out his right hand, and I suspected he'd been the one who'd gotten in the punch that had caused the break. I almost wanted to high-five him.

But nobody was moving. I shook the fire extinguisher as threateningly as possible in Augie's direction. "Get out!"

Pamela went to his side and led him to the door, Augie swearing about his nose until the front door opened and then closed behind them.

It was only then, in the silence that followed, that Banjo looked over at me.

I'd expected pain. Or confusion. Maybe even sorrow in his face.

But instead, he just stared at me still clutching the fire extinguisher like it was a knife.

He burst into hysterical laughter. Rafe followed quickly, and slowly, Selina joined in.

"It's not funny!" I wailed, the fire extinguisher slipping

from my fingers and clattering to the floor. But I couldn't help it. Their laughter was infectious. At least now that Augie was gone and neither Banjo nor Rafe seemed particularly hurt.

Selina's smile was the first to fall. She reached out and took Banjo's hand, squeezing it. "I'm so sorry. I had no idea what Pamela was doing with your brother...or that she was the one...I would have never brought her here if I'd known."

Banjo put his arm around Selina. "Hey, shh. It wasn't your fault. You've been nothing but amazing to me. And I've gone and ruined everything. Shit. Look at this mess."

"Doesn't matter," I told him. "Unless Selina's tennis buddies show up, it's just the four of us and Meredith anyway. She won't care. We'll just clean this up and pretend none of that ever happened. Augie who?"

He grinned at me, but Selina cleared her throat.

"Uh-oh," Rafe said quietly.

I knew exactly what he was talking about. Selina's face was swamped with guilt and worry.

Unease churned in my gut. "Why do I suddenly feel like we're headed to the gallows?"

She let out a long breath, then turned to me, as guilty as a toddler caught with her hand in the cookie jar. "For the sake of not losing any more serving bowls, I need to tell you something. It's not just us and Meredith. And I didn't invite anyone from tennis. Lacey, I invited your mother."

15

LACEY

Any trace of lingering humor disintegrated in the silence. "You what?"

Selina picked up my hand and pressed her fingers into my palm. "Sweetheart, I know I'm not biologically your parent."

I hated when she talked like that. "You're still my mom."

"And as such, I know you better than anyone. Your mother was taken from you before you were really even old enough to remember. Don't you want to know why?"

"No," I snapped. "Maybe I did back then, when I was a kid. But she hasn't been here, Sel. She's missed everything. She obviously wasn't being held captive in some slumlord's prison. She could have come back at any time. But she didn't."

"Sweetheart, you're eighteen. You have your entire life ahead of you. There's still time for you to know her if you want to."

"I don't."

"I don't believe that. I saw the curiosity in your face when she was here."

I didn't want to hear that. I tried so hard to hide it; I wasn't about to admit it now. "That wasn't curiosity, that was terror."

Selina sighed. "Maybe in the beginning. But she's the only one with the answers to your questions, Lace. I don't have them. Lawson is dead. Don't you at least want the opportunity to ask?"

"Where did you even get her number?"

"From her card."

"What card?" I growled.

Her eyebrows furrowed at that. "It was on a shelf in the pool house. I noticed it the other day when we were moving Rafe in. I thought she must have given it to you."

"I don't know what you're talking about."

Rafe groaned, still brushing fire extinguisher powder from his clothes. "Banjo, dammit. You didn't?"

Selina and I both whirled in Banjo's direction. "You didn't what?" I demanded.

Banjo's expression was full of sheepish guilt. "April and George approached us when we were playing football in the park last weekend. She gave me her card."

Rafe raked his hands through his hair. "I told you to just leave it be!"

"I know. And you were right." He focused on me again. "I'm sorry. I shouldn't have let her involve us. It's just...she wants to know you. I felt sorry for her, so I took her card."

Anger surged through me. A little of it directed at Banjo but most of it directed at April. How dare she go around behind my back, speaking to my friends about me. Who the hell else had she contacted?

He stepped in closer so I had to tilt my head back to look up at him. His green eyes were full of sincere remorse. "I'm sorry. I should have told you."

"Agreed."

"I just thought you might want her number. Not now, obviously. But maybe for sometime in the future."

The doorbell chimed through the house.

None of us moved.

"It could be Meredith," Rafe said quietly.

Selina shoved her hands in the pockets of her apron. "Meredith would have just let herself in."

"It's April," I said dully.

Selina crossed the space between us. "Say the word and I'll tell her to leave. The ball is in your court, Lacey."

A fierce determination shone in her eyes. I loved this woman. She was so incredibly selfless. It couldn't be easy for her, with my mother back in town. And yet here she was, putting me first. Always thinking about me before herself. She was the true definition of a mother. It didn't matter that we didn't share a single strand of DNA.

I couldn't be upset with her.

Especially when deep down, I knew she was right. I did want to know what had happened. What had made her leave? If it had been my fault, like I'd always quietly suspected. She'd left me behind. Forgotten me.

Only she could tell me why.

I pulled my shoulders back stiffly. "I'll add another place to the dining room table."

From between my spot in the middle of the long table, flanked by Rafe and Banjo, all I could do was stare at my plate. I slowly cut the food that someone had placed in front of me and chewed without tasting it.

I didn't need to look up to know that everyone was

watching me. Rafe and Banjo both periodically squeezed my leg beneath the table, a show of silent support, whenever they didn't need both hands for their food. From the head of the table, Selina's worry was evident in the tone of her voice. Meredith sat to her left, and the two of them kept up a constant stream of mindless chatter, which nobody else joined in with.

I couldn't lift my head, because George and April sat directly opposite me. George seemed happy to help himself to great portions of food, which he shoved into his mouth at rapid speed, like he hadn't eaten a home-cooked meal in a month. But I was well aware that April barely touched the tiny amount of food on her plate. She stabbed absently at it, while staring at a photo of Lawson and Selina in front of an old yellow sports car they'd owned before they'd taken custody of me. When I looked up, she caught my eye, quiet this time, instead of yelling demands like the last time we'd been in this house together. Not one person mentioned what had happened. It was the elephant in the room. A giant, gray, suffocating elephant that might as well have been sitting directly on my chest.

Meredith chattered on, filling the silence as best she could, even though she and Selina really only had so much in common. "So then my nail artist told me about this new brand they were using, but do you think it was even close to as pretty as the one—"

Rafe's phone buzzed on the table, and when he picked it up, he grimaced, flashing the screen at me. His mom.

"Answer it," I told him. "Take it in my bedroom so you can have some privacy. You're not missing anything here."

He seemed reluctant, but he went anyway, taking the phone, and my only distraction from the inane chatter with him.

After another minute, I couldn't take it any longer. I shoved my chair back, the legs scraping along the tiled floor. Banjo pulled his hand back into his lap. I picked up my empty wine glass because I'd already gulped down the entire contents and tapped it with a fork. "I'd like to make a speech."

The tinny pinging noise was effective at silencing Meredith's chatter. She nodded at me encouragingly.

I let out a long breath. "Since it's Thanksgiving, I feel like I should say what I'm grateful for, right?"

April's gaze was pinned to mine, but it was full of uncertainty. I suspected mine matched. I really had no idea what I was doing, standing up in the middle of dinner like this. All I knew was I couldn't continue to sit there and listen to nail chat. The tension in the air was so thick I could hardly breathe. Every muscle in my body was wound too tight. Something had to release the pressure.

And apparently, I was going to do it by running my mouth.

I focused on Meredith. "I'm thankful for my friend, who is making the best of this uncomfortable meal by attempting polite conversation."

Meredith grimaced but recovered quickly and let out a "Woo!"

It fell on deaf ears.

I turned to Banjo. "I'm thankful for you, and for Rafe. I hate the circumstances that have led to the two of you being here today, without your families, but I'm selfishly happy you're here with us."

Which led me to Selina. "And mostly, I'm thankful for you. For taking in Banjo and Rafe when their families cast them out." Anger bubbled up inside me as I turned to April. "And for taking in me, when mine did the same."

April shot to her feet. "Stop!"

"The truth hurts, huh?" I sank down into my chair and glared at her, well aware of the awkward stares from the other people at the table. But I didn't care. I was too angry. I just wanted her gone. I couldn't force the words from my mouth, but didn't she feel it? The animosity I had for her? I shrugged like I didn't give a shit. Though I did. I cared too much. I cared so much it was ripping me to shreds inside.

"You're right, Lacey. The truth does hurt. The truth has ripped me apart every day for the past thirteen years. But what you just said, about me abandoning you? That isn't the truth. That's complete and utter fiction. I never abandoned you. Not for one minute."

She paused, her bottom lip trembling. "Lawson and Selina stole you from me."

"What?" I choked out, but my question was overshadowed by Selina's shout of anger.

"April, what the hell?" She shoved to her feet so she and April were eye to eye, with only the humongous, now half-stripped turkey and a group of bewildered teenagers glancing between them like they were at a tennis match. "How dare you say something like that. After that stunt you pulled last week, you should be in jail. Yet I kept quiet. I opened my home to you, because I feel so desperately sorry for all the years you missed, and yet you throw out a ridiculous accusation like that? What kind of a woman are you?"

"One who doesn't lie, like you do." April swiveled back to me, voice shrill. "They stole you. He wouldn't let me see you. He set me up."

George reached over and put a calming hand on her arm. "We should go. This isn't helping."

But she shook him off. "No! I won't be silenced any

longer. What I did back then was wrong. It was illegal. We should have never used Lawson's health insurance—"

"What are you even talking about?" Selina asked.

My thoughts exactly.

"Don't pretend like you weren't in on it. You've held that over my head for the last thirteen years. Threatened to send me to prison over it multiple times. It's been a noose around my neck. How easy it was for the two of you to take advantage of the woman desperate enough to do anything to save her husband."

Selina's expression was as bewildered as mine probably was.

"I don't understand any of this," I muttered. "Can someone please explain?"

April opened her mouth to speak, but Selina got in first, silencing her with a look that could have killed. She turned sad eyes on me. "I never wanted to tell you. Especially not like this. Your mother was an addict. On the day you were brought to me, you were found in the closet of your bedroom. She'd locked you in. You'd been there two days."

I whirled on my mother. "Is that true? You were a junkie?"

Her eyes pleaded with me to understand. "Not like you're thinking. I wasn't shooting up or smoking. You father had just died. I was depressed. Lawson brought me pills—"

I held up a hand. "Stop. Just stop. I can't even hear it. You locked me in a closet?"

April didn't answer.

"You did, didn't you?"

She couldn't look me in the eye. "I put you in the closet, yes. But—"

"There is no buts. Get out."

"Lacey, no."

"You said you'd leave when I told you to leave. I'm telling you. Get out. Of my house and my life. Don't come back."

George stood quietly and put his arm around April's shoulders. "We'll leave."

"No," April said miserably. "No, no, no. Please, Lacey. Please!"

I couldn't stand to face her a moment longer. So many years I'd spent thinking about her. About why she'd left. Wondering what I'd done. But it hadn't been me. It was her. She'd chosen drugs over her daughter. I was as worthless to her as a used syringe.

Now I was just as empty. I stood and left the room, leaving my mother behind. As my heart broke in two, I wondered if she'd felt even a smidgen of this pain when she'd been the one to walk away. Because it was a pain I knew I wouldn't forget.

16

APRIL

Thirteen years earlier...

I may as well have had cement boots on. That's how heavy my feet were. My arms, too. The air seemed suddenly thick, my limbs too weak to stand and push through it. I just wanted to sleep. Forget. Ignore the fact Tony was gone, and I was here alone.

Not alone.

Lacey was still here. Where was she? My heartbeat picked up, turning into a stampede, but then her sweet little face poked around the corner of my bedroom, and she quietly said, "Mommy? Can you look at the picture I drew?"

"Sure, baby girl. Come here." My words were slurred like I was drunk. But I hadn't had any alcohol. Then why did my tongue feel like it was too big for my mouth?

Lawson, I remembered, as Lacey bounced on my bed, unaware of the mess my head was. She chattered on about the picture she'd drawn. Lawson had been here every day since the funeral. I'd been grateful for his support. For the way he'd helped with Lacey. For the pills he'd brought for me that made every-

thing seem easier. Lighter. The pills blocked out the pain, and the hole inside me that gaped, raw and full of an agony I didn't think I could survive. I'd only just got Tony back. And then he was gone.

"Mommy!" Lacey snapped.

I blinked at her, fighting against the drug haze, trying to make sense of what she was saying. "What, Lace? Tell me about your picture."

She smiled and then pointed to the piece of paper she was holding. "That's me. And Uncle Lawson."

I smiled at that and indicated to a stick figure drawing of a woman. "Is that me?"

But she shook her head, her dark, knotted hair falling around her face. I frowned, realizing I hadn't brushed it that morning. I struggled into a sitting position, the mattress shifting beneath me, and reached for the brush on my nightstand. I might have been a hot mess, but I wouldn't let that affect Lacey.

She was everything.

I pulled the brush through her hair and tried to keep my focus on her sweet voice, even though my brain wanted to drift.

"No, Mommy. That's not you. You have brown hair, not yellow hair. That's Aunty Selina."

I peered over her shoulder and noticed that indeed, the stick figure had yellow hair. "You know about your Aunty Selina?" I questioned.

She bobbed her head up and down rapidly. "Oh yeah. Uncle Lawson says I'll really love her. She has candy and bakes cakes, and there's lots of dolls at her place. See?" She pointed to a house in the background of her picture. "They have a big house. Really big, Mommy. Like a mazillion times bigger than this house. Lawson said I'll see it when I go stay with him."

My ears pricked up at that. "What do you mean Uncle

Lawson said you'd see it?" Lawson hadn't said anything of the sort to me.

"Yesterday, when he brought you your medicine. He said if I was a good girl, I could go with him to his big house. Maybe today! He said he has a pool. And he's going to teach me how to swim."

Alarm bells went off in my head. Over the last two weeks, in moments of clarity, I'd tried to understand why Lawson was always here. Why he was suddenly so interested in Lacey and me, when he'd never wanted anything to do with us before. Something about it set off my motherly instincts. Something didn't feel right, even though I couldn't put my finger on it exactly. "Lacey," I said slowly. "What else did he say?"

"He said he was going to paint a room for me. Any color I liked."

"What?"

She shrugged, losing interest, and jumped off my bed, running across the hall to her own bedroom.

But I couldn't shake the sense of unease. Lawson had been giving me pills, telling me I needed them to rest. I'd believed him. It was so much easier to let them numb the pain. How many times had he sent me to bed, while he played downstairs with Lacey? I'd trusted him, because he was my older brother, and I had nobody else to lean on. But now my skin prickled. I didn't know my brother anymore. And I'd gone ahead and left my baby with someone who was virtually a stranger.

"Mommy! Uncle Lawson's car just came into the driveway," Lacey singsonged, skipping into my room again. "Should I pack my bags? He said I could go to his house for a long time, so I'll need my pillow, and my Barbie T-shirt, and my rainbow unicorn...."

Fear wrapped itself around my heart. Why on earth would he have told her that?

"Mommy? What's wrong?"

I shook myself out of it and plastered a bright smile on my face. "Nothing, baby girl. Actually, why don't we play a game with Uncle Lawson?"

She clapped her hands happily. "Tag? I'm a fast runner."

"I know you are. But I think Uncle Lawson's favorite game is hide-and-seek. And I have the best spot for you." I led her quickly into her bedroom and pulled open the closet door. "Can you squeeze in there?"

She nodded enthusiastically. "I'm really small!"

"Good job." I plucked a drink bottle of water from her bedside table, thankful it was still mostly full from when I'd filled it up for her last night. She got dry mouth at night sometimes, so I was always sure to leave a drink for her. I gave it to her, along with her favorite doll. "You stay there until we find you, okay?"

She grinned up at me, her big eyes so full of innocence it broke my heart.

I hoped I was wrong about her uncle. But I couldn't ignore my gut. And with Mommy instinct screaming at me to protect my child, I shut her inside a closet.

17

RAFE

In the quiet of Lacey's bedroom, I answered the call, guilt eating away at me at the name flashing on the screen. Mom. It was early evening on Thanksgiving, the first we hadn't celebrated together, and I hadn't even called her. I was a shitty son. The fight I'd had with Dad had nothing to do with her. But deep inside, I knew why I hadn't called. I was angry. Angry she'd stayed when I'd left. She could have come with me. I could have taken care of her, if she'd just let me. But she'd chosen him. Again.

The thoughts were selfish. I knew that. I just wanted her to choose me for once. Hell, not even me. To choose herself.

I still should have called. She didn't deserve my silence. "Hey, Mom," I said softly, sitting on the edge of Lacey's bed. "Happy Thanksgiving. We're just in the middle of..."

Weird noises on the other end of the phone caught my attention, and I realized she hadn't even said hello. I frowned. "Mom?"

She didn't say anything. But the noise came again, and I squinted into the empty room, as if that would somehow make me hear better. Sharp intakes of breath, I realized. Like she'd been running and was puffed.

The line went dead. "Mom?" But she was gone. I hit the button to call her back, my heart rate rising. A prickle of worry rolled down my spine. Maybe it had been an accidental call. Maybe she'd pocket-dialed me. But something didn't feel right. I'd heard her breathing. I wouldn't have heard that unless the phone had been pressed to her ear. "Pick up. Pick up. Pick up," I muttered.

The phone rang out. She didn't have voicemail for me to leave a message, so I hung up, cursing under my breath, and made a decision. Lacey was downstairs, with a meal she'd slaved over all day. She'd been so excited about it, and I didn't want to be the one who ruined it. But something in my gut told me I needed to check on my mother. I typed out a two-word message.

I'm coming.

It was only then I registered the sounds of arguing in the dining room. Selina yelling. Lacey yelling. What the fuck? I hightailed it down the stairs just in time to see George and April leaving in a hurry. April glanced up at me with watery eyes. Our gazes clashed, but I was no Banjo. I held no sympathy for a woman who could abandon her child the way she had. So I let them walk out the door without saying a word.

In the dining room, Selina, Meredith, Banjo, and Lacey sat around the table in silence. My gaze strayed to the two empty chairs that George and April had occupied. "What happened?"

Lacey pushed to her feet wearily, as if the weight of the world had suddenly crashed down on her in the few minutes I'd been gone. She wandered to my side as if in a daze, and I automatically put an arm around her shoulders, protectively gathering her to my chest.

She laid her head over my heart before turning into my embrace. "I don't want to talk about it."

I smoothed my palm over her back in calming circles, while I shot Banjo a look over the top of her head. He made a face that told me exactly how well things had gone since I'd left the room, though I'd already guessed by the sudden departure of two of the guests. Well, this was turning out to be a fun little Thanksgiving, wasn't it? And I was about to make it worse.

I dropped my chin so my lips were closer to her ear. "I have to go, princess."

"What?" She clutched me tighter. "I don't want you to leave."

I didn't want to leave either. Hell, running back to Saint View to clean up whatever mess my father had made was the absolute last thing I wanted to do. But my mother's call had me spooked. My throat was tight with all the words she hadn't said. "I need to go home. I think...I don't know. Something isn't right. I need to check on her.

"Is she hurt?"

I grimaced. "Knowing my dad? Probably. I couldn't tell how bad, she wouldn't talk." My anxiousness grew with every second we stood here talking about it. I kissed Lacey's head. "I'm sorry to skip out on Thanksgiving."

"Thanksgiving is a bust anyway." She took my coat from the rack and passed it to me before grabbing her own. "I'm coming with you. I've lost my appetite."

Banjo shoved his plate away. "I'll come, too."

But I shook my head, surveying the huge table of food. Selina had gone to all this trouble, and now it was going to waste. "Stay. Help Selina clean up. I'll call you as soon as I know what's going on."

Banjo pressed his lips together, but he was also the sort of guy who took people at their word and didn't argue. What I wanted in this situation was more important than what Banjo wanted. Instead of pushing back, he strode around the table and engulfed us both in a hug. A tremble shuddered through Lacey's body. Or maybe it was mine. I didn't know. All I knew was neither Lacey nor I had it in us to be the rock at that moment, and this was Banjo giving us every last drop of his strength.

He stared me straight in the eye. "You call me if you need me. I'll be there."

I wrapped my free hand around Banjo and hauled him in, planting my lips on his, hard and fast. With Lacey held tight in my other arm, this was the shot of confidence I needed. I breathed deep for a moment, their scents mingling in my nose, calming me.

"You've got this," Banjo said quietly. "Go get it sorted, then come back. I'll wait up. No matter what time it is."

Our embrace unraveled, and Lacey and I rushed for the door. She headed for the passenger seat of her car, and I was grateful. I needed to drive and burn some of this extra energy coursing through me. I couldn't just sit there, waiting to see what we'd find when we got back to Saint View.

I slid behind the steering wheel, finding the key left in the ignition, and drove home like I wasn't even attached to my own body. My foot pressed down on the gas, my fingers turned the wheel, but it was all on autopilot. My head, or maybe my heart, had skipped ahead to the little house I'd grown up in.

My mother had never called after an argument with my father. That wasn't what she did. Her usual response was to clean up any mess as quickly as possible, cover her bruises with makeup, long sleeves, or scarves, and sweep the entire thing under the rug, trying to hide the evidence so I would never know.

I always knew. Everybody knew. The neighbors had to have heard her cries. Have heard him yell and swear. The broken glasses and plates. They knew. But nobody did anything. Because this was Saint View, and domestic violence was about as common as the fleas on the mangy dogs that roamed the neighborhood.

I didn't speak until we were just streets away from my house. "It feels different this time."

"The call?"

"She doesn't do that. She always tries to hide it. Tries to cover for him. Do you know how many times I've heard her say that she walked into a cupboard? Or fell down the stairs? Jammed her fingers in the car door? He broke her arm once, and yet she still didn't call me." I voiced the fear that had been curdling in the pit of my stomach. "What if he's really hurt her? Hell, maybe I should have just called an ambulance? What if we get there and—"

"Hey. Stop thinking like that. She's alive. Conscious enough to make the phone call. That's a good thing. Maybe it's not as bad as you think it is."

I ground my teeth as something new occurred to me. "Or maybe it's worse. Maybe it isn't her who's hurt this time."

Lacey's mouth dropped open. "You don't think...?"

I shot her a tortured glance. "What if she's only calling me because he can't? What if she snapped and—"

She gripped my thigh. "Hey, shh. Stop. Don't let your head get carried away. Let's just see what we find when we get there."

If my mother had finally snapped, then my father

deserved everything he got. If she'd slammed her fist into his face, then I hoped he felt the pain he'd inflicted on her more times than I cared to count.

If she'd done more than that, if I walked inside those doors and saw my father's body lying cold on the living room floor, I wouldn't cry for him. I wouldn't cry for a man who made himself feel big by making others feel small. By beating them down until they snapped and took a life.

It would be the justice my mother deserved.

Even still, when I pulled into my parents' driveway and Dad's car wasn't there, I breathed a sigh of relief. "He isn't here."

I hadn't realized how tightly Lacey held on to me until she unclenched her fingers from my leg. "Thank God."

We both got out and ran to the front door, the knob twisting easily in my hand and allowing us entry.

"Mom," I yelled.

We took two steps inside, and I blinked at the carnage laid out in front of me. "Shit, were they robbed?"

The last time I'd been here, the house had been sparkling clean, with not so much as a speck of dust on the bookcase. Everything had been neatly sitting in its designated place, the air scented with the chemical lemon of cleaning products.

Today, it looked as if a whirlwind had whipped right through the house. The couch had been slashed with something sharp, the stuffing spilling out of the cushions. Side tables had been upended. The large-screen TV had a huge crack spiraling from where someone had thrown something at it.

Ahead of us, in the kitchen, a feast was laid out on the kitchen table. A perfectly browned turkey. An array of sides in matching bowls, spread out around it. The table set for two.

But only one sat at the table.

Mom's dress was royal blue and long-sleeved. A strand of creamy pearls rested around her throat, matching earrings glinting at her ears. Curls of dark hair stuck up in odd angles around her head, and when she looked up, she had black mascara tracks running down her face and an open cut oozing blood from a split in her lip.

"Shit, Mom!" In a burst of speed, I rushed to her side. "What happened? Where's Dad?"

I threw panicked questions at her, one after the other, but she just stared at me blankly. When I shook her, her head bobbled back and forth limply. Panic set in. I'd never seen her like this. Never seen that blank look in her eyes.

I glanced to Lacey. "What's wrong with her? Should we call an ambulance?"

That seemed to shock Mom out of her daze. "No ambulance."

The relief I felt at her actually speaking was short-lived. Something was very wrong here.

"Might be shock," Lacey said quietly. "Where's your first aid kit?"

"Beneath the bathroom sink."

She disappeared upstairs, while I hovered over my mother. My attention slid to the family photos on the wall behind her head. Happy smiling family photos of the three of us throughout the years. What lies they told. There was no happiness here. There never had been. He'd destroyed any chance of that the first time he'd laid a hand on her.

Lacey reappeared with the kit, and I riffled through it, finding some gauze to dab at the cut on Mom's mouth. It probably could have used a few stitches, and the expression of concern on Lacey's face said she was thinking the same thing. But neither of us voiced it. I stuck a Band-Aid to the cut, hoping that would be enough, and pulled up a seat at the table. Lacey did the same thing. The turkey hadn't even been cut into. That was two Thanksgiving meals that had been lovingly prepared, only to go to waste. Burned-down candles still flickered with orange flames, the wax dripping onto the tablecloth.

"Mom," I said quietly, as if I were speaking to a skittish horse. "What happened? Where's Dad?"

"I don't know."

At least she was talking. "He just trashed the place and then left?"

She turned watery blue eyes on me. "No. I did that."

Shock punched through my gut. That didn't compute at all. My mother was a quiet, timid, well-put-together lady who had married a monster. Trashing a house did not at all seem within her capabilities. She was house-proud, though whether that was because she liked to keep her house clean, or because she was too scared of my father not to, I didn't know. "You smashed the TV?"

Lacey seemed just as shocked as I was. "And slashed the couches?"

"I hate this house," she whispered brokenly. "I hate everything about it. There are no good memories here. He's ruined them all. Overshadowed anything good with his hate and anger and jealousy." She blinked, becoming slightly more lucid. "I'm going to burn it. The whole thing. I just need to find a match." She took my hand and squeezed my fingers. "I just wanted you to be able to get anything of yours that you wanted first. Your things from your bedroom..."

Lacey glanced at me, her worry etched deep into the creases across her forehead.

"I moved out, Mom. Remember? I took my things already. They're at Lacey's place."

For the first time, she seemed to register that Lacey was even in the room. "Oh, right. Of course. I guess it's time then. Where are the matches?"

Lacey and I watched wide-eyed as she stood and crossed the kitchen, digging out a box of matches from a drawer.

"There's gasoline in the shed." Her voice was far away, like she was not fully aware of what she was saying.

True fear for her spiked and mixed with sorrow. He'd pushed her one step too far, and this was where she'd gone. To some place where she wasn't the weak-willed, mild-mannered, neglected wife of Todd Simmons. She'd turned into someone I didn't recognize. Hell, maybe this was her all along. The true version that wasn't stifled by evil. Or maybe he'd pushed her to the brink. I understood. I hated him, too. He'd hit me. Belittled me. Shamed me for my entire life. It could have so easily been me, standing here with a match, asking for a can of gasoline.

I couldn't let her do it. She wouldn't come back from something like this. And I wanted her back. The mom I knew she could be, without his iron fist.

I snatched them from her hand. "Mom, no. You can't."

"It's the only way to get rid of the memories." She grabbed at the matches again, but I held them out of her reach. She held my gaze for a moment, and for a single instant, I saw the woman she'd been before she'd met my father. I saw the strong woman inside her, who was brave enough to endure years of abuse, and then finally say enough was enough. I saw the fire in her eyes that yearned for revenge. For retribution. To make Todd Simmons feel even an ounce of the hurt he'd inflicted on her over the years.

But then it crumbled. Her shoulders shook. Lacey wrapped an arm around her and led her to the door.

"It's going to be okay," she mumbled, soothing a hand down her back like I'd done to Lacey back at the house. "You don't have to stay here. We'll find you somewhere safe, where he can never hurt you again. Let us help. Please."

"Yes." Her voice was tiny. Resigned. "I just want it to end."

Relief filled me.

Lacey grabbed the purse hanging from a hook by the door, and the only woman's coat on the rack, and helped Mom into it. She didn't protest. She didn't change her mind. She was doing it. Leaving, with nothing. But not with no one. She had me. And Lacey.

I flipped the box of matches over in my hand, surveying the destruction. With my toe, I nudged at an overturned chair on the kitchen floor. I'd lain there once, when I was about ten, after he'd backhanded me for getting a B on a math test. He'd hit me so hard it had knocked me right off my feet.

I'd been too young to fight back. Too small. Too helpless.

He'd liked that. I'd seen the power gleam in his eyes as he'd yelled at me to stand up and be a man.

I wasn't a man then. I was ten. A child.

I wasn't that child anymore.

"Rafe?" Lacey asked from the doorway. "Are you coming?"

I turned the matchbox over again. Then placed it down on the table beside the candle. I met Lacey's gaze.

Then tipped the candle, so it fell to its side.

I watched the flame. Watched as it burned, like the hate in my heart. When the cheap synthetic tablecloth lit up, I did nothing to stop it. I walked out of the house, closed the door, and let the fucking thing burn.

18

LACEY

The first fire engine sped past us, sirens wailing. I twisted in my seat as it flew by, heading in the opposite direction. The second followed in its wake, a blur of red and blue lights, glinting in the dark night.

"Guess it took," Rafe said quietly, flatly, his voice completely without emotion.

I reached across the center console and stroked my fingers down the back of his neck. He didn't glance over.

"Where are we going?" Mrs. Simmons asked from the back seat.

Rafe glanced at me, questions in his eyes.

"My place," I said, without hesitation. "You can stay as long as you need to. We have plenty of room."

Rafe shot me a thankful look.

"No," Mrs. Simmons said quietly.

Rafe jerked, peering over his shoulder at his mother before turning his attention back to the road. "Mom, it's a nice place. Lacey's aunt is amazing and—"

"Rafe, no. I can't." Her voice sounded stronger with every passing mile we put between her and her burning house.

She straightened, then leaned forward, grasping the back of his seat. "There's a women's shelter on the corner of Durley Street. Please. Take me there."

I stayed quiet, knowing this needed to be between the two of them, even though I wanted to insist she come home with us.

"I want you with me, where I can take care of you," Rafe said stubbornly.

"Rafe, no. Stop. Pull the car over."

Rafe seemed surprised but did as he was asked, then twisted so he faced his mother.

She pressed her fingers into the sturdy foam of the seat. "I love you. But I don't want you hovering over me. That isn't your job. I've already failed you as a parent, in so many ways—"

"No, you haven't," he protested.

She silenced him with a surprisingly strong look. "I have. I don't need you to make excuses for me. But I can't be with you while I get myself back on my feet. I can't let myself rely on you. That isn't the way this is supposed to be. You aren't supposed to parent me. So please. Drop me at the shelter. Let me do this my way. I need to. I need to prove it to myself. And to you. And to your father."

Rafe ground his molars at the mention of his dad. "You'll need support. Help with money and—"

"I agree. And I'll have that. But it won't come from you. When I see you next, I want you to see the real me. The woman I was before him. You'll like her better, I promise."

"I like you just fine..."

But it was clear for all to see that she had made up her mind. She waited patiently.

Slowly, Rafe nodded. He turned around and started the car again.

It was only another two blocks to the women's shelter. Rafe parked between white lines, slowly lining the car up, delaying letting his mother go. I sat in the car and watched through the windshield as Rafe delivered his mother to the door, met by an older woman with a long silver braid hanging over one shoulder. They chatted for a moment then Rafe engulfed his mother in a hug. She held him for a long time; the sort of hug you gave when you knew you might not see the person again for a while.

Tears pricked the backs of my eyes. I hoped this was it for her. I hoped this was the end of one life and the beginning of the other. I could only imagine how many women fell back into the same old routines, after escaping abuse like the kind Rose Simmons had endured. I didn't want that for her. I hoped she was strong enough to make it out the other side. And despite what she'd said about not wanting Rafe's support until she was on her feet again, I knew he'd be there for her, checking in every day, doing whatever he could to make sure she thrived.

He walked slowly back to the car, gaze to the ground, and when he got back in, he looked so thoroughly defeated. I threaded my fingers through his, wanting to offer some tiny bit of comfort, but he soon untangled them in order to drive.

The trip back to Providence was silent. Neither of us uttered a word, both of us lost to our thoughts. I should have been tired, so much had happened today. Too much. But adrenaline still filled my veins, and I had a feeling I'd be awake most of the night, replaying the argument with April, and Rafe tipping over that candle then walking out the door. I wondered how much of it had gone up before the fire trucks got there. I wondered if his dad had come home. Had he even cared his wife had left him? Or did he care more about the charred remains of his home?

Rafe's voice after so much silence was startling. "I set my house on fire."

"Yeah, you did."

"Shit. I can't believe I did that."

I unclicked my seat belt so I could twist to see him better. He stubbornly stared out the windshield, staring up at the house.

"Hey, look at me for a second. I'm proud of you."

The laugh that spilled from his mouth sounded near hysterical. "How? I've lost my fucking mind. Everything was in that house. Their clothes. Their photos...."

"Photos no one can bear to look at. You made a stand tonight, whether your dad ever realizes that or not, doesn't matter. You got your mom out."

He finally turned to face me, his expression bleak. "What if I'm like him?"

"You're nothing like him."

The pain in Rafe's eyes was a like a serrated knife, stabbing me over and over. I loved this boy, and he was in so much pain, it was tearing me in two.

"What if I am, though?" Rafe asked. "You heard my mom. I just tried to own her the way he does. I wanted to drag her back to your house and force her to be where I could see her and take care of her. What if I do that to you?"

"That wasn't trying to own her. That was being there for her. When she told you what she needed, you gave it to her. Even if you wanted to drag her here, you didn't. You listened. You followed her lead. That's how you love someone, Rafe." I swallowed down the lump in my throat and brought a hand up to his cheek. "That's how I love you. That's how I know you're good. And kind. And that you're nothing like your father. I love you because you're everything he isn't."

My heart pounded, and I was suddenly nervous I'd said this all wrong. Timed it badly. He'd just suffered a trauma, a life-altering event, and here I was, throwing in another. "I'm sorry," I whispered. "It's too much for tonight. I know that. I've just wanted to tell you for weeks—"

His lips met mine, soft and slow.

I stopped talking. Stopped thinking. He nipped at my mouth, and I opened for him, his tongue sliding in leisurely, meeting mine, melting my protests. I slid my fingers into his hair, tugging him closer, breathing him in, holding him tight.

When he pulled away, he pressed his forehead to mine, our gazes locked, and for the longest moment, we just sat there, drinking each other in.

"You have no idea how much I love you, Lacey," he said finally. "You say you've known for weeks? I've known since the minute I saw you."

I stepped in again, relief and excitement and leftover adrenaline all crashing together and mixing in a way that went straight to my head, spinning it in circles. I kissed him hard this time, morphing it into something more similar to the other kisses we'd shared. Branding. Scalding. Owning. I went to climb over the gearshift, wanting to get closer to him, wanting to feel him beneath me, his arms holding me tight. I wanted to tell him with my mouth, and show him with my body, exactly how much I loved him.

But to my surprise, he slowed me down again.

I pulled back and tilted my head to one side. "Don't tell me you suddenly want to wait for marriage?"

He chuckled low and swiped his thumb gently over my lips. "No, princess. I think that ship has well and truly sailed.

But I don't want to fuck you hard and fast in the back seat of your car either. Tempting as that might be."

I pouted. "Sounds pretty fun to me."

God, his grin was delicious. It lifted one side of his mouth, showing off his teeth, and when he ran his tongue over his lips, Jesus Christ, I thought I'd self-combust.

Hot guy moves. He had them down pat. I don't think he was even aware of it.

He leaned in close so his breath misted over my lips. "I just told you I love you, princess. I want to lay you down and do this right."

My nipples beaded at the thought, and I wasn't sure if the wetness between my legs was from me turning into a puddle or if I was just really turned on.

Both, probably.

We reached for our door handles at the same time, suddenly eager to get inside, and when he rounded the car, he grabbed my hand, our fingers linking together as easily as they always did. He'd salvaged this day for me. He was the one bright spark in a day that had been otherwise an epic disaster. But the two of us were anything but. With my fingers wrapped in his, every horrible thing fell away, and he and I were all there was.

We stumbled through the front door, a tangle of arms and legs and searing kisses that made me impatient to get through the lovemaking so he could fuck me up against the wall.

A cough came from the living room on the left, followed by Banjo's laughter. "I think you two are making Colt uncomfortable."

Rafe and I both spun in their direction.

Colt was sprawled in an armchair, jean-covered legs spread wide. He rolled his eyes, as if Banjo's comment was ridiculous. But I suspected he might have been right. There was a tenseness to his shoulders that wasn't normally there when he was just being his usual arrogant self.

Banjo came over and put one finger beneath my chin, tipping it up so he could kiss me. He tasted sweet, and I suspected he'd been getting into the desserts Selina had baked this morning. Good. At least some of the food hadn't gone to waste.

"You two okay?" he asked before brushing his lips over Rafe's as well.

I shot a glance at Rafe. I knew he'd tell Banjo everything in time, but it wasn't the moment. For now, we both just nodded.

Colt watched the three of us with interest, only the tiniest bit of jealously sparking in his midnight gaze. I kind of liked that.

I dropped Rafe's fingers and crossed the room to stand in front of Colt. "I thought you had family stuff to do today?"

He stared up at me, unfazed by the fact I'd taken the more dominant position. "I did."

"But..."

"But nothing."

I folded my arms over my chest. "You're here. Even though your lawyer told you not to."

"You gonna kick me out?"

I leaned down, grinning at him. He grinned right back, then stole a kiss.

It was nothing more than a brief press of lips, but it sent a jolt of lust down my spine. "Kiss me properly and I'll consider letting you stay."

His left eyebrow rose, a challenge we both knew he'd take. He shifted closer, moving his ass to the edge of the seat, and tucked his finger around the music note necklace Rafe had given me for my birthday. He tugged it gently, guiding me down. My lips met his, and within moments, his tongue pressed inside my mouth, giving me exactly what I'd asked for.

"I wanted to see you," he whispered when we broke apart. "I know it's late. And I know I missed the meal…"

I shook my head. I was just happy he was here. I'd missed him. But I was still itching to get upstairs with Rafe. "Rafe just told me he loved me," I admitted to Colt.

Banjo rammed an elbow into Rafe's side. "'Bout fucking time."

Rafe shoved him back. "Fuck off. I do things at my own pace. We don't all have to start throwing around I love you's in the first five minutes of meeting someone. Not like you do, Mister 'I wear my heart on my sleeve like a sap.'"

I sniggered at that, feeling playful. "Yeah, but Rafe, you took so long that even Colt beat you."

Rafe and Banjo went bug-eyed at that revelation.

"You lie," Banjo accused, "Colt couldn't even love a teacup pig. And they're the cutest, most lovable things in the world."

Colt pulled a face at him. "A teacup pig? What the fuck would I do with a teacup pig?"

I shrugged. "Put it in a teacup and love it? They are pretty cute."

He pushed to his feet and stretched like he was completely bored with the conversation. "I told Lacey I love her. Get over it. All of you."

Banjo and Rafe were grinning at him like fools, and it was getting on his nerves, I could tell. But I was warm and fuzzy inside.

Rafe wandered over and wrapped his arms around me from behind. "Fine. We're over it. We'll never mention it again. You can keep all your I love you's for when we aren't around."

Colt tracked Rafe's movements possessively, but he was going to have to get used to this, if this were truly going to work. And it had been working so well with just Banjo, Rafe, and me. The addition of Colt could either ruin it entirely. Or make it so much better. I wanted the latter. I needed to show him how good it could be, if he let it. Our families were imploding one by one, but this, the four of us, could be the phoenix rising from the flames.

I rested my head back against Rafe's chest, and he pressed his lips to the side of my neck. "I haven't forgotten what I wanted to do to you, Lace," he said in not all that quiet a whisper. The touch of his lips on my neck turned into an open-mouthed kiss, his teeth nipping at the sensitive skin beneath my ear, his tongue smoothing over the tiny stings.

I couldn't help it. He'd already got me riled up in the car, and the feel of his tongue set off that need in me again. My breath came out in a pant, and he worked his way down my neck, edging aside the collar of my dress to make his way lower.

I didn't need to look in Banjo's direction to know he was okay with this. I knew what would happen if the three of us went upstairs to my room or out to the pool house.

But Colt was the unknown.

The two of us alone were dynamite. I'd had one of the most earth-shattering orgasms of my life when it had been just me and him. But if this was going to work, we needed to find our boundaries. "Colt." My voice came out huskier than normal, but Rafe's tongue was wickedly good, and heat was building inside me.

Colt watched, his hot gaze pinned on mine.

He was hard to read. I wanted to think that was heat behind the black depths of his eyes. But I really wasn't sure.

"I should go," he said, gaze not leaving mine.

A shot of disappointment coursed through me. I didn't want him to. I didn't want to make him uncomfortable either, but I wanted this. The three of them. I loved all three, in such different ways, and yet, I never felt completely whole without them all here. Right now. They were perfect. They were everything. And I wanted to show them. I wanted to prove to them that this could work. It had to. I needed it to.

"Or you could stay," I invited.

Colt stiffened. Then he let his guard down. He shifted, but his movement was in my direction, not away. Heat flared in his eyes. This time, there was no mistaking it.

He wanted it, too.

I held out a hand out, and to my relief, he took it. I disentangled myself from Rafe, finding his hand, too, and with a grin at Banjo, led all three toward the doors, so we could make our way out to the pool house.

I had a feeling tonight was not the night to sleep in the main house, where Selina could hear every noise we made.

19

———————

LACEY

My heart skipped a beat as I led the guys down the garden path to the pool house we'd claimed as our own. With my fingers entwined between both Colt's and Rafe's, I let Rafe open the door and followed him in, Colt close behind, Banjo bringing up the rear.

The main room, which doubled as a bedroom and living room, was a little messier than usual, since Angelique had been off today to spend Thanksgiving with her family. A hoodie lay discarded on the couch, and nobody had bothered making the bed. Not that it really mattered. I was pretty sure we were about to mess it up again.

Rafe pounced on me as soon as we were all inside. I dropped Colt's hand, wanting to give him the chance to decide for himself how involved he wanted to be. Instead, I concentrated on Rafe. He cupped my face with both hands, forcing my sole attention onto him.

"Remember what I said in the car?" he asked.

"I remember."

"You still want that?"

I nodded. I did. I wanted a moment with him. Some time to explore his body, and this new realization that he loved me the way I'd always loved him. It didn't matter to me that the others were in the room. Rafe commanded my attention. I let my gaze drift over his too handsome face, then lower to the button-down shirt, open at the neck. I placed a kiss to his collarbone and slowly undid the buttons one by one, exposing the bare skin of his chest. I let my fingers graze over his biceps, enjoying the way his muscles rippled as he shrugged off the shirt.

His skin was velvet softness over hard muscle, and I trailed my fingers over his pecs and abs, unable to get enough of him. "You're so beautiful," I whispered, leaning in to press a kiss to his chest.

"You are." He traced his finger over the necklace he'd given me, then leaned in, so his lips were close, a secret only for me to hear. "I'm glad you wore that tonight. I want that to be the only thing you wear when I'm inside you."

A delicious shiver of expectation ran down my spine. My lips parted, a pant coming out needy and breathless. He had a filthy mouth when he wanted to. All these guys did.

Lucky me.

Rafe's fingers found the zipper on the back of my dress and tugged it down. There was nothing else holding it to my body. Once he pushed it off my shoulders, it pooled at my feet, and I knew I wouldn't be back in it before morning.

He drank me in, giving me the chance to see where the others were. Banjo had taken up residence on the couch. Colt leaned back on the door, arms crossed over his chest. His position by the exit made me think he might run at any moment. But his gaze was full of lust while he tracked my movements, and I suspected he was waging an internal war between his head and cock.

I wanted him to stop thinking. I met his gaze, letting any guards I still had in place drop. He needed to know I wanted this. Wanted him. Them.

Rafe hauled me into a kiss, hot and searing, one hand to the back of my head, the other on my hip. His finger ran over the lace of my panties, but he didn't try taking them off, content to leave me in my underwear for now.

I wasn't so patient. We pulled apart, and I found his belt, undoing the buckle before gently guiding it through the belt loops and tugging it free.

The button and zipper on Rafe's pants came undone beneath my fingers, but Banjo standing up from the couch, shedding his shirt, and making his way over to us, caught my attention. I smiled softly at him as he pressed up behind Rafe and dropped a kiss on his bare shoulder.

Colt let out a possessive growl, closer than I expected him to be, and it sent a thrill through my body. Then he was there, mirroring Banjo's position with Rafe, pressed against my back and brushing my hair to one side. His lips on my neck seared, taking my already heated blood to boiling. When his fingers found the clasp on my strapless bra and freed my breasts, I was grateful for one less article of clothing.

Rafe's fingers found my nipple, tweaking it hard, so that a jolt of pleasure made me wobble. But Colt's big body kept me steady. I hated that he was still in his clothes. I wanted to feel him, skin to skin.

"Take your shirt off," I whispered to him.

In typical Colt fashion, he ignored me. Instead, he dragged my panties down my legs, waiting for me to step out of them. His lips trailed down my spine, and I pulled Rafe in for another kiss, his bare chest to mine, needing the contact Colt refused to give me. My tongue tangled with Rafe's, the kiss deep and possessive, while Colt palmed my ass cheeks, squeezing them until I squirmed with delight.

Rafe's erection prodded at my belly, hot and thick. He'd shed his underwear, perhaps at Banjo's hands, I didn't know. I'd been too lost getting into the feel of Colt.

He needed to be naked.

The crack of Banjo opening a tube of lube broke the silence, but I was on a mission. I twisted and stared up at Colt, not asking for his permission anymore, but demanding it. When I grabbed the hem of his long-sleeved T-shirt, he didn't stop me.

He didn't exactly help me though, either.

Asshole.

He smirked at me struggling to get it over his taller frame, but fuck if I was going to give in to him. I hadn't seen him naked in weeks, and never properly. It had been so dark on the beach. I wanted to see him now. As soon as his shirt was off, I went for his pants, wasting no time undoing them and shoving them down his muscular legs, until he stood before me, completely naked.

He'd gone commando. I should have known.

His erection jutted from his body, long and thick and proud. I wanted to drop to my knees and fit my mouth over him, but fuck, I just wanted to look at him, too. To drink him in and commit him to memory.

But Rafe pulled me tight to his chest, his erection prodding my ass cheeks, and reminding me that I'd wanted this to be about him first. I tried to turn, but his arm was like a vise around my waist, holding me in place, while his other hand dipped low between my legs.

"Ohhh," I moaned, helpless to stop the sound as his finger touched my clit. I was already so wet for him, and for Colt, that Rafe's finger slid through my folds without resistance, gathering my arousal and spreading it over my nub. I spread my legs a little wider, giving him better access to the places I wanted him most.

Rafe let out a groan of pleasure, his breath quickening in my ear, his erection hard at my backside. He'd gone from in control to trembling, but I'd barely touched him, so I suspected Banjo had worked some magic on him from behind.

"I want you, Lacey," he moaned into my ear. "So bad."

The ache inside me grew, and with every rub of my clit, it got worse. Colt met my gaze and instinctively knew what I needed. He went to the edge of the bed, and I followed, Rafe close behind. Colt reclined against the headboard, a pile of pillows at his back; his hands tucked behind his head, glorious cock on display like he didn't give a shit who saw.

But Rafe wanted my attention. And I wanted to give it to him. When he spun me in his arms so we were face-to-face, I didn't resist. His fingers dug into my hips once more, and then he lifted me onto the bed, depositing me between Colt's widespread legs.

The two of them exchanged a look before Colt dragged me up the bed, so I was reclined back against him. He was hard beneath me but didn't try to get his dick in the right position. Instead he reached around, massaging my tits while Rafe hovered over me. I moaned at Colt's hands working my nipples, and I stared into the depths of Rafe's blue eyes. He pressed down on me so his dick was notched at my entrance, slicking through the wetness there. I lifted my hips, getting the angle right, needing him inside me, and then groaned.

"Fuck. We are going to the doctor tomorrow and getting those tests. And birth control." I wanted all the barriers gone. I wanted these guys fully, skin to skin. I wanted them indoors, outdoors. I didn't want to have to stop and think about condoms every time. But for now, we needed them.

Colt distracted me with a hard pinch to my nipples, and then Rafe was there, between my legs and kissing me hard. "I love you, Lacey," he whispered. And then he slid inside me.

I moaned softly, the stretch around his thick length delicious. I leaned back on Colt's chest, and wrapped my legs around Rafe, our hips meeting in slow, mind-blowing thrusts. He kissed me softly, his tongue delving into my mouth as I pushed my fingers into his hair. I loved him. His body. The way he made me feel.

"You're what I'm thankful for, Rafe," I whispered before moaning at his change in angle, the tip of him hitting that spot inside me so perfectly. I rocked with him, scratching my nails down his back and pulling him closer, wanting more of his mouth and his kisses that spun my head. It didn't matter Banjo was in the room, or that Colt still clutched me from behind. I'd needed this tonight. This connection with Rafe, and it built with every kiss, every thrust, every press of his fingers and tongue. The need to come spiraled inside me, until I was gasping with desire. "Rafe! Please!"

He reached between us, finding my clit once more, right as Colt squeezed my nipples.

An explosion of sensation cascaded over me. "Oh!" I yelled, orgasm barreling into me like a freight train. My walls clenched down around Rafe's dick, and he quickly followed me over the edge. He groaned my name, burying his head in the spot where my neck met my shoulder, thrusting into me until he couldn't take it anymore.

He shuddered over me, his lips finding mine. "I love you, Lacey," he murmured, and I whispered it back. For that moment, it was just me and him in the room. He was all I saw, all I felt. I kissed him soft and slow, loving the weight of him on top of me, completely blissed-out from the orgasm.

But eventually, he rolled onto the bed, and I became aware once more of Colt. He lay completely still, but the rapid rise and fall of his chest and his erection like stone, prodding into my back, told me exactly how turned on he was. I flipped over onto my belly, so we were face-to-face, and crawled up his body. I spread my knees either side of his hips, hovering just over his erection.

His eyes flared, drinking me in. His gaze rolled lazily over my sex-mussed hair, my nipples erect from his attention and straining for more. He paused at my slit, and it throbbed for him. Begged for his touch. His cock. The mattress dipped behind me, and then Banjo was there, trailing a hand down my spine, making a beeline for my ass. I moaned when he got there, pressing back on his hand, telling him what I wanted. One finger slid between my ass cheeks, finding the entrance.

"Fuck," Colt grit out. His dick kicked beneath me, so close, but I kind of loved taunting him.

"What's wrong, Colt?" I asked, the question laced with amusement. I knew exactly what was wrong. I reached between us and stroked my hand down his impressive erection. Precum wept from the tip, and he hissed when I smoothed it down his length.

His black gaze slammed into mine. One hand went for the back of my neck, grabbing me roughly, but damn if that didn't just make me wet for him.

"You like that?" he asked. "Being touched there?"

He meant where Banjo was touching me. Banjo lubed me up while he palmed my ass cheeks, massaging them, dipping in between every so often. God, it was good. I ground back against him and moaned deliberately, letting him know I wanted more. But my eyes were on Colt.

He hauled me in for a rough kiss, our lips smashing together, the tip of his dick sliding through my arousal. "Tell me, princess. Do you like it?"

Banjo chuckled, pushing the tip of his finger inside me.

I let out a deep-throated moan of pleasure, gaze locked on Colt, telling him exactly how much I liked it.

"Fuck," Colt groaned. He grabbed a condom, ripping it open and rolling it down his dick.

Neither of us could hold out a minute longer. He thrust up, and I plunged down. The effect was mind-blowing. He filled me so well, so fully, that I howled out his name. He set a punishing pace, thrusting into me, but I met him stroke for stroke, fucking him as much as he was fucking me. I dropped forward, my hands either side of the bed, simultaneously kissing Colt while giving Banjo better access.

I chased down a second orgasm, grinding with Colt, kissing him, wanting everything I could get, but knowing this wasn't it. "More. Banjo, please. More."

"Lacey...fuck," Banjo murmured, adding a second slicked finger.

I groaned at the intrusion. It was too good, riding Colt's dick, with the added sensation of Banjo's fingers. It felt forbidden, but it wasn't. Not here, with these guys. I trusted them with everything I had.

Banjo moved in behind me, and when I glanced over my shoulder, I saw the question in his eyes.

"Yes," I moaned, so close to coming I could barely stand it. "Banjo!"

He withdrew his fingers, and then the blunt head of his cock was there, pushing inside me. My orgasm barreled down on me, and I clenched around my guys. Colt kissed me harder and took over where I couldn't anymore. He worked me through, he and Banjo in tandem, sparks going off behind my eyes.

Colt lifted his hips, slamming them against mine, until his eyes rolled back and he came, his groans stifled by my mouth that couldn't get enough of him.

"Fuck," Banjo groaned from behind me. "So fucking tight." He picked up the pace, no longer scared of hurting me, until he abruptly stilled, shuddering as he came buried deep inside, where no one else had before.

His fingers gripped my hips tightly, holding on while he came, his dick spasming, setting off a new wave of pleasure ripples through my entire body. It was too much. When Banjo withdrew, I fell on top of Colt, resting my face against the light sheen of sweat covering his chest.

I needed to get off him and clean up, but when he tightened his arms around me, I let him. He probably needed that moment. He'd never had to share me like this, and though he'd obviously enjoyed himself, this was still unfamiliar territory.

I lifted my head wearily and focused orgasm-blissed-out eyes on him. "Are you okay?" I whispered.

He didn't open his eyes, but a small smile pulled at the corner of his mouth. "I just had a threesome. A foursome? An orgy? What is what we just did even called?"

"A forgy!" Banjo yelled from the bathroom.

Rafe, Colt, and I looked at each other, and then burst into laughter.

"A forgy," Colt sniggered. "Fuck. I wish I had someone to brag to, but all my friends are here."

Rafe snorted at that.

I stayed quiet, listening to their easy chat, wondering how the hell I'd been lucky enough to find them.

20

LACEY

The long weekend passed in a blur of sex, leftover food, and music. As we'd lain in bed on Saturday morning, Banjo and I had come to the startling realization that the recital was Friday night, and we'd barely practiced at all.

Weeks ago, when we hadn't really been speaking, we'd picked "One Last Night" by Maroon Five. It had been a song that felt easy, because there was no emotional attachment. I'd been too hurt to consider something with more meaning. But now, the song didn't fit right. It sounded decent with just my piano and his drums, but sounded a whole lot better when Colt picked up my guitar and joined in.

We were in my bedroom, Rafe lounging on the window seat watching Netflix on his phone, headphones over his ears to drown out our practicing. But even he popped one speaker from his ear and said we sounded awesome as a trio.

I sighed, flopping down on my bed. "That just means we suck as a duo."

"Agreed," Banjo said. "This song isn't us."

"Can't Colt just play with you guys on Friday night?" Rafe asked.

Colt plucked a low tone string that made a 'Buh buh' noise. "Nope. Gotta do my piece with Gillian. Which, hate to rub salt in the wound, is a hell of a lot better than what you two have."

I glared at him. "Thanks. Super helpful, six days before we're supposed to perform it."

"Quit whining. Six days is heaps of time to write something."

I bit my lip. But when I looked at Banjo, he was watching me closely.

"What?" I asked him. "You think we should write something? Do you even do that?"

He lifted one shoulder. "Not really, but I know you do. And I can add a beat."

Rafe went back to watching his phone, and Colt started playing something I didn't recognize. They'd both moved on like it was a done deal.

"Why don't you want to write, Lace?" Banjo asked.

I shrugged. "I don't know. I haven't written anything since my uncle died." I shot a worried glance at Colt.

He shook his head. "Don't."

"Don't what?"

"His name is going to come up. You and me? We won't work if you're always trying to stop yourself from mentioning him in my presence."

"And you're just going to be okay with that?"

"I'm just going to pretend you're talking about a different Lawson. Fuck, Lacey. The Lawson you know probably was a different guy to the one who attacked my sister. How do two such different people even live inside one body?"

"I don't know," I said quietly. "That's exactly what I've

been trying to work out."

Colt turned his gaze on me. "Use it. Write it into a song." He set the guitar down and pushed to his feet. "I gotta go to work, and I'm working tomorrow, too."

I pouted at that, and he reached across the bed and pulled at my bottom lip. "Whiner."

"Jerk."

Banjo rolled his eyes from his perch on my desk, but this was what Colt and I did. Taunting each other was our love language, and just because we were together now, didn't mean we could just suddenly switch it off and start being cutesy. He hadn't told me he loved me again, and I didn't expect that he would. Hell, maybe he'd tell me once a year, and somehow, that would be enough. He was never going to be like Banjo, or even Rafe, who had an easier time with words. But that was part of what I loved about him. I didn't want to change him, just because it meant I'd hear him say those words more often. I didn't need to hear it. I felt it in the way he touched me. In the way he got protective. In the teasing banter that might have sounded cold to someone else but told me he couldn't wait to rip my clothes off.

He swiveled in the doorway, leaning on the frame so his shirt rode up just a hint. "Hey, are we still doing the test thing on Monday?"

I nodded tentatively, peeling his hand from the frame and linking it through mine. "You still want to?"

His grin was devious. "You think I don't want to fuck you bare, Lacey Knight? If that's all it takes to make that happen, I'm there with bells on."

"Ditto," Rafe called from his position on the window seat.

I glanced at Banjo.

"Have I ever said no to you? Monday we go get our dicks

swabbed!"

Colt stared at him in horror. "Wait. Fuck. What? Is that what they do? Nobody said anything about a dick swab. What the fuck is that?"

Rafe chuckled. "It's where they get a tiny Q-Tip and ram it up your pee hole to check you don't have some nasty-ass infection."

Colt's hand hovered around his junk, his expression full of horror. He turned to me. "Sorry, babe. I don't want to fuck you bare that bad."

I chuckled and stepped in, pushing up on my toes to kiss him. It took a moment for him to move his hands away from his dick, and I had to really work at him, pressing my body against his and sliding my tongue over his lips until he finally gripped my hips, hauling me in and kissing me properly.

"They're pulling your leg. It's just a blood test. Think you can handle that, or do you have a needle phobia, on top of your Q-Tip phobia?"

"As long as they aren't inserting it into my penis, I've got no phobias at all."

Our appointment at the doctors' wasn't until five, to accommodate for Banjo and Rafe's after-school football practice. Colt had skipped last period, and I'd received a text message telling me to pick him up. I'd shot back a snarky reply, saying he could drive himself since he didn't know how to say please. But then he'd sent me back a really dirty message about all the things he'd do to me once we got these test results, and I changed my mind.

With some time to kill, I detoured past Rafe's house.

He'd filled Colt and Banjo in on what had happened there Thanksgiving night, but none of us had brought it up again. I'd heard him on his phone to his mom, checking in with her each evening to make sure she was okay, but anytime I'd tried to ask him about his house, he clammed right up.

But I had to know what had happened. Principal Simmons had been at school today, acting completely normal, his clothes as impeccably ironed as ever, his hair combed neatly. Not a trace of worry on his handsome face to belie his wife and son had left him, or that his son had set his house on fire like a common pyro. Not that anyone but Rafe's mom and I knew that.

I pulled onto their street and parked a few houses away. It was enough. I didn't have to go any farther to see that the house still stood. At first glance, you wouldn't have even known anything had happened. But on closer inspection, little details told the story. From my viewpoint farther down the road, I could see the charred edges of the dining room window where the flames had tried to take the house. And when I let the car roll down the hill, slowly rubbernecking as I went past, police tape covered the front door, forbidding entry.

A sick sense of satisfaction seeped through me. The fire had obviously been put out before it could do extensive damage. But a stand had been made. I just hoped it wouldn't come back to bite Rafe, or his mom, on the ass.

A few streets away, I navigated into Colt's driveway and beeped the horn. Willa's car was missing from its spot, and I guessed she was at work. Aria was probably home, though, and that made me super reluctant to go to the door. But when Colt didn't come out or answer his phone, I didn't have much choice.

Grumbling beneath my breath about him being an

inconsiderate douchebag, I grudgingly took the steps to the front door. My knock was timid, and I prayed that it would be Colt who answered.

As if I could ever be that lucky.

Aria scowled from the other side of the doorway. "What the fuck are you doing here?"

I gave her a sarcastic smile and quipped. "Good afternoon to you, too, sunshine."

She blinked at that. I probably did, too. I was as surprised as she was about how sharp my tone was. But fuck. I was sick of being her punching bag. And we couldn't keep this up. I was in love with her brother. We were going to run into each other from time to time. We needed to sort this out.

"I'm not getting him for you." She crossed her arms beneath her breasts defiantly.

I sighed. "Okay. Fine. That's your prerogative. And if you want, I'll just go sit in the car and ring him a million more times until he wakes up, or pulls his headphones off, or stops doing whatever the hell it is he's doing. But there's something I want to say first."

She bristled, and I could see it in her eyes. She was gearing up for a fight.

She wasn't going to get one from me.

"I believe you."

Her confusion flashed across her face. "What are you talking about?"

"I believe you. About my uncle. And I'm sorry. Not for what he did. I won't apologize for that, because what he did isn't my fault, any more than it's yours. But I am sorry for not being there for you. I'm sorry I don't remember how things were when we were kids. And I'm sorry for not making the time to get to know you when you came to Providence.

Those things are on me. And I can own them. You deserve that apology, and I've been slow in giving it."

Aria's expression gave nothing away. She didn't suddenly crumble and forgive me. I didn't expect her to. She simply turned her back and walked away from the door.

But she left it open.

And that felt like something. A tiny inch given on the road to building a bridge between us. I stepped inside, closing the door quietly behind me. Music blared from upstairs, and I took the stairs two at a time, passing the closed door of Aria's bedroom and taking another flight up to the attic. The music was louder up here, covering the squeak of the stairs beneath my feet.

Colt looked up from his guitar as I entered. "Could have knocked. I could have been jacking off." He grinned, teeth white behind his full pink lips.

I turned his speakers down so we didn't have to yell at each other. "Shame you weren't. I could have helped."

He groaned at that and tossed his guitar to his bed, reaching for me simultaneously.

But I danced out of his way. "Nope. Doctor appointment, remember?"

He glanced at his phone, hitting the home key to light up the time. "Shit. Yeah, okay. Why didn't you just beep? We're gonna be late."

I stared at him. "We need to get back to fight training, so I can punch you in the face for saying dumb shit like that."

"Oooh. Big words. Keep going. It's hot."

I shoved him out of the way, but we were both smiling as we ran downstairs and got into my car.

Ten minutes later, we pulled up outside a building with a sign declaring it a medical center. Banjo and Rafe lounged on the wall outside, cigarettes dangling from their fingers.

"You know there's a building full of doctors right there, probably just dying to lecture you about lung cancer," I told them.

Banjo grinned around his cigarette. "Yeah, but we look good doing it, right?"

I hadn't seen him smoke in ages, but I had to admit, it did bring back memories of the first night we'd met, which sent tingles down my spine.

He stubbed his cigarette butt out with his toe. "Plus, I needed it. I'm really frigging nervous."

I side-eyed him. He hadn't been nervous about it over the weekend when he'd been teasing Colt. "That you have an STD?"

He shook his head. "About the penis scraping."

Colt and Rafe both groaned.

"You said you were just joking about that," Colt complained.

Banjo shrugged. "How the fuck would I know?"

All three of them turned to me.

I threw my hands up in the air. "Do I have a dick? I just assumed it was a blood test. Why are you looking to me for answers?"

I took the initiative and headed for the glass doors, pulling them open, not waiting for the guys to follow me. I knew they would, even if their dicks were probably shriveling in fear right now. I sniggered at the thought. I kinda hoped there would be a penis scraping, just because they were being such crybabies. Try being a female. We got all the shitty, invasive tests. One wouldn't kill them.

Sure enough, the three of them dragged in after me and waited while I told the receptionist our names.

She pointed to the far end of the room. "Testing clinic is

down the corridor, second door on the right. Just wait there, someone will call you in when it's your turn."

Her gaze slid to the three guys behind me, then back to me. I could tell exactly what she was thinking. That I was some slut who'd slept with all three and now we all had to get tested. But then she surprised me by winking. I'd read her completely wrong. A small grin tugged at the edges of my mouth, and I led my guys to the testing waiting room.

The four of us took up half the seats in the otherwise empty space, so we were spared any further judgment when two women in doctors' coats called Banjo and me in.

Mine held a hand out in my direction. "Hi, Lacey. I'm Dr. Keller."

Banjo's doctor introduced herself, too, but Banjo stood a little warily, like she might suddenly poke him in the ribs or something.

She frowned at him. "Are you okay? I don't bite."

I rolled my eyes. "They're scared you're going to swab their junk with something sharp and pointy."

My doctor tried to hide her smile, but Banjo's frowned at him. "Got any open sores?"

His eyes went wide. "My dick is pristine!"

Colt, Rafe, and I all sniggered.

"Then you'll be just fine. Come on."

Despite his 'pristine' appendage, Banjo looked like he was being taken to the slaughterhouse.

I followed my doctor into her room and closed the door. "Do you think we could just take a little longer, so they're all done by the time I get out? The other two are being just as precious."

She chuckled quietly. "I think that can be arranged. We have more to talk about anyway." She pulled out an iPad and tapped the screen a few times while I shifted uncomfortably on my seat. She asked my full name and date of birth and she went through my different birth control options, before she asked, "You've been sexually active with all of them?"

Awkward. "Yes."

"In the last six months?"

"Yes."

"Any unprotected sex or touching of the genital areas? Of any kind. Anal, oral, vaginal?"

Uggghh. We'd been mostly good, but I remembered my slipup on the beach with Colt. And there'd definitely been some unprotected touching of genital areas. "Yes," I admitted.

The doctor simply ticked a box on her form and continued on with her questioning until she lifted her head and smiled at me. "Okay. That's it with the third degree. We just need to take some blood and then you get to pee in a cup, but after that, you're all done."

She sent me to the bathroom with a cup, and when I returned, she filled several vials with my blood. She stuck labels on each, explaining that they'd test for an array of diseases and conditions, and passed the tubes to me to check my details before storing them away.

When the last one was complete, she smiled at me. "You're all done. Hopefully your guys are, too. I worked as slowly as I could."

I hopped off the stool, taking my birth control prescription, and thanking her. The guys all stood as I walked back into the waiting room. I eyed each of them. "Good to go?"

They each showed off matching Band-Aids, where they'd had their blood taken.

"Good to go," Banjo said. He grabbed my hand and towed me to the door. "Let's just hope Colt's mangy dick hasn't given us all bunyip-itis or something."

21

LACEY

*D*ark thoughts intruded through the night, scaring off sleep. I'd managed to fill my brain with other things for the last few days, trying to write a song with Banjo. Though nothing we'd tried had come together, it had been the distraction I needed. But lying in bed, squished between him and Rafe, my mother pushed her way into my head again. I hadn't heard from her since Thanksgiving. She hadn't tried contacting me. Why would she? I'd told her to leave.

I tossed and turned, and eventually, not wanting to wake the guys, I slipped from bed and went up to the main house. In the kitchen, Selina's sleeping tablets lay discarded on the countertop, a half-empty glass of water sitting beside them. I emptied the glass into the sink and put it away in the dishwasher before tucking the packet of prescription pills back into a cupboard.

She'd taken them every night since Thanksgiving. That just made me feel worse. I knew she was struggling with the accusations April had made. I blocked them out with sex; she blocked them out with medication.

I took the stairs up to my bedroom and flopped across the neatly made bed. But it wasn't long until the lure of my keyboard called me. Selina would be dead to the world by now. She wouldn't hear me if I decided to play. I still needed to write something for the recital on Friday. I'd heard what Colt had said, about using my confusion over my uncle and my mom. But I hadn't been willing to let my guards down and allow those feelings in. They hurt too much.

But in the silence of my bedroom, the walls of resistance began to crumble. One by one, I let the bricks tumble down, and when I finally got up to sit at my keyboard, it was with cheeks wet from tears.

I put my fingers to the keys and played.

What came out was beautiful, a haunting melody mixed with the piece I'd been working on the night my uncle had been murdered. My fingers remembered the patterns, even though my brain had tried to force them out. I hadn't wanted to play it again. And it was different to how it had once been. But so was I. I was no longer that naïve girl who thought she knew everything.

All I knew now was that I knew nothing at all.

The music flowed around me, captivating me, and when the bedroom door opened and closed, I didn't even open my eyes. I knew who it was. Banjo sat and listened for a moment, and then he added a beat, which somehow grounded the piece, making it edgier, grittier.

The song was me. Too sweet. Too innocent at the beginning. A song that could get carried off in high notes and lost to the wind. Banjo's beat represented everything he was. Everything all my guys were. Everything Saint View. When the two sounds mixed together, they became a perfect representation of us both.

My fingers fell from the keys, and Banjo put his sticks down. We both just stared at each other.

"That's it," he said quietly.

I nodded. "It's perfect."

We played it over and over all night long, committing it to memory, recording it so we could play it back, tweaking it here and there. And when the sun came up, and Banjo kissed me softly in the warm light of the new morning, I knew we were ready.

Maybe I was ready, too.

I'd come to Saint View for answers. But I needed to look closer. Look back. I needed to find my mother and hear it all. The good. The bad.

I was ready for the truth.

22

LACEY

*M*eredith and Jagger lay on my bed, watching me frantically throw clothes out of my wardrobe. The pile on the floor grew bigger by the minute, but nothing was right, and I was panicking. "Are you two even going to help me?"

Meredith twisted lazily onto her side. "You've discarded fifteen already perfect outfits. What's the big deal? It's just a school show."

"Maybe so, but I haven't gotten up on a stage to play in over a year. And this song..."

"What about this song? You still haven't let us hear it." Jagger put a large pink lollipop back in her mouth, rolling it with her tongue.

"It'll be better if you just hear it live. But I'm never going to get to play it if you don't find me something to wear."

Jagger finally got up and eyed my wardrobe critically. She yanked a black dress from a hanger and thrust it at me. "This."

I groaned. "I can't. Tried it on yesterday. Thanksgiving leftovers has it like a second skin."

Jagger waved a hand like that was unimportant. "This is Saint View. We're all about dresses that cling. Put it on and then show us."

I did as I was told because I really did love that dress. It was expensive, and not something I would have normally worn to a Saint View function, but this was a special occasion, and I wanted to look nice. I knew Banjo was wearing a button-down shirt and tie, albeit he wasn't planning to actually knot it. It was more of an accessory, hanging around his neck, the top few buttons of his shirt undone. He was a drummer after all. But that was kind of our thing. He was the rough. I was the smooth. I needed a classy dress to pull off my half of the act. But everything I owned that cost more than fifty dollars had been bought months ago before I'd started at Saint View, and before the four days of Thanksgiving leftovers. Damn those pumpkin pies.

I slid the dress up over my hips and winced as I pulled up the zipper in the back. It gathered tightly across my belly and hips, the low plunging neckline showing off a lot of cleavage. I stepped tentatively out into my bedroom, already full of excuses. "See? It's too much."

But Jagger stuck two fingers in her mouth and let out a piercing wolf whistle. "Not even. Holy hell. That looks smokin'. It's perfect."

I glanced at Meredith. "What do you think?"

Her blonde curls bounced up and down at crazy angles when she nodded. "Only problem is, we're gonna need to hustle you out of here with a bag over you or something. Those boys aren't gonna let you out of the house like that. What bra are you wearing? The girls are looking good. I need to get me one of them." She peered at my chest.

I laughed and shoved her away. "I'll lend it to you. If

you're sure this is okay, I'm gonna grab some heels and then we'll go, okay?"

A horn beeped from outside, and Jagger squealed excitedly, running to the window. "It's here!

By 'it' she meant a long, sleek black limo, which Selina had ordered as a special treat so we could all go to the recital together. It seated ten, so I'd asked Meredith and Jagger if they wanted to come, too. Jagger had brought Aaron, and Meredith had brought Trenton, the guy she'd met at the Saint View bonfire party. They were down in the pool house hanging out with the boys.

We clomped down the stairs in our heels, and Meredith ran outside to tell the guys the limo was here. She came back with big eyes and grabbed my hand. "Uh, did you know that Colt brought a date? I thought he was part of your posse now?"

"It's a harem," Jagger stage-whispered, watching the guys traipse around the pool toward the sliding glass doors.

I shushed them both. "She's his sister, not a date. And don't let Banjo hear you trying to put labels on this thing. He's been calling it a forgy."

Meredith and Jagger both burst into laughter, and I couldn't stop the grin from spreading over my face. I turned it on Rafe and Banjo, looking hot as fuck in their version of evening wear. But my gaze slid quickly to Colt, and I went to his side.

Aria stood slightly behind him, looking decidedly uncomfortable.

"I'm really glad you came," I said to her.

"Hello to you, too," Colt grumbled.

"Shut up, Colt," Aria and I said in unison.

Our eyes met, and the tiniest of smiles lifted the corner of her mouth. She wiped it away with a scowl, but I'd seen it.

It made her beautiful dark eyes crinkle slightly at the corners, in a way Colt's didn't because he was such a damn grump. I'd thought Aria was similar, but now I wondered if there was a happy young woman beneath her frowns, who'd just been too beaten down to show her true face for the last few months.

Selina rushed down the stairs, wearing a completely over-the-top dress with a fascinator-style clip in her hair. She looked ready for the opera, or perhaps a day at the races, not a public school function. But I wasn't going to rain on her parade. Not after she'd gone to the trouble of trying to make tonight into something special. I knew she felt guilty about how awful Thanksgiving had been and was trying to make up for it. It was completely unnecessary, but it was nice all the same.

She took a ton of photos and then shooed us all out the door, claiming we'd be late.

Outside, parked on the road because the driveway wasn't long enough, a smartly dressed man held open the back door of the limo. He greeted us in a friendly tone, introducing himself as Bernie. Banjo slapped his hand, and Meredith slipped him a large tip as we all squished in, giggling and sliding across the seats, each of us finding a place for ourselves.

"Please tell me there's alcohol," Colt said, zeroing in on the minibar tucked away in one corner.

But Selina stuck a foot out, blocking his path. "You might be eighteen, but eighteen isn't twenty-one, and there's not a chance in hell I'm taking nine drunk teenagers to a school function. What would the PTA think?"

"Do we even have a PTA?" Banjo wondered out loud.

"Yes, ma'am," Colt said so respectfully my eyes bugged out. I'd never heard him speak like that to anyone, apart from his own mom. It made me happy that he was making the same sort of effort with mine.

He sat next to me, and I leaned in and whispered, "Yes, ma'am. No, ma'am. Three bags full, ma'am?"

"Watch yourself, princess. The night is young." His voice was full of promise, his gaze drifting from my face, and lower over my cleavage.

It heated my skin, but I faked outrage. "Hey. Eyes up here."

"Nah, they're good where they are."

I elbowed him, and he chuckled, stretching to put his arm around my shoulders. I nestled against his side, excited butterflies swarming around my belly and we cruised the streets to the high school.

We pulled up out the front and got out to stares and whispers from the other kids. There were only a few dozen actually performing, but most of the school seemed to have turned up, either to support friends or to make fun of those they weren't as close with. I wrapped my coat around me a little tighter to ward off the chilly night air, not worried by their stares for once. My friends snapped selfies and group shots with the limo in the background, wide grins firmly in place. I took in their smiling faces and my nerves ratcheted up a level. I hadn't even known half these people a few months ago, and yet now, here I was feeling like they were the most important people in my life. Three of them looked a whole lot like my future. Not a future I'd ever dreamed of, but it was ours, and it was there for the taking.

"Can we go inside?" Meredith asked.

Aria nodded. "Where are the bathrooms? I need to go before the show starts."

"I'll take you," I offered. "Come to the ones backstage.

They don't get used half as much as the main ones. They'll be cleaner."

Aria seemed like she might refuse my offer for a moment, and Colt glared at her.

I was trying. That was why I'd asked him to invite her to come with us tonight. None of these Saint View kids had ever seen a limo, let alone ridden in one. While fancy cars weren't anything particularly exciting to me, I knew that was privilege.

She reluctantly gave in. "Okay, thank you."

I said goodbye to the others, who went to line up outside the main doors of the gym. It had been converted into our theatre for the night with rows and rows of cheap folding chairs and a makeshift curtain around the stage. Banjo, Colt, and I led Aria to smaller door at the back of the building marked 'staff only.' Miss Halten, our music teacher, stood there letting students in. She didn't even give Aria a second glance, since there was more than just our class performing tonight, and she probably didn't know every student.

On the inside, I tapped Aria on the arm, not game to grab her hand like I would have had it been Meredith or Jagger. "Bathrooms are just down this hallway."

Banjo planted a kiss on my cheek and pointed to the backstage gathering area. "I'm going to go make sure our instruments are all set up properly. See you in a bit?"

I agreed, and he and Colt turned in the opposite direction, joining the flow of other kids who were all doing the same thing.

"Twenty minutes until showtime," someone called over the top of the din.

That set me hurrying. I knew the guys would check out the ancient piano the school had moved in. And Miss Halten would have had it tuned. But I wanted to make sure for myself, too, so this bathroom detour had to be a quick one.

Thankfully, there was no line for the girls' bathrooms, so Aria and I walked right in. At the sinks, Gillian scowled at her reflection, peering into the dirty mirror and frantically dabbing makeup on her cheeks.

She jerked upright when we entered, shooting me a look of annoyance before she realized I wasn't alone. "Aria?"

"Oh my God, Gilly!" Aria pushed past me, and the two of them threw their arms around each other like long-lost besties. A tiny flicker of jealousy wormed its way in. Colt's sister and his ex obviously had a very close relationship. I knew it was early days for us yet, and that he'd been with Gillian for years, so she'd had time to build that relationship with Aria. But it was still a little hard to realize there was a bond there that I may never have with her.

Instead of being a bitter bitch about it, I tried to smile. Aria squeezed Gillian tight, a squeal of happiness bursting from her chest.

But the noise that came from Gillian was anything but happy. She let out a sharp yelp of pain, letting go of Aria quickly and stepping away.

"Are you okay?" I asked her.

"Like you care," Gillian snapped.

"Of course I care. I'm not a monster."

"Just a cheating whore."

I rolled my eyes. "Get some new lines. I've already heard that one a million times—" My gaze narrowed in on her arm. In particular, the black bruise that crept out from beneath the sleeve of her dress.

There was no mistaking a bruise like that. It was distinctly finger-shaped, from somebody grabbing her with force.

Or somebody holding her down.

Dread filled my stomach. The same sick, creeping feeling that had swarmed me every time I'd seen her with Owen. Without even thinking, I yanked up her sleeve.

Aria gasped at the clear calling card of abuse.

"Hey!" Gillian protested, batting away my hand. "What are you doing, you crazy bitch?"

But I wouldn't be put off by her acid tone. Not this time. Not when the evidence was right there in front of me. "What are *you* doing, Gillian? That's the question. Why are you with him?"

Aria's worried gaze darted between the two of us but settled on Gillian. "Who are you with?"

"Owen," I supplied when Gillian didn't say anything.

Gillian refused to look at either of us. She tugged her sleeve down and went back to applying her lipstick.

Aria grabbed Gillian's lipstick from her fingers and hurled it across the room. It hit the wall and fell to the tiled floor with a clatter. "You need to break up with him. Damn it, Gillian. You need to report him."

My mouth fell open at Aria's sudden burst of aggression, though in hindsight, it shouldn't have been a surprise that her worry had morphed into anger. A burning rage turned her black eyes bright.

For a moment, I thought Gillian would deny it again. Or get angry with Aria, the way she would have with me. But then her gaze flickered, meeting mine in the mirror. And I knew she'd realized the same thing I had.

There was no reporting Owen Waller. He was the true untouchable.

People had said that about Rafe, Banjo, and Colt. They might have managed to rule the school, but Owen held a power that none of us could get close to.

I was so fucking sick of it.

I took her hand, surprised when she let me. "Please. Let me help. I'll work something out. There's got to be someone we can go to."

But then Gillian dropped my hand, her vulnerable expression morphing into one of indifference. "I don't know what you're talking about. Just leave me alone. Don't you have half the school outside the doors just waiting to pound your pussy? Worry about your own love life."

Aria blanched, but Gillian's words didn't faze me. Because now I saw them for what they really were. Armor.

She'd need it. We both would.

Because I was done. I was so fucking done. Owen couldn't be allowed to do this anymore, no matter who his father was.

I was declaring war.

And Owen had no idea what was coming.

From the side of the stage, I watched Colt and Gillian perform. To her credit, she was the ultimate professional. To look at her now, with her head held high and her shoulders pulled back, you would never realize the pain she was carrying. Or the secrets. The lies.

When she opened her mouth to sing, and her high, sweet voice filled the gymnasium, a hush fell over the crowd. She was dynamite.

Colt sat on a stool beside her, playing his acoustic guitar, every part the quiet, brooding, sexy-as-fuck rock star.

"They're good," Banjo admitted, slinging his arm around my shoulder. "But not as good as us. You've got the solo in the bag."

I shrugged. "I haven't even prepared anything," I said truthfully. And after watching Gillian perform, I knew that wouldn't be a problem. She'd get the solo.

I hadn't forgotten how much I'd once wanted it. But now, in the wake of everything else, it just didn't feel important. That goal to get up there by myself and blow everyone away had been based on spite. I'd known Gillian wanted it, and so I did, too. At the time, she'd had Colt, and I hadn't.

The tides had turned. The wave had crested with me on top, and her pummeled into the sand, thrown about by the force of the ocean.

It didn't sit well with me.

I didn't want this. The solo was the least of my worries.

Clutched in my hands, my phone flashed at me, distracting me from the performance. Thank God I'd put it on silent. I frowned at the number I didn't recognize.

Banjo glanced over my shoulder, then leaned in closer so only I would hear him. "It's the clinic. They just called me, too. STD free, baby."

With the knowledge the call wasn't anything important, I sent it to voicemail and turned into Banjo's side, wrapping my arms around his waist. "Good to know."

He nuzzled into the spot behind my ear. "Hopefully the others got their results today, too...because I spoke to Bernie—"

"Bernie?"

"The limo driver? And we've got it until one a.m. So I was thinking, that after we drop everyone else home...."

I giggled. "You wanna do it in the back of the limo? With poor old Bernie up the front?"

"There's a privacy partition."

"Oh, because that makes it okay?"

He grinned devilishly. "If I fuck you with my tongue, just the way you like, does that make it okay?"

A blush heated my cheeks, even though he'd said it too quietly for anyone else to hear. "He's probably used to it, right? Probably has people messing around in the back all the time."

Banjo sniggered and threw my own words back at me. "Because that makes it okay?"

I elbowed him, but then Colt and Gillian finished their song, and the crowd broke out into thunderous applause. Banjo and I joined in, Banjo letting out an earsplitting wolf whistle.

Gillian came off stage as the curtains closed temporarily. It was our cue to go out and set ourselves up, but I hesitated, my gaze meeting Gillian's. "That was amazing," I told her honestly.

I expected one of her usual biting remarks, but for once, it didn't come. Instead, her voice was soft when she simply replied, "Thank you."

Fighting back surprise, I followed Banjo onto the stage, but when I glanced back over my shoulder, Colt wasn't the only one standing there watching us from the wings. Gillian watched me, too, her expression a confusing mixture, but not full of anger and hate the way it usually was. That gave me hope that maybe she'd let me in. Let me help.

Let me do what I should have done in the first place.

I'd been scared.

I wasn't anymore.

"Lacey," Banjo said quietly, as the crowd beyond the curtain began to settle. "You ready?"

I was ready. For everything.

When the curtain slid open, I blocked out everything else. Gillian. Owen. My need for revenge. Even Colt watching me with an intensity that made me tremble. I couldn't think about that right now. All that existed was Banjo, me, and the song we'd written together.

I sucked in a deep breath and held it while I touched the first key.

That was all I needed to fall into the song. My fingers raced over the old piano, pulling out the soaring, sweet melody that held the audience quiet. I built it high, the notes pinging around the silent gymnasium, gathering anticipation.

From the corner of my eye, I saw Banjo spin his drumsticks. And when he came in with a crashing beat, the crowd cheered.

It fueled me. I let it in, using their enthusiasm to push the now faster beat that Banjo set. And when I touched the last key, the silence that settled was for but a moment. Then the crowd went wild. From the back of the room, Rafe, Meredith, Selina, and Jagger were all on their feet, cheering our names. I grinned out at them as Banjo came out from behind the drums and grabbed my hand, tugging me toward the front of the stage.

"Take a bow, princess," he said over the cheers. "You killed it."

"We did," I corrected.

We both took our bows, like Miss Halten had instructed us to. I suspected Banjo might have stood there all day, lapping up his moment of glory, but then the curtains slid shut, and we stepped out of the way.

I looked for Gillian on the wings, wanting to try to talk to her again, but she'd disappeared. Colt had his arms crossed over his chest, cocky grin in place.

I stopped in front of him. "What? No congratulations?"

"Nope. Because that was so fucking good I'm scared you're gonna beat me."

I grinned up at him. "Hate to break it to you, but I think Gillian has both of us beat." I'd finally spotted her to my left, standing beside Miss Halten with a massive shit-eating grin on her face.

She ran over to us and threw her arms around Colt. "I got the solo!"

"Congratulations," I said sincerely, meaning it. "You deserved it."

She eyed me cautiously, perhaps looking for some sign I was being sarcastic.

She wouldn't find any.

"You were okay," she conceded.

Colt snorted at that, but I knew that was about as close to praise as I'd ever get from Gillian.

She took to the stage again, and I stood between two of my guys, watching her set herself up.

"So, not to be a bitch," I said quietly. "But do we really need to stay for this? I'm kinda dying to get back into that limo..."

Banjo threw a look at Colt over the top of my head, and then I was hauled out of that gymnasium quicker than you could say "limo sex."

23

LACEY

It took too long to drop everyone else home. We did the rounds of Saint View, returning Aria, Jagger, Aaron, Meredith, and Trenton to their homes, before cruising back to Providence to deliver Selina.

She slid from the car with a smile, then leaned back in the open door. "I'm really proud of you." She started by looking at me, but then turned her warmth on Banjo and Colt, too. "All three of you were amazing. I wish I had even a tiny bit of your talent."

Colt said a polite thank-you, but Banjo crawled across the seats and planted a loud kiss on her cheek. "You're the real MVP," he declared.

Selina smiled at him. "Don't think I don't know you're buttering me up because you're about to take my daughter out for a night of backseat debauchery."

Colt choked on that, and Rafe mumbled something awkwardly under his breath.

But Banjo grinned. "It's like we share one brain, Sel. You just get me."

Selina shook her head at him, then turned to me. "Have fun. Behave yourselves. I'll see you in the morning."

I blew her a kiss from across the other side of the limo, and then she was gone, walking up the driveway in bare feet, her heels clutched in one hand. Banjo pulled the door shut and grinned at us wickedly. "All alone." He gave an overexaggerated wriggle of his eyebrows.

"Not quite," Bernie called from the front seat. "Where do you kids want to go?"

We all looked at each other, then Colt sidled over to the window. "You can't see in these windows from outside, right?"

"No, sir."

"And is this partition soundproof?"

Bernie chuckled. "No, but don't worry, I can't hear a thing once it's up and I have my music on."

Colt's grin widened. "Let's go to the city. And here." He passed Bernie a generous tip, which I suspected was probably an entire day's pay at the gym. "Just keep driving, okay? We'll tell you when to stop."

Bernie took the cash and pocketed it. "You got it. One nighttime tour of the city, coming up."

Colt slid the partition closed and went straight for the minibar. "This shit is included in the price, right?" But he didn't stop to wait for an answer, just pulled an array of little alcohol bottles from the fridge and handed them around. The boys all took scotch, while I went for tequila, letting the pleasant burn slide down my chest and settle low in my belly.

"You were so fucking hot up on stage tonight," Rafe said. "One day, the three of you are gonna be up there for real. Playing to sold-out concerts around the country." He took another sip of his scotch. "And I'll be your groupie."

Banjo grinned at him. "That mean you'll be outside my dressing room, ready to drop to your knees whenever I want you?"

The heat that flared in Rafe's eyes matched the heat flaring deep between my legs. I loved the dynamic between the two of them. It was always playful, yet somehow so masculine and just...hot. It never failed to get me going.

Colt shifted in the seat beside me. Rafe caught it, too, and cocked his head to one side. "I'd do it now, if Colt wasn't here."

He was goading him, pushing him. Or maybe just giving him an out, if he didn't want to watch his best friends get down with each other. Sure, we'd all been there, in the pool house, but that had been very focused on me. I knew how hot Banjo and Rafe were together, but Colt hadn't seen that yet. Not like this.

Colt spread his legs a little wider and reclined on the seat. "Don't let me stop you."

The interest in his voice belied his casual pose.

Rafe chuckled. "You just gonna sit there and watch?"

"That was my plan. "

"Hot," Banjo muttered.

He was right. It was.

Rafe turned to Banjo. "Come here."

Banjo slid along the seat, until they sat side by side. Rafe gave Colt one last, challenging look, and then grasped Banjo's chin and kissed him. Banjo opened for him immediately. Without breaking the kiss, Rafe reached for Banjo's fly, undoing it with deft fingers and sliding down the zipper.

"Last chance to change your mind, Colt," Banjo taunted with a cheeky grin.

Rafe didn't give him a chance to voice a complaint, not that I thought Colt had one. Like mine, his breath had quickened, just watching Rafe and Banjo kiss. The two of them were so in tune with each, their bodies so responsive, that it was hard to ignore the heat they generated.

Rafe freed Banjo's dick from his pants and ran a hand over his hard length. Then he leaned over and sucked him into his mouth.

Banjo's head dropped back, and he let out a groan of pleasure. One hand fell to the back of Rafe's head, Banjo's fingers sliding into his hair, gentle pressure guiding his movements.

Colt's hand landed on my thigh and squeezed. Then it walked slowly down my leg, finding the bottom hem, before wandering back up my bare skin, taking my dress with him. My breath hitched, and I shifted so the gathered material could pool around my waist.

Colt's fingers moved to my inner thigh, inching higher and higher, to the place where a pulse had taken up, throbbing with a new need.

Colt wasn't quiet with his demands. "Take your panties off, Lacey. I want to see you."

Banjo lifted his head and opened his eyes at that. They connected with mine, a fire burning there. I shifted again, hooking my fingers in the lace at my hips and pulling it down my legs.

Rafe took a break from working Banjo's dick and glanced up, too. His gaze slid right from my face to the bare mound between my legs. My nipples beaded, and I knew all three of the guys watched me. God, they were so hot when they stared at me like that. Like I was the most desirable thing in the world. When Colt's fingers pushed my thighs apart, I let them fall shamelessly.

There had never been any shame here. They had never made me feel anything but wanted and adored. Cherished.

The fact I turned them on, just by looking at me, was such a heady feeling that I just wanted it all the more. I wanted to put on a show for them. I wanted them to watch me come. Watch me fall apart.

With the outside world flashing by at speed, and the soft hum of Bernie's music muffled by the partition, I turned to Colt and kissed him. He tasted of mint, his tongue slicking into my mouth, devouring and exploring, matching the pace his fingers set below. He trailed over my mound, stroking me, massaging me, until I was breathing hard and kissing him with urgency. It was pure relief when he finally found the arousal building inside me and coated two fingers with it, sliding it up over my clit for a long, delicious moment, before pushing them up inside me.

Like Banjo, I dropped my head to the back of the seat, closing my eyes and letting the pleasure wash over me. Across the limo, Banjo's groans intensified, taking me higher right along with him. Colt kept up a constant rhythm with his fingers, urging my thighs wider and spearing up into me to touch that spot deep inside that had me clenching with need. He nudged the strap of my dress off one shoulder, exposing my breast, and I moaned as his hot, warm mouth closed over my nipple.

I rolled my hips, aching inside; dying to get just that tiny little bit more of Colt so I could fall over the edge.

"Not yet," he murmured.

I opened my eyes to find him and Rafe grinning at each other.

"You fuckers and your delayed orgasms," Banjo complained. But his heated gaze was trained traveling over one naked breast and my dress pooling around my waist. "Though this time, I'm not going to complain, because at least I'm still hard to do other things." He crawled across the floor of the limo and settled himself between my legs. "And there's definitely some other things I want to do." He palmed his dick, stroking it slowly while his gaze rose from my pussy to my eyes. "Did you get your test results tonight?"

"Got mine," Rafe said. "Clean as a whistle."

"Ditto," Colt replied.

All three of them turned to me. "I missed the call," I admitted.

I was sure Bernie heard the groans of frustration that echoed around the limo, even over the bass of his 90's hip-hop.

"How many condoms do we have?" Rafe asked. "Did anyone even bring one?"

Colt flipped open his wallet and came out empty-handed. "Shit. Didn't restock it after that night on the beach." He ran a frustrated hand through his hair, the bulge behind his pants noticeable. "Oh well, guess we're sticking to third base tonight."

"Third base is still good," Banjo said.

Rafe's gaze rolled over me. "But how fucking good does home base look right now?" He flung an arm over his eyes, making me laugh. "Quit laughing, Lacey. You have no idea what you're doing to me right now. And the fact I'm not gonna get inside you tonight is killing me."

With amusement twinkling in my eye, I casually picked up my phone, tapped the voicemail the clinic had left earlier, and pressed the phone to my ear.

"Who you calling, princess?" Banjo asked. He was still on the floor between my legs, but now he was gazing at me like I was some forbidden fruit he wasn't going to get to taste.

"Test results are on my phone. I'm just checking them so you can stop missing the obvious fact that we could just stop at a gas station for condoms. Honestly, you're all such drama llamas."

Banjo glanced at the others. "Do you hear this? She thinks she's funny." He pushed my knees apart once more and ran his tongue up the inside of my thigh and over my mound. "Still funny?"

I groaned in response and he wasted no time, his tongue slicking straight through my center. It was so good I nearly dropped the damn phone. With my concentration more on Banjo's mouth at my core than on the doctor prattling on in my ear, I shifted to give Banjo better access and grinned as Rafe came to sit by my side. He leaned in and sucked the delicate skin at my neck. Not to be outdone, Colt went back to sucking my nipple.

When I froze, all three looked up at me curiously. "You good?" Banjo asked. "Did I hurt you?"

I cancelled the call and shook my head quickly. "God, no. Of course not."

Banjo raised one eyebrow. "Don't tell me you have gonorrhea or something?"

Colt groaned. "Way to kill the sexy vibe, dickhead." But then he winced at me. "You don't, right?"

I shoved him in the shoulder. "No! Of course not. I'm STD free."

All three of them suddenly looked relieved. "So we're good?" Rafe asked, excitement building like it was Christmas morning and he'd just seen his gifts. In this case, his gift being bareback sex.

Banjo didn't wait for any such confirmation. He simply put his mouth over my clit and tongued it until all talk of doctor's messages and STD tests fell away. Rafe undid the zipper on my dress, and between the three of them, they tugged it off me, the slinky material just getting in the way of what everyone wanted. Completely naked and with Banjo moving between my legs, I reached for the others. With their help, I freed their erections, working them both up and down while the smaller towns outside gave way to the twinkling lights of the city.

Banjo's mouth was magic. A pure God-given talent, and he drove me higher and higher, until my rhythm on Colt and Rafe's dicks became sloppy and uneven. They moved away, letting Banjo lay me down across the bench seat.

"Kiss me," I whispered, not to any one in particular.

Rafe was closest, and he claimed my mouth with his tongue, and the sweet way he gripped my face like I was everything. Banjo shifted so he was between my legs, and when his warm, thick cock slid inside me, there were no barriers between us.

"Fuck," he groaned, going still. "Fuck, Lacey."

His hips reared back, before thrusting into me again. My thighs clenched around him, wanting more, not wanting him to leave, but Banjo wasn't going anywhere. He moved himself in and out of me so deliciously I could barely stand it. Colt found my nipples, squeezing them roughly, each one shooting pinging darts of pleasure through my already needy body. He squeezed my breasts, massaging them, working my nipples into stiff peaks that he then covered with his mouth, sending me even higher.

Rafe devoured my mouth, his dominant side claiming me for his own, even as his best friend plowed between my legs, building me up to an orgasm that was going to blow my mind. The pleasure pushed out all thought. All worries. There was no room for anything but Banjo inside me, my breasts in Colt's hands, and Rafe's mouth that turned my insides to liquid heat.

"I need to come," I moaned uselessly, well aware they already knew it.

But I needed them to feel it, too. To feel the same way I did. I twisted my head and pulled Rafe in, whispering into his ear, "I want you in my mouth."

He groaned so loud I thought he might have come. But then his erection was at my lips, and I wrapped them around him, sucking him in.

"Fuck, I love when you talk like that," he murmured.

Colt snorted. "Bet you're loving that she can't talk at all right now, too."

Through my blissed-out haze, unwilling to take my mouth off Rafe's dick for even a moment, I flipped Colt the bird.

He caught my finger, sucking it into his mouth, our gazes clashing. We held the look, Rafe thrusting into my mouth, Banjo between my legs, Colt and I staring each other down, because that was just what we did. He slowly took my finger from his mouth, shiny from where he'd licked it, and guided it between my legs.

I didn't need any further instruction from him. I knew what I needed as much as he did. With my wet finger, I rubbed tight little circles over my clit until I couldn't stand it anymore. My eyes rolled back, and I came so hard I saw stars. I moaned around Rafe's dick, swallowing him down when my pleasure set him off. Banjo stilled between my legs, his body tensing to pour inside me with a yell, my name mixing with Rafe's groans of ecstasy.

Banjo moved away, and Rafe pulled from my mouth. I still pulsed and ached, not ready for the void they left behind. But then Colt was between my legs, urging my thighs wide again and covering my body with his own. His dick hovered at my entrance, his abs to my belly, my breasts crushed beneath his chest. He licked up my neck and nipped at my earlobe, kissing me there straight after to soothe the sting. His dick bobbed lower, slick with his own arousal, and probably Banjo's, too, but neither of us cared. I moaned loudly as he prodded at my back entrance, nudging his way inside.

"Gonna fuck you here, princess. I want you tight around my cock when I come inside you. Get on your stomach."

I've never flipped over so fast in my life. He barely gave me any room to move, his body pressing my stomach and breasts to the leather seat. I twisted my head to one side so I could see Rafe and Banjo watching us.

But this was all about Colt. And what he could make me feel. He dragged his hand down my spine, and then over the globes of my ass cheeks, squeezing them hard before gripping my hips and guiding them up so my knees sank into the soft leather.

My clit throbbed, aching with the new need building inside me, and the anticipation of having him. I jolted when he sent a stinging slap across my ass cheek, but God, the pleasure it set off inside me was delicious. With his slick cockhead at my entrance, I pushed back, taking control of what I wanted.

And what I wanted was him. Them. Everywhere.

He was gentle, fucking me slowly, giving me time to adjust, but all too soon, the pleasure was overwhelming. He leaned over me, hips working, his erection pumping inside me. His fingers reached around to find my clit, and there was no holding back. I fell over the cliff again, my pussy spasming in on itself, my ass clenching around his cock, my legs trembling with ecstasy.

"Colt!" I screamed, pressing back harder, taking everything he had and yet wanting more. I wanted him. Needed him to come. Needed him to feel the same way I did.

When he came, he was loud, roaring my name, groaning out his pleasure, hot and thick and fast inside me. He pumped in and out, drawing out our orgasms, torturing us both in the most perfect way, until neither of us could take it a moment longer.

We crashed down onto the seat, completely and utterly spent. Everything tingled, from my toes and fingertips, up my limbs, and circling through my body like firelight dancing beneath the moon. Our chests rose and fell in unison while he kissed the back of my neck sweetly and helped me up. Rafe and Banjo had made some makeshift wipes from napkins and a bottle of water, and I cleaned up as best I could, wriggling back into my underwear and then my dress. Rafe and Banjo pulled me to sit between them, and I cuddled into them, wishing the afterglow didn't have to fade.

Because without it, everything came back. My conversation with Gillian in the bathroom, and my suspicions Owen was hurting her. The phone call from the doctor. And finally, the one thing I hadn't told my men, preferring instead to let them touch me until it had gone away.

It couldn't go away forever.

Into a quiet limo, I told them my truth. "I'm pregnant."

24

LACEY

Three sets of eyes swiveled in my direction. One set blue, one green, one almost black. All equally wide and full of confusion.

"What?" Banjo asked.

I bit my lip, turning to him first. He was the most laid-back of the three of them and seemed the easier subject to focus on. I was scared to look at Rafe or Colt, but Banjo was always sweet and kind and calm. But right now, his face was completely blank. There was nothing but shock in his expression, the blood drained from his face, leaving him unusually pale.

"Banjo," I said quietly.

But he just shook his head. And then he lunged for the partition, yanking it open. "Stop the car. I need to get out."

"Banjo!" Rafe barked. The car slowed to a crawl and then parked on the shoulder.

But Banjo yanked open the door and let himself out into the night, stalking away down the road. I watched him go, too shocked by his reaction to even move. I glanced down as Rafe picked up my hand and squeezed it. Something silent passed between us, and I nodded. "Go after him."

Rafe hesitated, but we both knew he had to. Banjo had done this once before. Run when it had gotten too hard, and we'd spent the next twenty-four hours terrified he was dead in a ditch somewhere. I couldn't do that again. And neither could Rafe.

"Please. Go talk to him."

"I love you," he murmured.

The door slammed behind him, leaving me alone with Colt. His black eyes burned, but I couldn't read him. I had no idea if he was upset, or angry, or just in shock like I thought I was. I'd gone from feeling everything, to feeling absolutely nothing in the space of minutes. And maybe that's why I'd done it. Had sex with them instead of telling them straightaway. Because I knew this was where we'd end up. From the moment I'd heard the words on that message, everything had changed. Yet all I'd wanted to do was keep it the same.

"Lacey. We have the results of your STD tests, and they all came back normal. However, I'll need you to stop the birth control I prescribed at your appointment. Your blood test showed an elevated HCG level, that indicates early pregnancy. Congratulations. I'd like you to call on Monday morning and make an appointment..."

I hadn't even listened to the rest.

"Is it mine?" Colt asked. "We had sex bare that night on the beach, but I didn't finish inside you..."

"I don't know," I said honestly. "That was one stroke. Maybe it was that. Maybe a condom split and we didn't notice. It could be any of you."

Shame washed over me. Unwanted and unwarranted, but it was there anyway. I had no idea who the father of this baby was, and there were names that went along with girls in my position. Horrible, hateful names, I would have never called someone else, but now dark voices whispered in my ears, labeling me with the same slurs. "Slut," they whispered. "Whore."

"Stop it," Colt said, reaching across the limo and grabbing my hand. He said it so viciously I wondered if I'd said the words out loud. He pulled me onto his lap and wrapped his arms around me so tightly I could barely breathe. And when I trembled, he buried his face in the crook of my neck and replaced the dark thoughts with his own sweet whispers.

"It doesn't matter whose it is. I fucking love you, Lacey Knight. That baby is mine. You're mine. And if Rafe and Banjo feel any differently, then I'll still be here. I'll always be here."

That was all it took for me to break down and cry. I clutched him in the dim interior of the car, holding him tight, because he was the only thing anchoring me right now. I sobbed into his shirt, crying out all the fear instead of letting it consume me. The dark whispers went away, chased off by his love.

"Everything okay back there?" Bernie asked through the open partition.

"Everything is going to be fine," Colt said firmly, gaze locked on mine, his words more for me than our concerned driver.

Colt's phone rang, and he frowned at Rafe's photo on the screen. "Fucking hell," he mumbled as he answered the call. "What, Rafe? Did you get him?"

I couldn't hear the conversation, but Colt swore again, and when he hung up, he leaned toward the partition once more. "Bernie? Could you take us home, please?"

My mouth dropped open. "What? They aren't coming back?"

Colt's eyes were dark. "No, they aren't."

I was near asleep when Bernie dropped us at the end of my driveway. Colt bundled me into his arms to carry me inside, and I didn't protest. He took me upstairs to my bedroom, ran me a warm bath, and slowly stripped me of my clothes, dropping tender kisses over my skin as he went. They weren't particularly sexual. They were softer and sweeter than I'd ever seen him before.

"You okay?" he asked, perching on the edge of the bathtub, watching me carefully.

I nodded, even though I wasn't. I was worried about Banjo and Rafe. I wanted them here with me so we could talk this out. Not roaming around the city streets in the dark. Were they coming back at all? Rafe would, I was fairly confident. He'd said he loved me as he'd left. But Banjo... My heart broke all over again as I remembered his expression. He couldn't get out of that car quick enough.

My hand drifted to my belly. But there was no sign of the baby who grew inside me. My clothes all felt a little tighter, but I was still convinced that was the work of Thanksgiving food, rather than the microscopic baby inside me. "What am I going to do?" I asked Colt quietly.

"We," he said firmly, pushing a damp lock of hair from my face. "You aren't alone in this. And what we do is up to you."

I shook my head. "This affects you, too. All of us." I swallowed down a lump in my throat. "Maybe all of us."

We fell quiet. Because this wasn't a decision we could

make tonight, or without the two other people in this relationship.

The water grew cold, and eventually a soft knock came from the bathroom door. Relief poured through me when Rafe stuck his head in. He and Colt exchanged a look, and Colt kissed my forehead. "I'm going home. I've got work in the morning, but we can catch up after. You guys need to talk." He tilted my chin up so our gazes met. "Hey. I love you."

My heart squeezed, because I knew they weren't the easiest words for him to say, but he'd said them because I'd needed them. "I love you, too."

He left the room, and Rafe took his spot, pulling a towel from the rack by the door. He held it up as I stood, the water falling from my body, and I let him wrap me in the fluff. He kissed me softly and I fell into his arms. "Is he back?" I murmured against his broad chest. I held my breath, waiting for his answer.

"Yes. He's downstairs in the pool house."

"Is he okay?"

Rafe paused, and when I looked up into his face, it was full of confliction.

"I don't know," he said honestly.

My heart sank. This wasn't like him. Banjo's heart was so big, so wide and open. Logically thinking, I would have expected his reaction from Colt, or maybe even Rafe, but Banjo should have been the one who'd immediately jumped to my side and told me everything was going to be okay.

It hurt that he hadn't.

I didn't bother with pajamas, too exhausted to care. I dried off and slipped beneath the blankets, closing my eyes as soon as my head hit the pillow. The mattress dipped as Rafe sat beside me, smoothing my hair off my face.

"Do you want me to stay?" he asked.

I did. But I had a feeling Banjo might need him more. "Go," I mumbled sleepily. "I'll be asleep in thirty seconds anyway."

He hesitated for a moment, but then he stood and moved to the doorway.

"Rafe," I said before he disappeared into the hall.

"Mmm?"

"Don't let him go, okay? I love him. I can't do this without him."

If Rafe responded, I didn't hear it. I was already asleep.

25

BANJO

"**W**here the fuck are you going?" Rafe demanded.

I sighed, halting in the doorway. "I thought you were asleep."

Rafe sat up, the sheets falling off his broad shoulders, exposing his chest and biceps. Any other time, I would have taken all that in, and maybe crawled straight back into bed with him. But not tonight.

He scowled at me in the darkness, the only light from the lamps around the pool outside. "You run, and I swear to God, Banjo, we're done."

I cringed at the aggression in his tone. It brought back too many memories from when he thought I'd been the one to make the sex tape that was played at my and Lacey's eighteenth birthday party. I'd hated those weeks, where he'd refused to speak to me. I'd been lonely and miserable. I couldn't go through that again.

"I won't," I promised him. And I meant it. "Go back to sleep."

He looked ready to launch off the bed and block the

doorway, but I slipped out before he could. The cold air was a shock to my system after the warmth inside, and I hurried across the lawn to let myself in the back doors of the main house. On silent feet, I crept up the stairs and let myself into Lacey's bedroom.

As soon as I stepped into her space, her scent engulfed me. The pounding of my heart and the fear that had exploded inside, worming its way into every fiber of my being, began to disintegrate. I sucked in a greedy lungful, using it to calm my nervous system.

Her forehead was furrowed, even in sleep, and I hated that it was me who'd put it there. I slipped into bed behind her, fitting my front to her back, curling myself around her and locking my arms tight around her waist.

"Banjo?" she mumbled sleepily.

"Yeah, princess. It's me."

Her body relaxed in my arms. God, she was beautiful, with her halo of dark hair and moonlit features. Too beautiful to belong to some kid who'd grown up in the slums of Saint View, bouncing from foster home to foster home until his cold-as-stone brother had taken him in.

She twisted in my arms; her long dark eyelashes fluttering open. For the longest moment, we just stared at each other.

"I'm sorry," I whispered. "Fuck, baby. I'm so sorry I reacted like that."

She put a finger to my lips. "Shh. It's okay. You're here now."

But it wasn't okay. "That's not who I want to be. I don't want you to think you can't depend on me."

She traced the curve of my mouth with her fingertip. "I was worried you'd run again."

"No. I just needed..." I didn't think I knew what, but

there, in her arms, I realized I did know. "I needed a minute to let the fear go."

"I'm scared, too," she admitted. "Terrified."

That was crazy. "But why? You'll be an amazing mom. You're smart and kind and beautiful. And I know you. You'll be the mom who's in the front row at recitals. Or the mom cheering from the sidelines on Saturday mornings."

She smiled softly at that, but then her smile fell. "But that's not what you want, is it?"

"It's not that. God, Lacey. I'd kill to have all that with you. With Rafe. Hell, even with Colt if he promises not to punch anyone at peewee football games. But that isn't in my DNA."

Her soft breath mingled with mine as she inched closer. "What do you mean?"

"I've never had parents. Not ones I can remember. Mine left when I was so young, and that was it for me. My foster parents weren't anyone I'd want to be. And you've met Augie. He has the emotional availability of a peanut. That isn't a way for any kid to grow up."

"And that's a good argument for not having a baby with your brother," she said quietly, "but it has nothing to do with you."

"I don't know how to be a parent. I don't know how to give that unconditional love this baby will deserve. I feel like I should just walk away and leave it to you and Colt and Rafe. And go somewhere I can't screw the poor kid up."

She sat up abruptly, the sheets falling around her waist and exposing her perfect, high, tight breasts. She didn't even seem to notice. "Are you done?'

I sat up slowly, blinking at her response. "Done?"

"Are you done with that bullshit? Because I don't accept that. Not for one moment. You, Banjo Mitchell, are the sweetest, kindest, most openhearted man I've ever met. I saw it in you from the very first day we met, when you stepped in front of those police officers only knowing my name. This baby would be lucky to have you in its life. I'm lucky to have you. Everyone who knows you is lucky to have you. So yeah, tell me when you're done with that bullshit, and start telling me how you really feel."

Her words punched me right in the gut. "I want that baby," I whispered honestly. "I want everything we've built. I love you so damn much; I don't want to leave. But I don't want to ruin what we have or disappoint you if I can't be the man—the father—that tiny baby deserves." I clutched at her fingers, as if she were already slipping away.

"This is what I mean about your heart being too big, Banjo. We haven't even talked about what we're going to do, and you're already ten steps ahead, worried about what sort of father you'll make. I'm still selfishly thinking about myself. I hadn't even considered if I'd be a good parent." She leaned in and kissed me softly. "See? That's how I know you'd be the best damn dad on the block. You already are, because you care enough to be worried about it. You don't have to be your parents. None of us do."

She looked a little wistful about that, and it tugged at my heart. "Are you thinking about your mom and dad?"

"I know I told her to leave, and I didn't want her in my life. So I shouldn't be surprised that she did, right? I mean, it's what I said I wanted."

"But you don't anymore?"

Her brown eyes shone in the moonlight. "Every time I'm around her I just get so confused. I don't know what I want or what to believe. I just want to know the truth."

"Do you, though? And that's not a judgment," I rushed to add on. But hell, someone had to say it. "April tried to talk to you at Thanksgiving, and you shut her down the minute she said something you didn't like about Lawson."

She sighed. "I know. But he was the only dad I remember. And he was a good one, Banjo. Everything a dad was supposed to be. How am I supposed to sit there and listen to her trash his memory? I'm already struggling to hold on to the man I knew after what happened with Aria."

I squeezed her fingers with mine. "I don't know. But at least let her tell her story. Whether you believe it or not, well, that's up to you. But you gotta listen."

She snuggled in closer. "And you're worried about your ability to parent? You have absolutely nothing to worry about in that department." She pressed her mouth to mine, her eyes wet with tears. "Banjo Mitchell, if we have this baby, I hope he or she turns out exactly like you."

I kissed her back softly, but when she reached inside my sweatpants, I froze. I was suddenly all too aware of exactly how naked she was. "Wait, stop. Are you even allowed to have sex right now?"

She raised an eyebrow. "Have you already forgotten what we did in the limo? I think that ship has sailed."

That was true but... "What about vitamins? And ultrasounds? I know we haven't decided what we're doing yet, but shouldn't we be doing all that, just in case?"

She smiled softly and kissed me. "You're back."

"Huh?"

"This is how I thought you'd react when I told you I was pregnant. I expected the terror from Colt. But this? The worrying about the baby and me? This is the real you."

"Is that a good thing?"

"It's a very good thing. But right now, it's killing my buzz. I'm really naked beneath these sheets, you know, and you're still cockblocking me."

I grinned at her. "Can't have that. Nobody likes a cock-blocker."

I grabbed the back of my shirt and hauled it over my head, letting her deft fingers undo the drawstring on my sweatpants. I was hard in an instant beneath her gentle hands, so I pushed her onto her back, covering her body with mine, and kissed her. "Thank you for never giving up on me."

"Never," she agreed.

Then she tilted her hips, letting me sink inside her warmth, and that was the end of any protests I had.

26

LACEY

I took my time driving through Providence, admiring all the decorations. With Christmas only three weeks away, the town was full of festive spirit, even without any sign of snow. A crowd of people was gathered at the park as I drove by, a fat Santa in the middle of it all, taking photos with the kids.

It was startling to think maybe that would be me next year. Taking a small baby to have his or her first Santa photo. My heart rate sped up at the thought, and I wiped my clammy palms on my jeans.

In a way, I wanted to fast forward a year and be there now. I wanted to know that all of this was going to work out, and that when I stood in that Santa line, I'd be surrounded by men who loved me, all of us happy with the decisions we'd made. But there was more than just that. None of us were close to done with our educations. There was still college and opportunities for Banjo and Rafe in football, and for Colt and me in music. A baby would change all of that. We'd need more money than part-time jobs would bring us. Would Selina even let us stay in the house? It was one thing to take in a bunch of teenagers who were all old enough to look after themselves. But it was something entirely different to have a baby in the house full time.

I needed to tell Selina everything, but not until I'd seen the doctor again. Until then, it was better to just go on like everything was business as usual.

Which was why I'd told Banjo and Rafe to go for their extra practice this afternoon. They'd missed the game last night so they could be at the recital, and Coach had called an extra practice because of it. Both of them had declared they weren't going and had spent the morning hovering over me, until I told them I was going to Colt's and they weren't welcome to come. The pregnancy wasn't affecting me at all yet, so they could save their hovering for when it did. Even if it was a bit cute.

I got to Colt's just before three and debated over what to do. He didn't finish work for another fifteen minutes, and then it would take him a little longer than that to get his stuff together and get home. I probably had thirty minutes before he'd arrive. I could either sit here in my car. Or go knock on the door and ask his family if I could wait for him inside.

In the end, it was the cold that made the decision for me. Without the engine running, my convertible turned into an icebox rapid time. I strode up the path and knocked on the door.

Aria opened it. "Lacey. Hey. Colt's not home."

For the first time, there was no aggression in her voice. She didn't even sound upset. It was just a regular greeting that any younger sister would give her brother's girlfriend. Happiness at this new progression mingled with relief. Things were improving between the two of us.

"I know. But it's freezing. Would you mind if I wait inside? I won't get in your way."

"Yeah, sure." She stepped aside, leaving the door open.

I followed her, melting into the warmth of the house. It was delicious, and I shrugged out of my thick jacket, hanging it up on the hook by the door. The air was scented with cinnamon, and I followed my nose to the kitchen where Aria had a mess of bowls and spoons and an oven full of cookies.

"Baking?" I asked the obvious. "It smells amazing."

She shrugged. "Just something to fill the time. I'll package them up so Mom can take them to the hospital and give them out to the patients and their families."

I smiled at that. "That's nice of you. Is it okay if I sit and watch? Or I could help if you need an extra set of hands?"

She eyed me for a second, then opened a drawer and tossed an apron at me. "Sure, knock yourself out. The recipe is just there on my phone."

I tried not to fist pump the air. This wasn't just an improvement on our last encounter. This was a huge step forward.

The timer on the oven went off right as someone knocked on the door. Aria already had oven mitts on. "Can you grab that? It's probably Colt anyway, he must have forgotten his house keys."

I tied my apron in a knot so it wouldn't slide off my hips. "Yep, no worries. He must have gotten off early."

I hustled to the front door and pulled it open.

Gillian's cheeks were tearstained, mascara smudged, her arms wrapped around herself like she was freezing. "What are you doing here?" she snapped.

As always when it came to her, my hackles rose. "My boyfriend lives here. What are *you* doing here?"

She blinked, her shoulders falling an inch. "Shit. You're right. I shouldn't have come."

She spun on her heel and ran down the short flight of steps.

Fucking hell. I couldn't let her go. "Gillian. Stop. What's wrong?"

She just kept going.

"For fuck's sake," I muttered and ran down the stairs after her, grabbing her arm and spinning her around to face me. "Gillian, stop! Tell me what's wrong."

Her bottom lip trembled in such an un-Gillian like way that it shocked me. This was the girl, who, despite her tiny stature, had half the school terrified. She was like a Chihuahua in a bad mood, tiny but vicious, teeth always bared, barking and snarling.

She did yelling and swearing.

Not trembling bottom lips and vulnerability.

Yet right now, she was anything but strong. Her head dropped, and her shoulders shook. "I need help," she whispered. "I didn't know where else to go."

Without even thinking about it, I pulled her into a hug and held her tight. It was what I would have done for Jagger or Meredith, and it felt cruel not to do it for Gillian, too, even though I knew she wouldn't have done the same for me. She froze for a moment, and then she let out a sob so full of pain it broke my heart.

"Come inside," I said quietly, well aware it wasn't even my house, but I couldn't just leave her standing there on the curbside in this state.

She let me guide her up the stairs, and Aria met us in the living room. She did a double take when she saw the state Gillian was in and rushed to her, engulfing her in a hug. I stepped away, worrying my bottom lip with my teeth and wishing Colt would hurry up and get home.

"What happened?" Aria demanded, putting her hand in Gillian's and leading her to the couch.

I stayed back, leaning against the wall, not wanting to intrude. Gillian had been a part of Colt's family for years. And I was an outsider.

But Gillian looked to me. "You were right," she said quietly. "About Owen. I should have listened. But you had Colt, and I just..."

"You just wanted to get back at me?"

She lifted one shoulder. "Or at him? I don't know. Maybe I just convinced myself that because Owen had money..."

"That he was better?"

She didn't say anything.

I sighed and crossed the space to sit beside her. There was no point saying I told you so. "Did he hurt you?"

She lifted her watery gaze to meet mine. "We had sex. I agreed at first...."

Anger boiled in my blood. "You're allowed to change your mind. At any time."

"He's rough," she whispered. "So rough. It hurt, and I told him to stop. But apparently all us gutter trash girls from Saint View like it like that."

I was going to be sick. Memories of that night on the beach flashed behind my eyes. He held me down, his big body covering mine while I kicked and bit and fought to get away. I had six inches and probably thirty pounds on Gillian's little frame. She was lithe and strong from cheer-leading, but I hadn't stood a chance against Owen. He would have raped me that night on the beach if Colt hadn't stopped him.

I suddenly realized this would be triggering for Aria,

too. The way I felt about Owen was how she felt about Lawson. Bile rose in my throat. God. I could barely stand to think of his name anymore. I'd had to separate him in my head, into the Lawson I knew, and the one Aria had accused of doing such horrible things. But now I realized I'd given him a free pass he didn't deserve. Owen had two sides as well. The sweet guy who'd come to my uncle's funeral and hung out with me at parties. And the man who'd attacked me in the darkness, cold and callous. But that didn't make him two different people. It was still him. All of him. The good side didn't get to outweigh the bad. He didn't deserve that.

And neither did Lawson, no matter how much it hurt to realize it.

I glanced at Aria; wanting to make sure she was okay, ready to comfort her.

But in her expression, a fire burned. Her chest heaved, and the look in her eye was hard as stone. "You need to go to the police."

"We do," I agreed. "I'll go, too. I'll tell them what he did to me. Colt saw it; he'll back me up. The police already know that Colt was at the Providence fire, so Owen can't hold that over us anymore."

"His dad knows," Gillian said brokenly. "He heard it all and did nothing. When I left the house, he called me a Saint View slut and told me never to come back."

I couldn't breathe around my anger and disgust. It twisted in my throat, cutting off the air, choking me. "He'll sweep it under the rug without any solid proof."

"There's more," Gillian whispered. "The party…"

My eyebrows furrowed in confusion. "My party?"

But Gillian shook her head. "No, his. The one at the graveyard this weekend. I overheard him talking to his friends from Edgely Academy when he thought I was asleep."

"What about the party?" Aria asked, her voice low and sharp.

I was reminded again of how much like Colt she was. And even more so now that someone she loved had been threatened.

"They call it pills for pussy. It's this whole stupid game. They make colored shots. Most shots are green, with just straight tequila and food coloring. Those are the safe ones. But the other colors are assigned to each guy. And those ones are roofied. They pass them out at the party, and then whichever girl takes their designated color is theirs for the night. It's this whole big joke, because if an ugly girl takes your drugged shot, you still have to fuck her."

I sucked in a sharp breath.

"Fuck, I think I'm going to be sick," Aria said, standing abruptly and pacing the length of the living room.

"I didn't know what to do. If we go to the police, Owen will get wind of it and just call the party off. And then they'll play it again next time, but I won't be there to know the details and will be helpless to do anything about it. I thought Colt—"

"Colt can't know. He'll kill Owen. You two might be broken up, but Colt loved you for a long time," I said.

"And he's already out on bond. If he steps even a toe out of line, he could end up right back in jail," Aria added with a groan. "So what do we do? If we can't tell the cops and we can't tell the boys?"

"We deal with it ourselves," I said quietly.

They both looked to me, eyes wide.

"You got some sorta plan for that, princess?" Gillian

asked, but for once, the princess taunt wasn't said with malice.

"We let it happen. The graveyard party. It all goes ahead as planned."

"No," Aria said, shaking her head viciously. "What kind of fucked-up plan is that? We just stand by and watch a bunch of rich prick's date-rape girls for the fucking fun of it?"

I held a hand up, asking her to stop. "No. What's the one thing we've never had on Owen?" I didn't wait for an answer. "Proof. Solid, irrefutable proof that the police, even his sadist father, can't deny. Our word against his isn't enough. It fucking sucks, but it's not. We need video evidence."

"You're one of the targets," Gillian whispered.

My mouth dropped open. "Are you kidding?"

She shook her head. "Owen is obsessed with you. He talks about you constantly. About how you want him. How you tease him."

I balled my fingers into fists. "Good," I spat. "That only makes me want to do this more."

"So what's your plan?" Aria asked.

"Revenge," I said quietly. "That's all there is left."

27

LACEY

Thursday was the earliest I could get an appointment with the doctor. The four of us skipped school in order to make the ten a.m. time slot. Selina would have been suspicious if we'd left late, though, so we sat in the clinic parking lot, staring up at the building with all the time in the world to contemplate what we were about to do.

"Anybody else feel like they're going to puke?" I asked with a laugh.

Colt looked at me sharply. "Morning sickness or nerves?"

I had no idea.

"If it's morning sickness, I think I have it, too," Banjo said. He scrubbed a hand over his face. "How the hell are we going to explain this situation?"

"Do we even have to?" Rafe asked.

I shook my head. "She already knows. I talked about the three of you last time we came in."

Banjo rolled his head on his shoulders, as if trying to loosen tension. "Well, I suppose that's something."

We lapsed into silence again, lost to our own thoughts.

At five minutes to ten, Colt grabbed the handle on his door. "I can't stand it anymore. Let's just go in."

The rest of us were quick to follow. For me, the waiting had been the worst. We should have gone to school first. At least it would have made the time pass quicker.

On the inside, the receptionist directed us to a different waiting room. We followed her directions, but when we turned in, my stomach sank.

"Shit," I whispered, gazing around at the large waiting room full of pregnant women and small children. There had to be at least a dozen of them, all in various stages of pregnancy, judging by their rounded bellies. Some had partners with them; others were alone. Most rested their hands on their bumps, and with a start, I realized I was doing the same thing. I dropped my hands quickly, feeling foolish since my stomach was still flat.

"There's seats over there." Rafe headed for the corner of the room.

But it didn't matter he'd chosen seats in the most out-of-the-way spot possible. The entire room was watching us. Whether that was because we were so young, or because I was surrounded by three of the hottest men I'd ever seen in my life, I had no idea. I mean, I'd look at them, too. I did. Every day. They were beautiful. Inside and out.

Colt laced his fingers through mine and squeezed them supportively. "Fuck everyone else," he whispered. "Fuck them and their stupid boring marriages. I bet they're all miserable and cheating behind each other's backs. What we have is good. They don't get to judge."

The corner of my mouth lifted, and I glanced from Colt to Banjo and Rafe. "That going to be us in ten years? Miserable and cheating on each other?"

Colt's grin was cocky. "Not a chance you could ever be miserable with us, babe."

I rolled my eyes, even though I suspected he was right.

"Lacey Knight?" the doctor called, and the four of us got up and made our way into her office. It wasn't a large room, and I eyed the two seats opposite her desk with worry. She seemed to come to the same conclusion I did.

She gave us an apologetic smile. "Wait one minute."

She strode off before any of us could agree and came back with a chair under each arm. Colt and Rafe hustled to take them from her, and she shut the door. "Sorry there isn't much room. But I want you all to be comfortable. There's a lot to discuss."

The guys got the chairs in place, but then the doctor held out a hand to each of them, introducing herself and asking their names.

If I'd liked her last time, I liked her a whole lot more now.

She settled behind her desk and picked up a pen. "How are you feeling, Lacey? Bit of a surprise, I assume, since last time we spoke it was about birth control."

"Yes," I admitted.

"There's a lot of medical history I'll need to get from you, but first I wanted to talk about your options. You know them?"

I nodded.

"Have you talked about them?"

"Not exactly," I admitted. I knew Banjo's feelings, but we hadn't talked in depth, all four of us, about what we were planning to do. "I wanted to speak to you first."

"That's perfectly okay. Now the blood test did show that you were pregnant, and there's no fooling blood. So I don't think we need to test again. But we do need to work out how far along you are. Do you know the date of your last period?"

"Not exactly," I confessed.

"Any idea when the baby might have been conceived?"

Heat flushed my cheeks. "No, not really."

She smiled. "Stop looking so worried. Ninety percent of my patients say exactly the same thing. But that does mean I'm going to need to do an ultrasound. Are you okay with that?"

"Now?" Banjo asked.

The doctor nodded. "No time like the present."

She stood and wheeled a portable machine out from behind her desk. "Lacey, can you hop up onto the examination table over there? We'll start with an external ultrasound and see what we can see, but we might have to go internal if you're not very far along."

My pelvic floor muscles gave an involuntary squeeze of fear, which was probably a bit ridiculous, considering the guys I'd been having sex with were none too small in the appendage department.

I did as she asked, slipping off my shoes and then climbing up onto the vinyl-covered table and laid back on a scratchy pillow. My heart pounded, the nausea I'd been feeling earlier suddenly returning and attempting to send me running for a vomit bag. The enormity of the situation crashed down on me. I was about to see this tiny baby growing inside me. It was a part of me, and of one of the guys I loved so much.

Before she even put the wand to the lower part of my belly, I knew.

There were no other options. Not for me.

I was having this baby.

She slicked my belly with a thick gel then pressed the

wand into it. From the corner of my eye, I could feel the guys all inching in so they could see the monitor better. I craned my head to the side, gaze glued to the grainy black screen.

A rhythmic beat came from the speakers, and the doctor smiled. "Sounds good," she commented. "Strong heartbeat."

"That's it making that noise?" Colt choked out.

"Sure is. And that," she pointed at the blob on the screen, "is your baby."

It didn't look anything like a baby. But it didn't matter. That blob was mine. Ours. And right there, in that moment, I fell so deeply in love it took my breath away.

I glanced around at the guys, monitoring their expressions. Rafe had his head cocked to one side, like he was trying to figure out exactly what he was seeing. Colt stared dumbfounded, but with the corner of his mouth curled up. Banjo kept glancing at me, and then back at the screen like an overexcited puppy. He leaned in and put his hand on my leg, the only part of me he could reach from his seat. I grinned down at him, feeling his excitement, too.

The doctor noted down some measurements and then hit a button that made the image on the screen roll out of a printer beneath. She passed them to me. "Cutest six-week-old fetus I've ever seen."

Part of me knew she said that to all her patients, but I didn't care. It was my first taste of parent pride. And I liked it.

Obviously, Colt did, too, because he and Rafe high-fived like our little blob had just scored a touchdown. I wiped the gunk off my belly with some tissue and threw it in a trash can in the corner before sitting again.

"The scan indicates you're due in summer. Everything appears perfectly healthy for this early stage." She passed me some pamphlets, and I leafed through them quickly.

Most were things I'd need to do or not do while pregnant. But I hovered over the last one that was titled: *Adoption and Terminations. All the facts you need to know.*

The doctor must have noticed me hesitate, because she reached across the desk and took my hand. "You're young. And so this is where I'd normally ask if you have enough support." Her gaze bounced from Colt to Rafe to Banjo. "But I can see already that you have a lot of it right here in this room."

"I haven't told my aunt yet. She'll be shocked and probably upset. But she'll support me."

The doctor nodded and noted that down on her pad of paper. "Okay, well, I'll leave you to think about things and talk to everyone involved. But I'd like to see you again once you've made your decision."

"Okay."

"One last thing before you leave." Her hand hovered over a final pamphlet. "I wasn't sure whether you would want this. But there are tests we can do, either while you're pregnant or later, once the baby is born, if you want to know who the father is."

She looked to the guys, holding it out, waiting for one of them to take it.

None of them moved.

"I don't need it," Colt said. "It doesn't matter to me. I already told Lacey this, but I'm not going anywhere."

"Ditto." Rafe picked up my hand and threaded his fingers between mine.

"Me neither," Banjo agreed. "I already love him."

I elbowed him. "Might be a girl."

He shrugged. "As long as she likes football, we're all good."

28

LACEY

"Ugh, make it stop. Why do these movies always have some sickeningly sweet small town where everybody knows everybody? Or a meddling grandmother. Or a cowboy."

I threw a piece of popcorn in Colt's direction, amused when it bounced off his nose and onto his bed. "It's a Christmas movie. What did you expect?"

He picked up the popcorn, tossing it high into the air, and caught it in his mouth. "I never should have let you talk me into this."

"You have no Christmas spirit. Find some."

"Where? At a barn dance like these fools? Hard pass." He wrapped an arm around me and pulled me close instead. "How about I show you my Christmas spirit?"

I snorted. "Do you mean your spirit stick? I think it's already prodding me in the leg."

As if to prove my point, he rolled on top of me and ground it against me some more. "This one?"

"Mmm hmm. Feels big."

He sniggered. "Take your thirty layers of clothes off and I'll show you."

My phone buzzed with an incoming call, and when I retrieved it from the pocket of my pants, Meredith's name was flashing on the screen. I pushed Colt off me to answer it. "Mer? What's up?"

"Oh, nothing," she wailed, her voice high-pitched and squeaky, giving away that there actually was most certainly something. "My life is just over."

"So dramatic. Wanna spill the deets?"

"My beautician cancelled my appointment."

I raised an eyebrow. "Seriously? Okay, that's a little over the top, even for you. Just rebook it?"

"I can't! I need to be hair free by tomorrow."

"Why?" I gave Colt a warning look when his fingers tried creeping beneath the hem of my hoodie.

"Because tomorrow, I'm finally going to let Trenton pat the pussy."

I snorted, trying to hold back my amusement. "I have no idea whether to laugh or be shocked. Are you saying he hasn't seen it yet?"

"That's exactly what I'm saying. Hasn't seen it. Touched it. Licked it. Nothing!"

"Is he gay?" I asked seriously. Because this was unheard of behavior for Meredith, and Trenton not wanting to go there was the only explanation I could think of.

"What? No! I've just been trying to take it slow. I like him, Lace. I don't want to fuck it up. But…"

"But you're horny?"

She cracked up laughing. "Well, yeah. It's been weeks. And have you seen him? He's gorgeous."

I shrugged. He was all right, but he was no Colt, who was

currently kissing my neck, while his fingers ran the elastic of my sweatpants. I needed to wrap this phone call up. "Okay, so we've established that your vag will be the way nature intended when Trenton sees it tomorrow night. Is that really so bad?"

"Yes," Colt deadpanned, none too quietly.

I swatted him with the back of my hand, but Meredith squealed in my ear. "Was that Colt? See? This is an emergency. Trenton cannot see me with a full bush. Seriously, Lacey. Get over here and help me. I can't reach to do it myself."

"Oh Lord. Okay, okay. I'm coming. Be there in fifteen. Do not put hot wax anywhere until I get there."

Colt groaned and shifted off me. "Please tell me you aren't leaving?" He looked down at the erection straining behind his pants. "What am I supposed to do with that?"

I shrugged, getting off his bed, and picking up my car keys. "Jack off to the cowboys and meddling grannies?"

"You aren't right in the head, you know that?"

I leaned into kiss him. "You love it. I'll see you at the party tomorrow, yeah?"

"Are we seriously doing that? Who throws a party at a graveyard anyway?"

"Rich kids who like to think they're rebels, and poor kids who just wanna get drunk."

He shrugged. "I'll check my schedule."

I rolled my eyes because he was all talk. He liked a party as much as anyone else. But the guilt that I hadn't told him the whole truth was eating at me.

"Colt?"

"Yeah?"

"I need to tell you something, but promise you won't get

mad, hunt Owen down, and bury his body where no one will find it."

Colt's relaxed expression morphed into something savage. "What do you mean?" he growled, though I immediately knew his anger wasn't anything to do with me, but all about the mention of Owen's name. "What has that fucker done now?"

I went to the door and stood against it, blocking him from leaving. Then I explained everything that had happened with Gillian, and everything we'd planned to bring Owen down at the party.

When I was done, Colt's knuckles were white from gripping the edge of his mattress and keeping himself in place. "I'm going to kill him," he seethed.

"Or you could just be our backup. You heard the plan."

He raked a hand through his hair, indecision playing out all over his face. "Shit. The plan is good. But I don't want you involved. Rafe, Banjo, and I will do it. I don't want you anywhere near that party."

I crossed the room and sat back down beside him. "You know that won't work. I have to be there."

"The baby..."

I knew what he was saying. I was worried, too. But this was bigger than just us.

When I was sure he wasn't going to go digging through his garage for a hunting knife, I left him to his Christmas movie and ran outside to my car, taking the quickest route back to Providence and through the gates of Meredith's sprawling mansion. I tried to forget about everything that was going to happen tomorrow. Now wasn't the time. Not when I had a best friend in dire need of hot wax.

Meredith met me at the door, yanked me inside, and

dragged me upstairs to her bedroom, all the while wailing about how inconsiderate it was of her beautician to get sick on a Friday afternoon. "I bet she isn't even sick. She probably just wanted to go out clubbing. I bet her lady garden is neatly groomed and ready for plowing."

I bit my lip, stifling my laugh, and followed her into her bathroom, blinking in dismay at the array of products spread out on every available surface. "Jesus, Mer. It's like the health and beauty aisle at Costco threw up in here."

She looked insulted. "I'd never buy health and beauty from Costco."

I stifled a sigh. She'd been less of a snob lately, since we'd started hanging out with the Saint View crew, but it was never fully going to go away. At heart, she was still a rich kid with expensive tastes.

Despite the mess, Meredith knew exactly where the wax was. It was sitting above a little heater that kept it warm and runny. I picked up the stick poking out and watched the yellow wax slide off, back into the pot. "Okay, so what are we doing here?"

"The whole thing. It's all gotta go."

I cringed, eyeing her still-covered nether regions. "You're really gonna make me get all up in there, huh? You couldn't just shave?"

"And get one of those hideous bumpy shaving rashes that could be mistaken for an STI? Hell no. This is in the best friend rule book. Get in there and get the job done, soldier."

I snorted at that, giving her a mock salute and helped her pile towels on the bathroom floor, creating a makeshift beautician's table. She tossed me an extra towel to lean on, then ditched her sweatpants, leaving her in a black thong.

I indicated the pile of towels. "Please. Make yourself comfortable. This won't hurt a bit." I shrugged. "Actually, it probably will."

"Lacey!"

"Fine, fine. Come on." I turned to deal with the wax, while she settled herself into position. I swirled it, making sure it was properly combined, and then scooped some up on the wooden stick. "Dear Lord, please don't let this be a disaster that ends in a trip to the emergency room."

"Your bedside manner is so reassuring," Meredith deadpanned. She settled back with her hands behind her head. "Just do it already."

I went to smear the first line of wax, when I paused in shock. "What is that!"

Meredith's eyes flew open, and she glared at me. "Seriously? Not what a girl wants to hear when there's someone looking at her vagina."

"Not your vagina. Above it. When the hell did you get a tattoo?"

She flapped her hand around and lay back down on the towels. "Oh, ages ago. Come on, just get on with it, the suspense is making me need to pee."

"Ew." I so didn't need her peeing when my fingers were in that vicinity. I didn't give her a hard time about getting a tattoo and not telling me. She wasn't the only one who had kept a secret. I still hadn't told her I was pregnant. We'd talked about it some more, the guys and I, but nobody had mentioned announcing it to the world yet. I felt I owed Selina, Willa, and Rafe's mom, Rose, the courtesy of knowing first. But it was hard keeping things from Meredith. I smoothed the wax down over her, trying to emulate what my beautician did, wanting to do a good job for my friend. I pressed a clean white cloth to the wax, held Meredith's skin taut, and then ripped it back.

The string of expletives Meredith let out could have made a sailor blush. Coupled with the moaning, groaning, and grabbing of her nether bits.

This was going to take all night.

29

LACEY

$\mathcal{E}$arly Saturday morning, just as the sun was peeking out over the horizon, I waited in my car, engine off so as to not draw attention to myself. Two minutes before our designated meeting time, Gillian drove into the main drive of the graveyard, headed for me. Aria sat in the passenger seat, dark hair spilling out from beneath a winter hat.

Reluctantly, I got out and headed for their car. "Fuck you, Owen, for having an outdoor party at this time of year," I mumbled, and rubbed at my arms in an attempt to ward off the chill.

"It's too early for this shit," Gillian complained, handing me a cup of coffee.

I blinked at it in surprise, and then at her. "Did you poison it?"

She sniffed. "That's a bit on the nose, considering what we're here for, isn't it? Just shut up and drink your damn coffee."

Aria sighed, like the two of us were naughty toddlers.

"Not even five minutes before you started arguing. How unsurprising."

She had a point. I probably could have said thank you. But that wasn't my and Gillian's style. I could be the bigger person, though. I eyed her over the top of my cup of steaming coffee and nodded. She nodded back, and that was enough.

"Did you get the stuff?" I asked Aria.

She took out a small bag from the back of the car and passed me my credit card. "Yep."

I tucked it into the pocket of my jeans. "Let me see."

She handed over the bag. On the inside, half a dozen tiny spy-style cameras sat in their boxes.

"These will work?" I asked, skeptical.

"The guy at the shop said these were the only ones good enough for a dimly lit room, that also did audio. I figured a dimly lit graveyard was much the same thing."

I freed the first one from its packaging. "Perfect. Let's get this done before anyone comes looking to visit some dead relative."

Aria did the same with the camera she held. "Please tell me this is going to work."

Gillian followed us toward a group of headstones that were so ancient the writing on them was barely legible. "It'll work. It's simple and to the point. We just need to get them on camera, admitting to what they've done. There's no way they aren't going to be bragging to each other when they think no one is listening.

Aria pulled her shoulders back, determination straightening her spine. "Let's go."

Gillian took the lead since she knew where the party was being held. The family friendly vibe quickly gave way to the oldest section of the property, where few people ever went, judging by the untouched weeds and leaf debris covering the ground. It homed a group of crumbling graves and a mausoleum that had to be a hundred years old. The stone walls still seemed solid, but its looming presence and the silence of the morning air still gave me a creepy vibe I didn't enjoy. I shivered. Much of the early morning sunlight and warmth was blocked by the building. It cast long shadows that we had to follow Gillian into. The trees surrounding the perimeter had all lost their leaves for the winter, their branches stripped of color, adding to the overall dead feeling in the air.

"They're having it back here," Gillian said. "These graves are so old that all their immediate descendants have all passed on, too. Nobody comes back here unless they're history buffs. Plus, it has the added bonus of being creepy." She swung open a wrought-iron gate that, of course, creaked like it was straight out of a horror movie. I eyed the sky, just waiting for a one-eyed crow to show up, but it was free of birds.

I understood now why a party here was appealing. It was going to be scary as fuck in the dark. I wasn't looking forward to it. I was already itching to get out of here.

"Put one over there, behind the building. Another in that tree. Spread them out so we capture as much as possible." I took mine to the biggest headstone, thinking it would probably draw the attention of partygoers, just like it had drawn mine. "Sorry Herbert James Darwin," I muttered to the ancient headstone bearing the deceased's name. "Just gonna leave a little friend here for you..." I made sure my camera was on and pushed it into one of the cracks in the crumbling headstone, hoping it wasn't wedged in so tight that I couldn't get it out later. I stood back and surveyed my work critically.

"It'll be fine in the dark," Aria said, coming up behind me. "It's only obvious because you know it's there."

"Yeah, I guess so." I placed my second camera in a tree at the back of the mausoleum, thinking that the stone walls might offer some privacy from the main party, and therefore be a good place for Owen and his friends to congregate and brag about their conquests. Then I glanced around, searching for the cameras Aria and Gillian had hidden, but I didn't see anything. I met them back in the center. "Okay are we good? We all know the plan?"

They nodded.

I sucked in a deep breath. "Let's hope it works."

"It has to," Gillian said quietly. "Or he's just going to keep doing it."

I took her hand and squeezed it. "It'll work. I promise. Tonight we get the proof we need so Owen can never do this again. Not to you. To me. Never again."

"Never again," she agreed.

I made it home before Banjo and Rafe even woke up. I puttered around the house, doing nothing in particular, but too restless to sit and read or watch TV or even work on my music. Instead, I found myself staring out at the pool, watching the slight ripple that blew across the surface, while absently twisting the music note charm on my necklace. There was a niggle at the back of my mind, like I'd forgotten to do something important.

I jumped when the door to the pool house opened and Banjo wandered out, his hair still tousled with sleep. He jogged up, wearing Ugg boots and gray sweatpants, a hoodie stretching over his broad shoulders. He stopped a few inches in front of me. "Uh-oh. What's wrong?"

"What makes you think there's something wrong?"

"You're tugging your earlobe. You only do that when you're stressed or worried."

I blinked, realizing he was right. "Oh."

"Is it Rafe? The police would have come for him by now if they were going to. And his dad hasn't attempted to talk to his mom. He's got to have realized it's over."

"No, it's not that. Rose and Rafe are both safe. As long as he stays away from them, he's the least of my concerns."

"Then what?"

I could have blown him off, claiming it was worry over the party tonight. A million things could go wrong. What if they changed the location? What if they were more subtle than we expected them to be and they all kept their mouths shut? But it wasn't even really the Owen thing that was bugging me. We'd put those wheels in motion. It was done, no going back now. Something else danced at the edges of my memory, taunting me, flittering away before I could quite grasp it. "I don't know." I said honestly. And then I laughed; shooting a look over my shoulder to make sure Selina wasn't listening. "Is it too early for baby brain? I feel like I've lost something. Or maybe it's someone's birthday and I've forgotten."

"Wouldn't have a clue, but hey, run with it. It's a good excuse, and you'll only get nine months to use it." He kissed my hair and then stretched his arms up high above his head, linking his fingers together to crack them. His hoodie rode up, showing off a delicious set of lower abs, and those V lines running either side of his hips. The dark-blond thatch of hair above his cock was just visible above his low-slung pants.

It reminded me of what I'd been doing with Meredith last night. "Meredith got a tat," I said, stepping in close to him and running my finger over the edge of his hair. "Right here."

"Yeah?" he asked. "What of? Wait, let me guess. A dolphin."

"Ha, no."

"Butterfly?"

"Try again."

He mused on that as he moved around me and grabbed a box of cereal from the pantry. "Nope, got nothing. Tell me."

"It's script. It says forever."

He froze.

I peered at him curiously. "What? You don't like script tattoos either? It was pretty. It looked well done."

He shook his head rapidly, but the color had drained from his face.

Uncomfortable butterflies took off in my stomach. "Banjo, what?"

He glanced around, making sure we were alone. "Do you remember those photos we found on Lawson's USB stick? The ones with the woman..."

I closed my eyes. Because suddenly I knew exactly what he was talking about. It was the memory that had been fluttering at the edge of my subconscious all day. I shook my head hard. "No. NO, Banjo! I don't believe that."

Before he could say anything, I ran up the stairs and yanked open the top drawer of my desk, rummaging through it until I found the USB stick I was looking for. The one I'd tucked into my pocket when it had fallen from Lawson's pile of papers, the night of the fire at Providence. The same USB I'd gone to put a song on, when Banjo and I had been practicing, and found it full of underwear and nude shots.

Nude shots of a woman whose face had never been shown, but who had a script tattoo that read 'forever' across the top of her mound.

Tears built behind my eyes as I shoved the stick into my computer and blindly clicked around with the mouse, unable to properly see what I was doing. Banjo came up behind me slowly, putting his arm around my waist and taking the mouse from me calmly.

"No," I mumbled over and over.

"It might not be her," he said quietly, but neither of us believed it. And when he double-clicked the only folder on the drive, and the provocative photos flashed up on the monitor, I knew.

"It's her," I whispered, staring at the same tattoo I'd seen on Meredith last night.

Banjo bit his lip. "This doesn't mean anything. That could be a standard ink shop tattoo. One right off the wall that hundreds of people have."

I knew he was just trying to be kind. "It's her Banjo. You know it, too."

He didn't try to argue anymore, just wrapped me in his arms. "What do you want to do?"

My shock was already turning to anger. I grabbed my keys from my desk and pulled from his arms. "I'm going over there."

He raced after me, plucking the keys from my hand.

I whirled on him. "I'm going!"

"I was going to say I'll drive."

I didn't bother answering. Just stormed to the car, but I did go to the passenger side. Banjo shot me wary looks for the entire drive, and when we pulled into Meredith's place, I got out before he'd even fully stopped the car.

My first attempt at knocking on the door failed because my hand trembled so much I couldn't form a fist. But my second attempt was a bone-jarring pounding that sent vibrations up my arm. "Meredith!"

She pulled the door open, workout leggings hugging her lower half, and her cheeks flushed pink from whatever exercise she'd been doing. "Hey, Lace. What's up?"

I clenched my fingers around the doorframe. "Why did my uncle have nude photos of you?"

She balked at the accusation, but I didn't miss the flash of guilt in her expression that she tried to cover with surprise. "What?"

"Your acting sucks. Why?"

She bit her lip. "Lacey...you were never meant to know."

"Yeah, you don't say. You kept that conveniently quiet. Why, though, Meredith?"

"Because I was in love with him."

I blinked in surprise. Because for some reason, that was the last thing I'd expected her to say. I shook my head.

"And he loved me, too," she rushed on.

I snapped. "You're deluded. He was married!"

"I know."

"Were you even eighteen in those photos? When were they taken?"

She shook her head slowly, and I made a face. "Meredith! You know that's classed as fucking child porn?" I dropped the USB stick like it was hot, letting it clatter to the ground. I doubled over, sure I was going to vomit. "That day I met you for breakfast at the café, not long after Lawson died. You were crying over him, weren't you? The photos you were looking at, they were of him?"

"Him and I together, yes." Her voice was small, but it was still as sharp as a knife to my ears, stabbing at me over and over again.

"He raped you."

"No, it was consensual."

"You were seventeen. He was thirty-eight. And your teacher. That isn't consensual. Fuck. How many other girls are there? How many did he do this to?"

"What do you mean?"

"You know what he did to Aria."

"No. I told you, I don't believe that. He would never."

I laughed, the sound bitter and harsh. "Yeah, that's exactly what I used to think, too."

A tear dripped down her face. "Lacey, please. I'm sorry. There was just something between us that I couldn't deny... and when he liked me back...I never wanted you to know."

I was completely defeated, the energy suddenly drained from me. "Well, I do. And now I have to go home and tell my aunt what I should have told her from the very beginning. That her husband was a lying, cheating rapist who got everything he deserved."

She gasped, and somewhere deep inside me, a part of me did, too. But I couldn't bring myself to regret it. It was the first real truth I'd let in. The first real thing, I'd let myself say out loud. The man I thought I knew didn't exist.

This world was a better place without him.

30

LACEY

When yet another call went unanswered, I fought the urge to hurl my phone across the room. "Dammit, Selina!"

Rafe carefully pried the phone from my death grip before I did it permanent damage and searched my face with his intent gaze. "Hey. Stop. What's one more night going to hurt?"

I shook my head. "Why didn't I tell her about Aria?"

"Because you wanted to believe he was innocent."

"But I believed her. I said I did."

"Maybe a part of you didn't? Maybe part of you hoped it wasn't true? He was practically your dad, Lace. You could be forgiven for wanting to believe the best of him."

"I hate this," I moaned. I picked up the mask I was supposed to wear tonight. "I hate him. I hate Owen and Chief Waller. Augie. Your dad. Fuck!"

He wrapped his arms around me, until the trembles that racked my body disappeared. "We don't have to go tonight if you don't want to. We can just stay here and wait for Selina to get home. Or we can go find her..."

"No, I can't. We need to go through with this. There's nothing I can do about Augie, or your dad or Lawson. But there is something I can do about Owen."

Rafe didn't seem happy, but he just held out my leather jacket and helped push it up onto my shoulders. He retrieved a black lace mask from the bed, put it in place over my eyes, and tied the silky ribbons at the back of my head.

I critically studied my reflection in the full-length mirror. I'd gone with a more Saint-View-inspired look. Tight black jeans, with heeled boots, and deep-red lips to complement the dark eye makeup peeking through my mask.

Rafe's gaze raked over me. His hands skated up the back of my thighs to my ass and squeezed. "I can't wait to walk into this party with you dressed like that," he murmured. "And then take it off you once we're home."

I grinned over my shoulder at him. "Why wait 'til we're home? Being in public has never stopped any of us before."

He groaned. "You want me to fuck you in the graveyard, Lacey? That's kinky, even for us."

I giggled. "Let's just see how the night progresses, huh?" There were other things I needed to take care of tonight before I could even think about sex. Though staring at Rafe, when he looked at me like he was right now, made that infinitely harder. It would have been so much more fun to be going to this party without Owen and Meredith on my mind.

Colt picked us up once it got dark, seeming none too happy that Aria was in the seat beside him. He kept shooting her worried little glances that were adorable but just seemed to agitate both of them.

"Colt," I said quietly, pressed between Banjo and Rafe. "Stop acting like you want to tie her to the seat."

"That's exactly what I want to do. To both of you."

Aria gave an exaggerated sigh and got out the minute he parked the car, as if she suspected he might actually try it if given the chance. The rest of us followed her lead, getting out and adjusting our clothes. All of us wore dark colors to suit the mood of the party, with an array of masks. Aria's was made of black feathers laced with gold, and she'd worn a wicked cool gold glitter lipstick to match.

"Okay, so where is this party?" Banjo asked, gazing around.

We'd parked on a side street, since the gates of the cemetery were closed, but there was a section where the fence had come down, so I led the way, stepping around headstones and hoping I wouldn't break my ankle in the process. As we neared the back of the cemetery, music filtered through the air, and the paths became overrun with other kids coming in from multiple directions. A crowd gathered around the wrought-iron gates, and Gillian joined our group, a red devil's mask covering half of her face.

"What's going on?" I asked her quietly, hoping the music would cover our conversation.

Her gaze darted in my direction. "Shit. They're making everyone do a shot in order to get in. Make sure you take a green one."

"You think they've already spiked some?"

She lifted a shoulder. "I'm not willing to risk it, are you? Shit. We should have gotten here earlier so we could start warning people."

There was no point talking about the what-ifs. We hadn't known about the shots on entry. But I was uncomfortable with the fact that already something hadn't gone to plan. We hadn't even gotten inside yet. We inched forward as more people were let in. At the head of the line, a guy stood at the gates, blocking the narrow entryway. He had a huge tray full of shot glasses in his arms.

They were all red.

Gillian's panic was clear in the look she gave me.

"Entry fee is a shot," the guy said from behind a full-face mask.

I ran my gaze over him but quickly determined it wasn't Owen. He was tall enough, but my body didn't immediately cringe away in disgust like it did every other time Owen was around. I'd have to trust my gut on this one.

"No thanks, I don't drink," I said casually, trying to edge around the guy.

But the other one blocked my path. "Then no entry."

"You can't do that!"

He leered at me. "Can't I?"

I moved back, alarm bells going off in my head.

Rafe stepped in front of me and slapped the guy on the shoulder. "Let's get this show on the road, huh?"

Banjo and Colt both stepped up, too, pushing me, Gillian, and Aria behind them.

"Shots! Yes!" Banjo yelled, like he was already a little bit drunk. The three of them surrounded the guy with the tray, each of them jostling and grabbing a shot.

"Hey, settle down," he said, fighting to keep his tray upright.

I suddenly realized what they were doing and grabbed Aria and Gillian's hands, edging through the gates while the boys created a diversion.

"We can have more than one of these, right?" Colt asked, drawing the guy's attention in the opposite direction. "You don't mind? I love these things. What's in them?"

"Actually, yeah I do mind." The gatekeeper was clearly

annoyed, but we were already through and hurrying beyond into the darkness.

Rafe threw a glance in our direction, making sure we were in, and faked a stumble, which sent him right into the tray of drinks. It was well done, but I saw it for what it was. He didn't want anyone touching drinks that might have been spiked.

Colt and Banjo both jumped back as the hundred shot cups spilled all over the ground.

"What the fuck?"

At his yell, a bunch of other masked men appeared, all of them glaring at Colt, Rafe, and Banjo.

"Shit," Aria murmured. "Someone is gonna get their ass kicked right about now."

Rafe held up his hands in mock surrender. "Hey, man, I'm sorry. I've already had a few. I just tripped."

"He's off his face," Banjo agreed. He twisted to everyone gathering in the line behind them. "Sorry, guys, no shots tonight. Our bad."

The line groaned their disappointment, and I fought back the urge to roll my eyes at their stupidity.

"Get out," the guy said to Rafe. "All of you."

"Wait now," Colt said. "Kick him out, fine. But what the hell did I do?"

"All of you, out."

Colt went eye to eye with him. "No. We're here to party, and that's what we're going to do." His words held a barely concealed threat, and I knew it was fueled by the fact Aria, Gillian, and I were now alone inside. His protective nature couldn't handle that. Not with Owen around.

His gaze slid to mine for just a second, and I shook my head rapidly. It didn't matter if they couldn't get in. I retrieved my phone from my pocket and shot off a quick text. Colt's phone went off, interrupting the standoff, but he didn't look at it. I glared at him again, and finally, he took a step back, pulling Banjo and Rafe with him. "Fine. Forget it. This party is lame anyway. Let's go."

The three of them backed away, and Colt got out his phone to read the message I'd sent him.

We've got this. Meet us at the car.

He seemed ready to jump the eight-foot wrought-iron fence and drag us out of there by our hair. But then his fingers flew over his phone, and mine lit up silently with his text.

I love you.

Aria read it over my shoulder and groaned quietly. "You two are gross. Can we just get on with this and get out of here? I've got the heebie-jeebies already."

My gaze met with Colt's through the bars, then Rafe's, and finally Banjo's. They might not have liked that we were going to have to do this on our own, but we were going to get it done. I could see from the determination in their eyes, the guys knew it as well as we did.

This went no further. This had to be the end.

Without another word, I turned my back on the men I loved and disappeared into the darkened cemetery.

"This place is creepy as fuck," I said, as we wandered between graves.

"Made worse by the fact I can't tell who anyone is," Gillian complained.

Aria huffed out a breath. "Does it even matter? Let's just check the frigging cameras and pray we've already got something usable on them. We aren't here to socialize. The quicker we can get some proof to take to the cops the better. Getting the party and Owen shut down before they can hurt anyone is the aim of the game here."

"Fine. Each of us gets the cameras we planted, and we meet in thirty minutes. Then we get the hell out of here." Gillian rubbed briskly at her arms.

I wrinkled my nose. "I hate the idea of splitting up."

"We don't have time to hold your hand because you're scared of the dark," Gillian sniped.

I shot her a dirty look, but I knew she was right. I hated the idea that every minute we stood here, was another minute Owen and his friends had to play their vile games. "Fine. Spread a rumor that the shots were spiked, too, okay? Just in case."

Aria and Gillian both nodded, and the three of us separated. I headed for the gravestone, the one where I'd shoved my first camera. But somebody stepped in front of me the moment Gillian and Aria disappeared.

I knew who it was instantly. The blonde curls falling down her back were a dead giveaway. Meredith was the last thing I needed right now.

I spun on my heel and walked in the opposite direction, even though it meant I was going away from my target. There was a small crowd of people gathered beneath a copse of trees, and I hoped she wouldn't confront me when there were other people around.

"Lacey, stop, please. Can we talk?"

Irritation crept up the back of my neck. "You want to talk about the affair you had with my uncle? Here, in front of all these people?" I realized the gathering was the food and drinks table. My mouth was so damn dry; I picked up a bottle of water, checking it was sealed before cracking it open. I took a long, deep swallow as I waited for Meredith to respond. If other people were watching us, I didn't notice.

Meredith pulled her mask up. "If you want to tell

everyone what we did—what I did—then I'm not going to try to stop you."

"Good. Then maybe you won't try to stop me when I walk away from you either."

She grabbed my arm. "I don't expect you to forgive me. I know I fucked up. But you're my best friend."

I whirled on her. All I could think about was how Meredith had spent half her life at my place. Selina was like a second mother to her, and Meredith had knowingly slept with her husband. I knew it wasn't solely her fault, and Lawson was the real person I wanted to yell at, but he was buried in the ground only a few hundred feet away from where we stood right now. I couldn't scream or make him admit all the horrible things he'd done. I couldn't yell, or punch, or demand he apologize. All I had was Meredith. And I was angry. So fucking angry that my fingers trembled. The words punched from my chest before I could stop them. "Were you my best friend when you were riding his dick?"

Her mouth dropped open, and for the tiniest instant, I realized how cruel the comment had been. But it was too late to take it back. "Didn't think so. Bye, Meredith."

This time, she let me go. And I was grateful, because tears blurred my vision. I stumbled to the headstone where my camera was hidden and none too discreetly pulled it out, enclosing it in my hand so nobody would see it. Then I pushed through a group of people dancing and drinking in a clearing, heading for the back of the mausoleum where my second camera waited. With each step, the chilly winter air whipped around me, chilling me to the bone. I ducked instinctively at a flapping noise. When I looked up, a group of birds, or maybe bats, flew overhead. "Time to get the fuck out of here," I mumbled. Grass, leaves, and sticks crunched beneath my boots as I hurried to the other side of the imposing stone building. I stopped abruptly when there wasn't a soul on the other side. There was nothing but more graves and that wrought-iron fence that enclosed us in.

Well, that was a waste of a camera. I'd put one here specifically, thinking that it would be the perfect private place for people to be up to no good. But it seemed I was the only one who'd ventured this far. Glancing at the time on my phone, I noted that I still had fifteen minutes to kill before I had to meet Aria and Gillian, so I connected the camera I'd already collected to the micro USB on my phone and scrolled through the footage. It started early in the morning, right after we'd set them up, and I sped past hours of footage where nothing happened except for the sun moving out of sight. The screen eventually grew darker, afternoon turning into evening.

Night fell slowly and the activity on the screen picked up. Bodies walked past the camera carrying tables, chairs, decorations, and the big tubs of drinks I'd pulled my bottle of water from. I recognized some of them. Jordan. Anthony. Carter. All guys from Edgely Academy. Owen's friends and the guys Gillian had pinpointed as taking part in their twisted little game.

Anger boiled my blood, though they'd so far done nothing more than blindly walk past my camera. But they were predators all the same. Spoiled, selfish rich kids, who thought drugging women was a bit of fun on a Saturday night.

I hated them. Each and every one of them disgusted me.

A bat squawked overhead, drawing my attention, and I looked up, making sure it wasn't about to fly at me. But I was still alone, with the cold stone pressed to my back. I glanced down at my phone again and a gasp slipped from my lips.

Owen's face filled the screen. He was so close, I knew instantly, even before the screen went black that he'd seen the camera. "Shit," I whispered, yanking it from my phone and shoving it in my pocket.

"Shit indeed," a voice said from the darkness.

I dropped my bottle of water with chills skating down my spine. And not the good kind. Not the kind my guys gave me by whispering something dirty in my ear. These were the kind that spoke of danger. A threat lurking in the shadows. And when he stepped from them, the chills turned into a warning.

Run.

He caught me easily, his longer legs chewing up the small amount of ground I covered. I hadn't even reached the edge of the mausoleum, the ancient tomb shielding us from the rest of the party. His big hand clapped over my mouth before I could scream, and he pulled me roughly to his chest, squeezing me until I squeaked with the need for air.

"Ah, princess. So glad you could make my party. I threw it just for you, you know."

Despite his hand, I tried to scream anyway. I thrashed in his arms, throwing back elbows and my head, trying to connect with any soft body part of his I could. Anything that would distract him long enough that I could escape.

"Oh, I do like it when you fight," he purred in my ear. He pushed me up against the wall face first, using his bigger body to pin me there. "But we need to have a chat, you and me. So here's what you're going to do. I'm going to take my hand away, and you're going to keep quiet and listen. Capiche?"

I fought to slow my breathing, though the adrenaline crashing my system made it difficult. But I wasn't going to get anywhere like this. I couldn't overpower him. So I needed to be smarter. To be smarter, I needed a clear head. One filled with the oxygen I was struggling to get right now. So instead of continuing the useless fight, I reluctantly nodded.

His tongue darted out, licking the shell of my ear. It was slimy and wet, and I fought back a heave of disgust.

"You scream, I'll snap your neck right here."

The acid in his voice was terrifying. And perhaps for the first time, I realized Owen truly was completely unhinged. He wasn't just willing to drug and rape women. If his threats were to be believed, he was willing to kill them, too. My gaze lifted, spotting the camera I'd planted on this side of the wall. He might have found the one I'd put on the grave, but if he hadn't found the one out here, then this was exactly what I needed. The proof of who Owen really was.

His fingers peeled from my mouth one by one, but all that came out was my sharp breaths, as if I'd run a marathon. "I won't scream," I promised him, forcing myself to sound weak.

He cocked his head to one side. "No? Shame. I can't stop thinking about your pretty neck and what it felt like beneath my hands."

"You said you wanted to talk," I ground out, ignoring his psychopathic ramblings.

He eased the pressure on my back a little, enough that I could turn to face him, though he still pinned me in with his arms either side of me on the wall. His breath washed over my face, tainted with alcohol, but I tried not to cringe away, unsure of how he would react to my disgust. Would it anger him? Or would it turn him on? Either way, I didn't want to find out.

"How about you tell me what sort of game you're play-ing, Lacey? I had my own games planned for tonight, but then I got distracted by the revelation of a camera. I've been waiting all night for the trickster to show herself. How fun it turned out to be you."

There was no point denying it. He'd seen me with the proof.

I decided that going with the truth might just be the easiest way to get him to confess. "Fine. You got me, Owen. I put the camera there. You know why?"

"Please. Enlighten me."

"Because I know all about your games. You and Jordan and the others. Drug a shot, hand them out randomly, rape whichever unlucky girl was the recipient."

His smile was as genuine as the Joker's. "I've no idea what you're talking about. The only shots we handed out tonight were completely virgin. Not even a drop of alcohol in them, let alone any sort of drugs. What sort of man do you take me for?"

I snorted. "Right. Just like the drinks you fed me that night at the bonfire. Were they completely virgin, too?"

"If you're into underage drinking, Lacey, you can't blame that on me."

My patience wore thin, but I tried to hide it with a laugh of my own. "It's sad, Owen. Truly. You're such a good-looking guy, but your personality is so God-awful that you have to drug women in order for them to sleep with you. How does that feel? Knowing I put you in the friend zone? I chose *Saint View* guys—not one, but three of them—over you. Do you know how much their net worth is? Zip. But I still want them." I couldn't keep the seethe out of my voice. "I wouldn't touch you with a ten-foot pole."

Something flickered in his gaze, a tether letting loose on his short temper. "Slut."

Despite the murderous glare in his eye, and the direct

danger I was putting myself in, I had to keep pushing him, while praying that tape was still rolling. I shrugged like I didn't have a care in the world. "Fine. I'm a slut." I leaned in closer. "But I still wouldn't spread my legs for you. You had to force me onto my back, with me kicking and screaming and biting. You attempted to rape me, because even me, the Saint View slum-loving whore can't stand to be touched by you!"

His fingers closed around my neck faster than I could react, and he slammed me back against the wall. "That just makes tonight all the more fun then, doesn't it? I told you I planned this party for you."

"I heard," I snarled at him. "But I didn't touch your entry shots. So don't think I'm going down easy." I brought my knee up between his legs, aiming for his junk, but he dodged, forcing my knee into his thigh instead.

He chuckled darkly. "Oh, Lacey. Sweet, sweet Lacey. You think I underestimate you? Oh no. I know exactly how smart you are. Not smart enough to hide your cameras well, obviously. But smart enough not to touch the alcohol. So I brought a different surprise for you. You drank the water, right?"

What?

Dread crept down my spine. No. That bottle had been sealed. I'd checked. I glanced down at the bottle where I'd dropped it on the ground.

That was all the distraction he needed.

A needle pierced the skin at my neck, cold liquid filling my vein.

I passed out to the crunch of the camera beneath Owen's boot and his laughter ringing in my ears.

31

ARIA

I stomped back through the party, ignoring cries of "Hey!" and "Watch where you're going, bitch," as I shoved past other people. I snarled in the direction of the guy who'd sworn at me, and he backed off pretty quick.

Across the other side of the drinks table, I spotted Gillian's red devil mask and made my way over to her. "Anything on your tapes?" I asked quietly, though the music was so loud I doubted anyone would overhear us even if I'd yelled it. As it was, Gillian had to lean in and ask me to repeat myself.

Once she understood my question, though, she pulled off her mask, letting it sit atop her head. "No. Nothing on mine. I deleted and reset them. How about yours?"

I ground my teeth together. "Same."

"Dammit." Gillian kicked at the exposed roots of the tree we stood beneath. "Dammit, fucking, shit!"

I knew exactly how she felt. Owen might not have been my attacker, but this was the only vengeance I was ever going to get. I'd had nothing to do with Lawson Knight's downfall. I hadn't felt any relief in knowing he was dead, even though I was glad he wasn't able to hurt anyone else, the way he'd hurt me. In a way, his death had robbed me of so much. He'd gotten away with his crime, never having to face a trial or do time in jail. He'd gotten off so easy and died with his good reputation intact. I'd never gotten to say my piece.

All I could do was help Lacey and Gillian get theirs. And maybe somehow, in the process, I'd heal something broken inside me, too.

I grabbed Gillian's hand and squeezed it. "Maybe Lacey's camera's got something."

Gillian forced out a long breath, trying to calm herself. With her free hand, she pulled her phone from the back pocket of her skintight jeans, and the little screen lit up. She frowned. "She's late. We were supposed to meet back here five minutes ago."

I glanced in the direction of the headstone I'd seen her put a camera in, but she was nowhere in sight. "Her other camera was behind the mausoleum, in a tree. Should one of us go check?"

Gillian stepped a little closer to me. "Let's both go. I don't like that she's late. And I want to get the hell out of here before I run into Owen."

With her hand clutched firmly in mine, we headed for the creepy old mausoleum, skirting its edges. I flinched when a spider's web coated my face, dropping Gillian's hand to frantically wipe it off.

"Oh my God. I hope that's fake," I yelped.

I expected Gillian to sympathize, since she was more of a girly girl than I was, but she hushed me and pushed me up against the wall.

"What?" I asked, forgetting about the spider's web and focusing on Gillian.

"I don't know. I thought I heard something."

We both peered around the corner of the building, straining our eyes to see in the darkness. Gillian crept forward, then stooped to pick something up off the ground.

"Shit!" she turned to me with big eyes. In her outstretched hand, she held the remains of one of our cameras. "There's a used syringe on the ground, too."

I couldn't even process what that meant, if anything. But I doubted Lacey would have just dropped the camera on the ground for someone to step on. She was hardly that careless.

Unless she'd had no choice.

A roar of an engine cut through the music, and headlights lit up the dark. On instinct, I brought my hand up to shield my eyes. Tires crunched over gravel on the other side of the wrought-iron fence, swinging into a sharp U-turn and peeling away into the darkness. The taillights flashed devil red in the dark night.

Gillian ran to the fence, wrapping her fingers around the metal posts, watching it go. "That was Owen!"

Dread swamped me like a tidal wave.

She pulled her phone out again and jabbed at the screen. "Pick up, pick up, pick up," she yelled. I ran to her side, but she shook her head, stubbing out the call. "She's not answering!"

I ran the length of the fence, checking each post, searching for another way out. At the very end of the row, several posts were missing, plenty big enough for someone to walk through. "There's another exit over here."

What I didn't say was, it was plenty big enough for Owen to have dragged Lacey through.

But Gillian seemed to come to the same conclusion I did. She hit another button and pushed the phone to her ear. "I'm trying her again."

I grabbed my own phone and frantically hit my brother's name in my list of contacts. "Colt!" I yelped when he answered halfway through the first ring. He had to have had his phone in his hand, just waiting for one of us to call. "Something's happened. Lacey's missing, and she's not answering her phone. Owen's car just left. I think..."

"What? Where is he taking her?"

"I don't know," I yelled at him. "We found her camera, and there was a used needle, and then Owen's car..."

"Fuck! Where's Gillian? Are you both safe?"

"Yes. She's with me. She's been calling Lacey, but she isn't picking up."

"Ask her where Owen would go."

I repeated the question to Gillian, but she shook her head hard, confusion overwhelming her.

I dug my fingers into the fleshy part of her arm. "Think! Anywhere private that he ever took you. His house? Does his family have a weekend place?"

"I don't know! Maybe? They have enough money."

"Colt?" I said into the phone again.

But the line had gone dead. He'd hung up.

32

———

LACEY

*M*y leg ached, twisted at an unnatural angle. Moaning, I tried to straighten it, but it met with something solid and unmovable. Darkness surrounded me. So dark that for a moment, I didn't realize my eyes were actually open. I reached out; my fingers meeting a vibrating fuzz beneath me I couldn't comprehend.

The honk of a horn cut through the fog in my brain, rattling around my skull and pushing out some of the confusion. A creeping sense of dread filled me, and in horror, I stretched a hand up toward where I thought the sky should be.

I didn't get far. I hit metal before I could even straighten my elbow. A scream choked my throat, and I thrashed in the confined space, terrified for half a second that I was in a coffin. But no. The vibrating beneath me. The honking...

The trunk of a car.

I couldn't hold it back a second longer. The scream ripped from my body as if it had a life of its own, filling the small space, stealing the air I so desperately needed.

Owen's muffled chuckle had me stuffing my hand into my mouth in terror.

"You're awake, princess?" he called from somewhere inside the car. "Good. I was hoping you would be. We still have a ways to travel, though, so make yourself comfortable."

I thumped against the roof of the trunk, the hard metal bruising my skin, but there was no way of budging it. My chest heaved with the exertion and the terror of being enclosed in such a tiny space, being driven God knows where with a madman.

I was going to run out of oxygen if I kept sucking it in the way I was. That thought scared me almost as much as the realization that I had no idea where Owen was taking me. How long had I been out for? It could have been hours. Days. Would everyone be searching for me by now? Gillian and Aria would have noticed I was missing when I hadn't show up to meet them. They would have told the guys. But then what? By then, Owen and I were probably miles away.

My fingers shook, but I forced them down my body, patting my pockets, looking for my phone.

Empty. I searched the trunk the best I could in the complete darkness but came up with nothing. I twisted, kicking at the taillights, but the cramped space didn't allow me the leverage to get any sort of momentum up, and my kicks were as weak as a baby's from whatever drug Owen had injected me with.

Baby.

"Oh my God," I sobbed, hands falling to my belly. "Please be okay." Exhausted and groggy, I curled into a ball, protecting the little life inside me the only way I knew how. I squeezed my eyes closed, trying to block out the suffocating feeling of the walls closing in on me.

Images flickered at the edges of my subconscious.

Darkness surrounded me. Only a few gaps in the closet doors let in any light, but that was good. That meant no one would find me. All I could see was a piece of carpet, where I'd left a lid off my marker and it had leaked onto the carpet. I'd cried, but Mommy had said it was okay, and that she still loved me. I smiled at that.

I wondered if Mommy liked playing hide-and-seek, like she'd said Uncle Lawson did. I liked it, too. I wriggled in my hiding spot and took a sip from my bottle of water. It made a funny slurping noise, and I shut the lid quickly, not wanting to be found. I liked winning. And Colt had taught me how to be really quiet when we played hide-and-seek. One time, we'd hid beneath the bushes and we'd been so good our moms couldn't find us at all.

I strained my ears to listen. Downstairs, a door opened and closed.

"Where's Lacey?" Uncle Lawson asked.

"Next door," Mommy lied.

I clapped a hand over my mouth, holding in a giggle. It would take Uncle Lawson ages to find me if he thought I was at Colt's house.

"That's probably good. There's something I need to discuss with you," Uncle Lawson said.

"Okay." Mom's voice was slower than normal, like she was tired again. She was tired a lot lately. The door opened and closed once more, and then Mom said, "What is this?"

I wished I could see them, so I knew what they were talking about.

"This is Officer Waller. He's here to escort you to a rehabilitation clinic. A good one. I spoke to Selina, and she's agreed we'll pay for it."

"What? I'm not going to rehab!"

"April, look at yourself. You're high as a kite every time I come here. You're depressed. Grieving. You need help."

"I thought that's what you were giving me. The only thing I've taken is those sleeping tablets you brought me. But I'm done with them now."

"April, we both know you've been taking more than sleeping tablets. You aren't caring for Lacey properly. Last time I came, she told me she hadn't eaten in two days."

I frowned. That wasn't true. I'd told him I was hungry and asked if I could have a snack. But that was only because Mommy had told me no more snacks, or I'd spoil my dinner.

"Liar!" Mommy screamed. "I would never let Lacey go without."

I cringed, wrapping my arms and round my knees and tucking myself into a ball.

"Settle down now, ma'am," the man I didn't know said. What had Uncle called him? Officer Waller? "It'll be better for everyone if you come quietly. You don't want your child to see this if it has to get ugly."

"I'm not going," Mom screamed. "I have a child to care for. She has no one else. I already told you, I'm not taking the sleeping tablets anymore."

"I'll take Lacey until you're well again. Please, April. Just do it. Don't make me tell Officer Waller about all the other illegal things you do when you're high."

"What are you talking about? I'm a law-abiding citizen."

"How did you pay for Tony's treatments?"

I didn't understand what they were saying. But I didn't like any of it. I put my hands over my ears, but they were so loud. My hands did nothing to muffle their argument.

"You son of a bitch!"

There was a thumping sound, and then Officer Waller was yelling to stay on the ground.

A tear slipped down my cheek when I realized Mommy was crying. I wanted to run downstairs and comfort her, but I didn't *dare. She'd told me to hide from Uncle Lawson, and I didn't want to get in trouble.*

"Get the help you need, April. I'm just trying to do what's best for you and Lacey."

"You're a narcissist. You always think you know best. That what you want is the right way. You grew up here, Lawson. You think you're better than me now, because you married for money, while I married for love? You're not."

"Just take her," Uncle Lawson said, and the scuffling sound broke out again.

"At least let me say goodbye to my daughter! Let me explain that I'll be back to get her. She's upstairs, hiding in her closet."

"No," Uncle Lawson said. "She doesn't need to see this. Get yourself together. Don't come back until you do."

The front door slammed, and then there was the sound of footsteps on the stairs. Heavy footsteps, too big to be Mommy's. I sniffled and stared at the purple patch on the carpet until Uncle Lawson's shoes covered it. A tremble racked my body. I didn't want him to know where I was. I just wanted my mom. I made myself as small as I could, waiting for him to open the doors.

But he didn't. There was a scratching noise, and then he walked away. His footsteps went down the stairs, and the front door opened. Outside, an engine roared to life, then slowly faded into nothing.

Slowly, I uncurled from my ball and pushed on the door.

It was locked.

I blinked in the sudden light, Owen's face mere inches from my own. He shook me by the shoulders. "Wake up, slut. Get out and act normal."

"What?" I murmured. But then his punishing grip was wrapped around my arm, and he yanked me from the trunk. My muscles protested as he hauled me out, pain shooting up my thigh. My feet hit the ground, and my knees wobbled.

Whatever he'd given me wasn't as strong as the night he'd spiked my drink. But I still felt disconnected from my body. Like I'd been on an all-night bender and hadn't had time to sleep it off.

I blinked around in the darkness. A small cabin sat surrounded by woods, but it wasn't Owen's. This one was more rustic than his ultra-modern house in Providence.

"Owen? What's going on? What are you doing out here?"

I froze at the sound of Chief Waller's voice. It was ripped straight from my memories, and suddenly I was that scared little girl locked in that closet again.

Owen put his arm around me and half-dragged me to the door of the cabin. I let him, because my muscles were too locked up to fight.

Chief Waller stood on the porch, his belly straining at a flannel shirt. His gaze hardened as it met mine, disgust rolling off him. He looked to Owen. "What is it with you and these girls from Saint View? First the blonde. Now this one?"

"She's not from Saint View, Dad."

"Yes I am," I said slowly, forcing my lips to form the words I wanted to say. "You know it, don't you, Officer Waller?"

He puffed out his chest and narrowed his eyes. "Chief Waller to you, young lady."

I shook my head, the memory of his voice, his name, still fresh in my mind. "It wasn't back then, though, was it?"

His bushy eyebrows drew together like angry black caterpillars. "What are you talking about?"

"Back when you dragged my mother, kicking and screaming from my house. And then left me in a locked closet for days."

He shot a glance at Owen, then back at me. "She high?"

"Yeah," Owen answered.

"Not high," I spat. "Drugged by your son, and not for the first time. But don't change the subject." I strained at the hold Owen had on me, and his fingers bit painfully into my flesh.

It wasn't enough to stop me from what I needed to say. I'd remembered it all. Everything I'd blacked out because it was too traumatic for my five-year-old brain to hold on to it. But I remembered now. Remembered what this man had done.

"It was you who pulled me from that closet."

He huffed. "Fine. I pulled you from the closet your drug addict mother locked you in. You should be thanking me. I saved your life."

The rage boiled up and spilled over. "You knew what he did. You were there the day my mother left. I heard her tell you I was upstairs in the closet. Lawson locked me in. And then hours, or maybe even days later, when I was starving and thirsty, and had wet my pants and was crying for my mother, you came and let me out."

His eyes hardened. "How was I supposed to know he'd locked you in there? I'd already left the house with your mother. I thought he'd taken you with him."

"I don't believe that for a second. The two of you left me there and made it seem like my mother had done it. Then you delivered me into his care, like he was some fucking saint saving the day."

Chief Waller's eyes flashed with anger. "You disrespectful little bitch. We lifted you from the slums and gave you a better life. You should be thanking me!"

I launched myself at him, only to be jerked back by Owen's hold. "You never once looked into my parent's disappearance. And now I know why. Because my father was already gone, and the two of you kept my mother away with the threats of exposing the fraud she'd committed. I'm right, aren't I? Jesus Christ. April said Lawson stole me, and I didn't believe her." I laughed, the sound bitter and filled with disgust. "You're as corrupt as they come."

His meaty hand cracked across my cheek, pushing it in Owen's direction. The glint of enjoyment in his eyes turned my stomach. My cheek stung from the impact of the chief's slap, but it wasn't enough to silence me. "How did he get you? How much did he pay? Fuck, what kind of man are you? You already had all the money in the world and yet you needed more? You fat, greedy pig."

"You think a second-year officer makes good money, sweetheart? Lawson and I understood each other. We both did what we had to."

All I could think now, was what I would do if someone tried to take away the little life growing inside me. "You ruined April's life and stole my mother from me. You're evil. And you spawned more of the same."

Headlights flashed behind me, startling all three of us. They pierced the darkness, spotlighting us against the night. Chief Waller lifted his arm to shield his eyes from the glare.

I saw my chance. It didn't matter who it was in that car behind me. It could have been Jack the Ripper and he would have been preferable to the men who held me now. I struggled in Owen's arms. "Help me!"

"Fucking hell, get her inside and shut her up," Chief Waller hissed.

Owen dragged me toward the door, but I went dead weight, surprising him when I slumped to the ground to get out of his grip. I crawled across the porch, scrambling to get to my feet to flee to the safety of the car that had just arrived.

Owen's fingers speared into my hair, yanking me back so

hard I yelped in pain. I opened my mouth to scream, but Owen clapped a hand over my mouth and dragged me to the shadows of the porch.

The car door opened, and I squinted through the glare, trying to see who was on the other side, desperate for it to be someone who would help me.

"Chief Waller?" the unfamiliar male voice said.

"Officer Berlin. What brings you out here tonight? Is there a problem at the station?"

I struggled against Owen's hold, screaming from beneath his hand. His fingers snaked around my throat and squeezed, until I had no choice but to stop. I trembled in his arms. There was no way the officer hadn't seen me when he'd pulled up. His headlights had shone right on me.

"Uh," the young officer said. "We had a report about a potential kidnapping at this address..." His gaze darted from the chief to the darkness where Owen sat with me. I could only see the officer through the slatted porch rails and had no idea whether he could see me or not. I couldn't get a sound out. Owen's erection pressed hard into my lower back, and I shuddered at the realization he enjoyed cutting off my oxygen.

Chief Waller made a hearty, friendly-sounding laugh as if he were fucking Santa Claus at the department store. "I think somebody might be playing a prank on you, Officer. Or perhaps on me? Good one." He walked down the wooden steps slowly until he stood close to the younger man. Too close. The chief was taller, broader, and had probably a hundred pounds and thirty years on his subordinate who stood in front of him. The officer's fingers fell to his side, no longer hovering around where his gun was holstered by his hip.

"The young girl..."

"Oh her? That's my son and his girlfriend. They just got back from a party. I'm afraid they are guilty of some underage drinking. But he knows my stance on that, and I'll be sure to speak to him at length about it."

The officer nodded.

My heart sank. He was falling for it. And I was going to be left here, alone with a monster, and the man who created him.

Tears threatened the backs of my eyes.

"Well, there's obviously no problem here. I'll just call it back into the station and let them know."

"I'd appreciate that, son."

"Hear that, slut?" Owen whispered in my ear. "He'll be gone in a minute, and then we can have that party, just you and me."

I shuddered at the promise of violence in his voice, watching in horror as my only lifeline got back in his car and said something into his walkie-talkie. A sob built up in my chest, making it even harder to breathe.

The officer poked his head out the open door once more. "All taken care of, boss. Mind if I borrow your bathroom before I leave?"

Hope surged, but Owen was already dragging me backward through the house toward the rear exit, his anger mounting with every step. "Fucking rookie cops. Never mind. It'll be better if we play out here in the woods anyway. Then you can scream to your heart's content and no one will hear a thing."

I dragged my heels and blindly reached out, trying to get a grasp on the furniture, but he moved too quickly. I grabbed the doorjamb of the back door, positive that if I let him get me through it, that would be it.

They'd find my broken, beaten body somewhere deep in

the woods. Terror roared through me. All I could think was how I'd failed so miserably. Failed to find Lawson's killer. Failed to see the truth when it was right under my nose. Failed at protecting my unborn child.

The voice in the darkness was a shock to both of us.

"Let her go."

33

COLT

*E*very muscle in my body was primed to fight. Either side of me, Banjo and Rafe tensed, too.

I'd kill him. Slowly and painfully. I'd rip him limb from limb to make him feel the pain I was in right now, helpless to do anything but watch him drag Lacey while she fought to get away from him.

"Take it easy," Detective Jones warned us quietly, her gun aimed at Owen and Lacey.

I'd take it easy when Owen was six feet under.

Owen's gaze darted from the detective to the three of us standing slightly behind her, and his laugh echoed across the night air. "Oh, well, isn't this rich? The thugs have a new slut. You've been replaced already, Lacey."

"Detective Jones, Providence Police." The woman identified herself in a much different manner to how I'd met her, when she'd slid her card across the table after my arrest. She'd been kind that night. But there was none of that in her now. She stared at Owen with pure steel in her gaze and an unwavering tone of command in her voice. "Let her go and put your hands up."

If Owen was bothered, he didn't show it. "You know who I am, right?" His arrogance still rolled off him in waves. But I couldn't keep my focus on him for long. It kept straying to Lacey. Her body was weak, slumped against Owen, but a fire burned behind her eyes. They met mine.

I put everything I had into that look. Every ounce of love. Every promise for our future.

This wasn't where we ended.

"What's going on out here?" Chief Waller demanded, coming out behind Owen and Lacey. He glanced right over Banjo, Rafe, and me, his eyes widening when they landed on Detective Jones' raised gun.

"Now, now, there's been some sort of misunderstanding—"

Detective Jones gave her chief a sarcastic smile. "Really? You're honestly going to try to talk your way out of this one?"

The young officer we'd used as a decoy slipped out behind Chief Waller and pointed his gun at Owen's head. "She said let her go and put your hands up."

Owen froze, but his fingers loosened on Lacey. And that was all any of us needed.

Everything happened at once.

Lacey darted away from Owen. Banjo, Rafe, and I lunged for her. And the officer grabbed the back of Owen's shirt, spinning him around and shoving him face-first into the wall of the cabin. He made a satisfying grunt of pain.

Lacey flew down the steps, and we met her halfway in a tangle of bodies, her smaller one engulfed by the three of us circling around her, forming a protective barrier. "How are you even here?" she asked between sobs, clutching at Banjo first and then Rafe. They crushed her in their embrace before turning her over to me.

Nothing had ever felt so right as having my girl back in

my arms. I skated my palms over her hair, across her shoulders, down the sides of her body, searching for any injuries. I stopped at her belly. My hate for Owen grew even stronger, knowing he'd put her baby—our baby—in danger. She lifted her eyes to me, and I crashed my mouth down on hers, taking the kiss I needed. She clutched me tight, her fingers gripping my arms, while I wrapped mine around her body, never wanting to let her go.

Banjo and Rafe hovered protectively around us, their eyes trained on Lacey, but mine were drawn to Owen. Our gazes clashed, and the fury in his was unmistakable.

"Slut," he spat in our direction. "You filthy whore!"

I saw red. The officer pulled him away from the wall by the handcuffs slapped on his wrists. There was a small amount of satisfaction in seeing that, but it wasn't enough. Turning Lacey over to Banjo and Rafe, I stormed the space between Owen and me, getting right in his face.

"Colt," Banjo shouted, but it sounded far away. The red haze that engulfed me took over, until all I could feel was the adrenaline coursing through my system.

My fist met Owen's face with a satisfying crack. He let out a howl of pain like the pansy he was, blood spurting from his broken nose.

"That's assault," Owen screamed, blood coating his lips.

Detective Jones laughed as she put cuffs on Chief Waller. "It would be if it had happened. But I didn't see anything, did you, Officer Berlin?"

"Not a thing. Must have happened during the arrest."

There was no satisfaction in the punch, and despite the detective covering for me; she gave me a stern look that told me not to try it again. I nodded slightly, a silent thank-you for giving us back what we'd lost.

She shoved Chief Waller toward the house. "We're going

to take them in for questioning. Call an ambulance, okay? Get her seen to. I'll come down to the hospital as soon as I can."

She prodded an oddly silent Chief Waller in the back, and he went quietly, at complete odds with the way his son wailed and carried on as they were both put into the back of the squad car.

"Colt," Banjo yelled, the panic in his voice grabbing my attention.

I spun just in time to see Lacey's eyes roll back and her body go limp.

34

───────

LACEY

The bed beneath my tired body was soft as a freaking cloud. Clean, starched white pillows and blankets made it look like one, too. Huh. That was funny. I blinked around at the mostly white space, my gaze finally focusing on the only person in the room.

"Hey, Lacey. Good to see you awake. Do you remember what happened?"

I grimaced. "Can I just go back to sleep and pretend I don't?"

The doctor, with a stethoscope around his neck, smiled at me. It was a million-dollar grin, with teeth too straight and white to be real. He was young and handsome, his scrubs covering broad shoulders and a trim waist. Meredith would have been going gaga right about now. A stab of pain shot through me at the thought of my best friend. Or former best friend. I had no idea what we were anymore. I went back to concentrating on the doctor because that was easier to think about.

"Your friends are very worried about you," he said with a

smile. "They've been hovering over you like bees to the first spring flower."

"Three big guys, super handsome, probably gave you a hard time for kicking them out?"

He chuckled. "Fitting description. I thought they might riot for a moment." He perched on the end of the bed, his expression turning serious. "I can let them in, in a minute. But I just wanted to talk about the baby."

My hands flew immediately to my nonexistent bump. "Is he or she okay? Owen injected me with something…"

The doctor checked an iPad. "We ran some tests while you were out. It was a sedative. A mild one, judging by your toxicology reports. You won't have any lingering side effects once it's fully left your system."

An unspoken 'but' hung in the air.

"The baby?" I asked quietly. My heart thumped in anticipation.

He smiled tightly at me. "It's not a drug I would willingly use on a pregnant woman. But I don't believe the small amount you were administered will have any effect on the baby. We did an ultrasound while you were unconscious, and everything looked perfectly fine."

I bit my lip to keep from crying. "Okay. Thank you."

"One more thing before I leave you to rest. I thought I spotted a telltale gender sign on the ultrasound, and your blood tests confirmed it. Do you want to know?"

I threw a glance at the closed door. "No. Not right now. I just want to see my guys. It's enough that he or she is healthy."

He nodded and stood. "I'll send them in then?"

"Yes, please."

Excitement fluttered through me, and almost as soon as the doctor left the room, Banjo bounded in, rushing to my side, closely followed by Rafe and Colt. Banjo's gaze swept my body, coming back to focus on my face before he leaned down and pressed his forehead to mine. His hand cupped my cheek, and he closed his eyes. I did the same, just breathing him in, relishing his touch.

"I thought we were going to lose you." His voice broke. "Both of you."

I smiled and put my lips to his. "I'm made of tougher stuff than that."

He smiled against my mouth and moved back, letting Rafe in. Rafe just shook his head then kissed. "You scared the fuck out of me."

"I know."

"Don't even complain when I follow you around for the rest of your life, closer than your own damn shadow, okay? That isn't happening again."

I reached up and stroked a hand down his stubbled jaw. The pain in his blue eyes was startling, but I knew I had to set boundaries straightaway or the three of them would smother me with their love and protection. "You can't put me in Bubble Wrap."

"If he doesn't, I will," Colt mumbled from the foot of my bed. His black gaze bored into mine. The white bandage wrapped around his hand caught my attention, and he tucked it behind his back.

"Please tell me you won't need to. Is Owen in jail?"

A grin stretched across Colt's face. "Yep. Detective Jones called me just before. She's got some paperwork to do, but then she's coming over here to see you."

"But we have enough to make a case against him?"

"Gillian and Aria got your second camera from the trees behind the spot he attacked you. Everything he confessed is on there, along with him ramming that fucking needle in your neck." Colt's fingers squeezed around the metal rail on my bed. "There's more than enough proof to put him away."

"And Chief Waller?"

"Detective Jones has been building a corruption case for a long time. That's how she knew about his hunting cabin. When I called her from the graveyard and asked for her help, she put out an alert on Owen's car. When she heard he was traveling north, she knew exactly where to go. Rafe broke every road rule to follow her up here. No word yet exactly on what will happen to Chief Waller, but hopefully he'll be sharing a cell with his son. I should have asked for her help earlier. But even after my lawyer bailed me out, I still felt like Waller was going to keep coming at me until I went down for good."

He looked so full of regret that I nudged him with my foot. "You didn't know she was one of the good guys. None of us knew we could trust her."

I breathed out a sigh of relief when Colt nodded. The last thing I wanted was him, or any of us, shouldering any regret over the decisions we'd made. Owen was in jail and would face a trial for what he'd done. With video evidence, I doubted there was a lawyer alive who could get him off this time.

But my relief was short-lived. Rafe was the first to notice and smoothed his hand across my forehead. "Hey, what's wrong? Are you in pain? Is it the baby?"

I shook my head quickly. "No, no. We're fine, but I need to talk to my mom. My birth mom, I mean. April."

"You sure?" Banjo asked. "Last time..."

"Last time she told the truth, and I didn't want to hear it. I want to hear it now. Do you still have her number?"

Banjo nodded.

"Can you ask her to come in? I don't even know if she's still around, she might have left town..."

He stood, pulling his phone from his pocket, and headed for the door. "I'll call her now."

"Thank you. Did someone call Selina?"

"Yep. We've only just managed to get a hold of her, but she's on her way in." Rafe brushed a strand of hair behind my ear. "You're tired."

I was. "I'm sorry. I know you only just got here..."

Rafe brushed a kiss across my forehead and tucked the blanket tightly around me.

Colt squeezed my foot. "We'll let you sleep. But we'll be back. First thing in the morning, okay?"

"I love you. Both of you. And Banjo, too. Tell him?"

"He knows. Just rest so we can spring you ASAP. We need to get you home for Christmas."

Christmas. I smiled at the thought of waking up in my own bed, surrounded by people I loved, no fear niggling at the back of my mind. My eyes drifted shut before Rafe and Colt had even left the room, and for the first time in months, I slept without Owen plaguing my dreams.

***

When I woke up, Selina's long silky hair was splayed out across my bed, covering my blankets. "Hey," I murmured, mouth dry.

She was awake instantly, her head shooting up, blinking at me as she tried to clear the sleep from her eyes. "Lacey?"

"Yep."

She launched herself at me, wrapping her arms around my shoulders, and hugging me tight.

"I guess the guys filled you in, then?" My words were muffled by the fierceness of her embrace.

"Yes," she said eventually, pulling back. Her eyes filled with tears. "Sweetheart, why didn't you tell me everything that was going on? Owen and Chief Waller and...the baby."

My cheeks warmed. "They really told you everything then, huh?"

She lifted one shoulder. "Banjo hasn't got a very good poker face. And he was so worried about you. The tiniest bit of pressure, and he folded like a house of cards. Don't be upset with him. His honesty and his heart are what makes him special."

"I know. I'm not upset. I would have told you anyway. I should have said something before this. It was just..."

"A lot?"

"Yeah."

"So...I'm going to be a grandma?"

A tiny smile tugged at my mouth. "How do you feel about that?"

She squeezed me tight. "I still want you to go to college. All of you. And we're going to make that happen, no matter what. But a baby? You know how badly I wanted one. It broke my heart I couldn't have one of my own." She looked at me with so much pride in her expression. "But then I had you, and it didn't matter anymore."

My smile fell. "Selina...did you know?" I asked quietly.

A knock at the door interrupted before she could answer me. April stood in the doorway.

Selina frowned at her.

April focused on me, ignoring the chill frosting off Selina's rigid shoulders. "Banjo called and said I should come down. He said you wanted to talk."

"I do. Come in. Please."

Selina stood. "I should go. And let the two of you talk."

I grabbed her hand so she couldn't leave. "No. I think you both need to be here for this." She sat back down, but it was April I focused on. "At Thanksgiving, you said Lawson stole me from you."

Selina bristled at that once more, but I dug my fingernails into her palm, cutting her off. "Selina, stop. Last night triggered a memory for me. And I...I don't think she's lying."

"I'm not," April said quietly.

"I was in the closet. You told me to hide."

Her eyes went sad. "I should have never told you to do that."

"Lacey, she locked you in there," Selina insisted, her gaze full of anger, eyes flashing in April's direction. "I never wanted to tell you, but that's how they found you."

Relief rushed my system. "That's exactly what I wanted you to say. I wanted to look into your eyes and know that you had nothing to do with it."

Her brow furrowed, her eyebrows pulling together. "To do with what?"

"It was Lawson who locked me in that cupboard. They set April up."

She shook her head hard. "No. The social worker brought you to us."

"I remember it. I watched him through a crack in the doors. He locked the closet and walked away. Waller knew, too. I think Lawson might have paid him to keep quiet."

Selina's mouth fell open, and her gaze darted from me to April. "But...but why?"

"To keep you happy," April said sadly. "He couldn't give you a baby, so he stole mine for you. And I guess for him, too. He told me over and over how Lacey was better off with him, free from the life he'd hated as a kid. I think he actually told himself that so many times he'd come to believe it."

Selina scrubbed a hand over her face. "I don't understand."

"I didn't either," I said, squeezing her fingers. I knew this was a lot for her to comprehend. "Not until I remembered being in the closet and hearing the argument downstairs when they dragged April out."

I turned to my birth mother. "You never wanted to leave me."

"No," she agreed. "And I've thought of you every day since."

"Why didn't you come back? Once you were out of rehab?"

Her fingers fisted in the white sheets of my hospital bed. "I wanted to. God, Lacey. You think I wanted to leave you with that monster? But he had Waller in his pocket. And every time he came to see me in rehab, he lorded that over my head. He said I'd be tried for child abuse, and if they couldn't get me on that, there'd be the fraud charges from when we'd used his insurance card to get the help we needed for your father's illness."

Selina gaped at that. "I don't understand. Why didn't you just ask us for help?"

April blinked. "I did. He said you wouldn't agree to pay for it."

Anger burned behind Selina's eyes. "I would have helped. I would have helped then, if I'd known. But I didn't."

"Sel, it's okay. I believe you."

But Selina pushed away from the bed, mumbling to herself, before turning back to April. "He died? Lacey's father? He didn't just disappear?"

April shook her head.

"Why would Lawson lie about that? He said you'd both skipped town. All these years, that's what we'd told Lacey. I believed him."

April sucked in a deep breath, as if she were steadying herself for what she had to say next.

I just knew she was about to drop a bomb.

"I think Lawson murdered him."

My mouth fell open. "What?"

"There's a photo in your entryway, of Selina and Lawson in front of a yellow sports car. It was a yellow sports car that hit Tony outside our house. As far as I know, the driver was never found. Hell, I suspect it was never even investigated. It was just thrown in the 'I don't care' basket, like every other serious crime that happened in Saint View.

"I've thought about it so much over the years. I don't think he expected Tony to get better. He was so sick before we took him to the hospital. I was sure he wasn't going to make it. But then he got better, and Lawson wasn't going to get custody of Lacey with both of us still around." She gave a weird-sounding laugh and ran a hand through her hair. "God, I don't know. That just seems insane. Maybe I had it all wrong."

But the color had drained from Selina's face. "It was my car. He drove it one night, said he was meeting friends. And when he brought it home, there was damage to the front panels. Lawson had it replaced the very next day, and we sold it not long after."

April's mouth pulled into a straight line, but she remained calmly sitting in her seat. Selina paced the floor, but all I could think was one thing.

"Did you kill Lawson?" I asked April.

It was a completely emotionless question. And I realized I didn't even care if the answer was yes. Hell, I hoped she'd done it. Because I'd seen Lawson for the monster he was. It didn't matter any longer that he'd spent most of my life loving me. It had all been a lie. None of it felt real. He was a liar. A cheat. A narcissist. A murderer.

"No," April said quietly. "I wanted to. So many times. And I won't ever mourn that man's death. He ruined my life. But it wasn't me. I wish it had been."

"It was me," Selina said in the quietest of voices.

My stomach plummeted. "What?" I croaked.

April got up and closed the door.

"It was me," she said again, focusing watery eyes on me. "I didn't mean to. I swear it, Lacey. It wasn't why I was at the school that night."

"Why?" My head spun.

"I found videos. Photos. Women and...girls from his school. There'd been a rumor, whispered about in some circles just outside my own. Pamela had filled me in. Accusations he'd raped a girl. He thought he'd kept them quiet, but gossip runs hot. I'd heard what they were saying, and I had to know for myself. I searched his desk at home but found nothing. So I went to the school that night to search his office. It was all there, Lacey. Folders and folders of it. Disgusting images that made my skin crawl. Some of the girls had been in their uniforms."

"Meredith was one of them," I choked out. "She said they had an affair but..."

My aunt hovered a horrified hand over her mouth, eyes wide. "All I could think was that it could have been you. I couldn't see their faces. I didn't know if it was or if it wasn't. I couldn't bear the thought that he might have been hurting you, all these years, while you were underneath my roof. He walked in and realized what I'd found. We argued..."

I just kept shaking my head, unable to comprehend what she was saying. "You killed him?"

"There was a letter opener on the desk. He came at me. I didn't think. I just defended myself."

"Oh my God," I whispered.

She slumped down in the chair and turned to me with pleading eyes. "Sweetheart, I swear, I didn't know you were in the building when I set that fire. I had no idea. I just panicked. I didn't know what else to do."

"You murdered him, Sel!"

A tear rolled down her cheek.

"Colt could have gone to jail for what you did. You would have let him."

"No! I swear. I wouldn't have let that happen. That's why I sent him Liam. I knew Liam would get him off, if he hadn't, I would have confessed. I *am* going to confess."

"What?" I yelped, sudden panic flooding my system. "No. You can't! You'll go to jail."

She cupped the side of my face, brushing a thumb over my cheek. "I have to," she said in a broken voice. "I can't keep living like this. The headaches and the nightmares. They've all gotten so much worse. I need to own what I did. Stand in front of a judge and take my punishment so I can move on with my life. I just had to wait until I knew you'd be okay."

I couldn't stop the tears from falling down my face any longer.

Selina brushed them away and placed a kiss where they'd been. "You've changed so much in the last few months. I've watched you go from spoiled little girl, to independent woman, ready for a family of her own. You don't need me anymore."

"I do," I yelled. "Of course I need you. You're my mother."

She nodded. "Always. You'll always be my daughter." Then she glanced at April. "I'm sorry. I truly am. I know that must hurt to hear. But I can't be sorry for the fact I got to raise her."

April swallowed hard. "It wasn't your fault. And maybe I owe you a thank you. You raised her well. She's strong. And smart."

Selina grinned through her tears. "Independent. Feisty." She sniffed and wiped at her eyes. "And loved. So very loved. Not just by me. By those boys. By your friends." She leaned in and hugged me close. "You'll be okay," she promised.

But when Detective Jones arrived to take my statement, she took Selina's instead. With reluctance, she placed handcuffs over her wrists and led her from my room.

Selina didn't look back.

I was glad, because I didn't want her to see that I wasn't okay at all.

35

___

LACEY

I left the hospital a week before Christmas, but I'd never been less festive. The house was cold and empty without Selina, and so I went back to school to keep busy and slept in the pool house with Rafe and Banjo. Angelique had already started her holiday leave, so the big house sat untouched, some sort of shrine to the last day Selina had been there.

The morning of Christmas Eve, when my phone rang, I almost ignored it. It had been ringing almost constantly since news had broken of Selina's arrest, and I'd answered each and every call, hoping it would be Selina on the other end. Most of them had been journalists, though, and I'd hung up in their ear.

My breath faltered as the robotic voice identified a call from the Saint View Jail. I spun around, eyes wide, and made wild hand gestures in the air to Banjo and Rafe, who paused their video game and looked at me in confusion. "It's Selina!"

That got their attention. I accepted the call and held my breath until Selina's tentative, "Hello?" echoed in my ear.

I burst into tears. I'd been holding them in since her arrest, but now I couldn't hold them back a moment longer.

"Oh, sweetheart," she said sadly. "Please don't."

I straightened my shoulders and tried to pull myself together. Banjo gathered me into his arms, and I rested my head on his chest. Rafe eyed me from his perch on the bed, concern written all over his face.

I swallowed hard, trying to push down the ball of emotion clogging my throat. "I'm okay. Are you? What's going on? Liam won't tell me anything."

"I know, I asked him not to."

"Why?"

"Because I wanted to find out what was happening first, so I could tell you myself. I'm pleading guilty to the arson."

"What? No!"

"Sweetheart, I have to. I did that. But Liam says the murder charge will be downgraded."

"So what does that mean?"

She paused. "I'll do five to ten years."

"No," I moaned.

Banjo clutched me tighter, murmuring gentle words into my hair.

"But listen to me," Selina continued, urgency in her tone. "You need to go see Liam Banks. Today."

"It's Christmas Eve. His office will be closed."

"Not for you it won't. Just go. And Lacey?"

"Yes?"

"Merry Christmas. I love you."

"I love you, too, Mom," I sniffed.

The line went dead before either of us even got to say goodbye. Banjo and Rafe crushed me between them, stroking hands through my hair and down my back, comforting me in the only way they knew how.

I finally pulled away to fill them in on what Selina had said. Rafe's mouth morphed into a grim line, and Banjo looked as devastated as I was. But Rafe called Colt to update him, and even though he'd promised to spend the day at Coach's early family Christmas, he left and met us outside Liam's office in the city. We had to buzz to be let in, and I frowned when Liam answered it himself. He was waiting for us in the reception area as the elevator doors opened into his spacious offices.

Colt raised an eyebrow at him. "You double as a secretary?"

Liam grinned and crossed the office to shake Colt's hand. "Just for today. How you doing, Colt? Keeping out of trouble since I saw you last?"

Colt shrugged.

Considering everything that had happened with Owen, a shrug was probably the best Liam could hope for. I introduced Rafe and Banjo as he led us back to his office, and his ears pricked up at Banjo's name. "Good thing you came down too. You were on my list of people to call after Christmas."

Banjo's eyebrows shot up in surprise. "I was? Why?"

Liam settled behind his desk and indicated that we should take the seats opposite. "We'll get to that." He turned to me first. "Selina said she already told you the sort of charges she's looking at. I can get her off the murder. That can be easily downgraded to self-defense. But there's little I can do about the fire she set to cover it up."

"Can't you claim temporary insanity or something? That isn't something she would have done if she was thinking rationally."

Liam nodded. "I promise. I'll get her the shortest sentence possible. But she will still do some time. She knows that, and she's okay with it. You need to be, too. It will just make it harder for her if you aren't."

I wasn't okay with it at all, but I was also aware if there was nothing Liam could do, then there was nothing I could do either.

Liam unlocked a drawer in his desk and pulled out a folder. "But that brings me to why we're here today. Weeks ago, not long after Lawson died, Selina came to me, and we drew up papers. In hindsight, I probably should have known something was wrong. Though at the time, I thought she must have had cancer, and I didn't want to pry." He pushed a stack of papers across the table to me. "Selina signed her entire estate over to you, in the event of her death, debilitating illness, or incarceration. The house, her money, your trust fund. All of it. I think she was assuming she'd go away for life. But after she confessed, and I assured her I would get her out before her fiftieth birthday, I asked her if she wanted to change the papers." His gaze flicked to Banjo, and he handed another smaller set of papers to him. "The only change she wanted to make was in regard to you."

Banjo leaned forward and peered at the papers. "What is this?"

"A full ride to the college of your choice. Plus enough money to live on while you're there."

Banjo's mouth fell open in shock.

Rafe let out a laugh and elbowed him "You look like someone just slapped you in the face with a dead fish. Blink, man."

I put my arms around him, hauling him into a hug and kissed his cheek.

He turned to me in shock. "Why would she do that?"

I smiled. "Because that's who she is. She's a mother. You might not be hers biologically, but she loves you."

"Does that make the two of you brother and sister then?" Colt taunted.

We both shot him a dirty look that did little to dull his amusement.

Liam cleared his throat. "Lacey, Selina left a note that should Colt or Rafe not receive the scholarships they're expecting, she hopes you'll use some of your inheritance to pay for their college tuition, too. She was very adamant that all four of you have the opportunity to go."

I agreed, though I already knew Colt and his stupid pride would argue with me about it. But that was a problem for another day. A little of the weight lifted from my shoulders, while my heart expanded for the woman who had raised me. No matter what she'd done wrong, she was still the mom I knew. The one I loved. Even when she couldn't be here with me, what she'd done for Banjo just proved how big her heart was.

Liam passed me a pen. "All you need to do is sign."

I took it from him, the nib hovering over the line waiting for my signature. "She'll have nothing, though? When she gets out, I mean."

Liam lifted a shoulder with a smile. "I don't think you'd really let that happen, would you?"

I shook my head hard. "No, of course not."

"Then there's no problem. Sign it, Lacey. You'll need to be the one in control of the assets while she's inside. It's what she wants. And it's what makes sense for you all."

I knew my aunt trusted Liam, and so did I. So I picked up the pen and signed on the dotted line. And again, and again, in each spot that Liam pointed out to me. Banjo did the same with his papers, and then it was done.

Liam sat back in his chair. "That's it. Congratulations, Lacey. You just became a rather wealthy young woman."

I gave him a half-hearted smile. It was a relief to know that our financial future was secure, but my heart still hurt at the way it had happened. I went to stand, but Liam held up a finger that stopped me.

"Wait. One more thing before I let you go and enjoy your Christmas." He opened the top drawer of his desk and took out a white envelope. On the front, my name was scrawled in Selina's handwriting. "She wanted me to give you this. She gave it to me yesterday, when I had a meeting with her about her case."

I thanked him, taking the envelope from his grasp, and the four of us wished him a merry Christmas before piling back into the elevator. During the descent, I ran my fingers over the envelope, turning it over and picking at the seal.

"You going to read it, princess?" Rafe asked, watching me carefully.

"Can you drive home? I'll read it in the car. I suspect I'll need to be sitting down for whatever this is."

When we got to the car that we'd left on the street outside Liam's skyscraper office, Banjo and Rafe got in, but Colt had parked a way down the street. He pulled me into his arms, rubbing my back briskly. I pressed up onto my toes and kissed his lips, grateful he'd come all this way for me. I hated that he now had to leave again. I was so lucky to always have Banjo and Rafe so close by. Call me selfish, but I wanted that with Colt, too.

"Colt?" I said quietly. "I own a house now."

"Yeah, you do." His nose ran up my neck, sending a shiver through me.

"It's really big."

He snorted on his amusement. "That's an understatement."

"Plenty of room for one more..."

His breath hitched, and his black gaze bored into mine. "You talking about me or that baby in your belly?"

A small smile lifted the corner of my mouth. "It's a really small baby, and a really big house. I think we could probably find room for both of you."

My heart stopped when he didn't immediately say yes. "You don't have to," I added in a rush. "It's a lot, I know. I just...I hate it when you go back home. Selfish, I know."

He grinned at me. "Totally selfish. What a horrible person you are."

I shoved him again, twisting to break his hold on me, suddenly completely embarrassed. I should have waited. We'd been together only a few months, and things were already going so fast. This would probably send him sprinting for the hills.

But he pulled me back and put one finger beneath my chin, tilting it up so I couldn't look away. "Where are you running off to? You didn't even let me give you an answer."

"Because I didn't want it to be no."

He chuckled. "I love you, Lacey Knight. And I love that little baby growing inside you. Hell, I even love the two morons in the car, who seem to kinda like you, too. You really think I'd say no to being with you every day? Waking up beside you, and seeing our baby stretch your belly as he grows?"

"He or she," I corrected.

"He," he said with conviction.

I rolled my eyes. "So is that a yes?"

His mouth hovered over mine. "Hell yes."

I wrapped my arms around his neck and kissed him hard, my chest pressed to his, him tugging me closer until there wasn't an inch between us. "I love you," I whispered to him.

"Back at ya, baby momma."

I groaned. "Call me that again and I'll rescind my invitation." I stepped away. "Go home and pack. Then come back tonight so we can all be together on Christmas morning."

I rolled my eyes when he saluted me and left to go find his car.

The other two were grinning as I got into the passenger seat. "What?" I asked with a smile. "You heard that?"

"Every word. We're just discussing how we're going to fit enough beds in the pool house. Perhaps bunks?" Banjo asked.

I settled back in my seat with my letter. "Might be time for an upgrade, huh?"

I tuned out as the two of them argued over which room in the main house they were claiming. Instead, I ran my finger beneath the seal of the envelope. I pulled out a thin piece of lined paper that looked like it had been ripped from a notepad and unfolded it with trembling fingers.

Dear Lacey,

Sweetheart, by now you'll know that I've signed everything over to you. I know you'll manage it wisely and take care of those you love. Those boys adore you, and the four of you are going to be the best parents to that baby. There's a sentence I never thought I'd be saying to you. But the four of you work. I see it. And so will everyone else. Don't hide it. What you have is special. People won't understand it, but don't let that taint it. Love is love. And you, my daughter, are so very loved.

I hate I won't be there while your baby is young. I hate I won't get to hold her and squeeze her cheeks and spoil her by giving her ice cream for breakfast. But I know Banjo will probably do that last one, won't he? So at least she won't miss out.

Let April take my spot. I know, I know. I can already hear your protests and your assurances that no one will ever replace me. But that little girl will need a grandma who can be there every day. And I know another little girl who needs to know her biological mother. Now is your time. Yours and April's. Make the most of it. And once I'm free, I'll take my place in whatever capacity you'll allow me to have.

Forgive her, the way you've already forgiven me. She's been dealt a bad set of cards, with Lawson as her brother. He robbed her of the chance to know you. Don't walk in his footsteps. Let her in.

And while we're speaking of forgiveness, why haven't you spoken to Meredith yet? Whatever she did with Lawson is irrelevant. She was a minor, and he took advantage of her, whether she calls it consensual or not. She made a mistake. But don't let one mistake cloud all the years where she had your back. You're bigger than that. I know it.

You're the brightest star in my sky, Lacey. And I promise you, there won't be a day in the next however many years that I'm not thinking about you, and loving you from afar.

Love, Selina

PS - I hope childbirth doesn't hurt too much.

I stifled a laugh and blinked back the tears welling in my eyes.

"Everything okay?" Rafe asked.

I smiled at him and nodded. "Yeah, I think it might be."

36

LACEY

J woke up early on Christmas morning, before the sun even rose. I blinked around in the darkness of my bedroom, wondering what had woken me. There were no male bodies in the bed, and the bathroom door was wide open, so I knew there was nobody in there.

They were downstairs I determined, when odd noises started up again. Some bumping, some scratching, and the not-so-quiet sound of Colt telling one of the others to shut the fuck up. Not very Santa-like.

I snorted and got out of bed, wrapping a robe over the top of my long-sleeved nightshirt. The robe touched the floor, and I was grateful that it engulfed my bare legs. It had gotten cold throughout the night, and I bumped the thermostat up when I passed it in the hall.

The noises increased as I went down the stairs, and I stopped dead in the entranceway to the living room.

All three guys spun around to face me.

"Well, shit. There goes the surprise. That's your fault, Banjo. You're so fucking loud," Colt complained.

But I had nothing to complain about. I just blinked

around at the living room in awe. Fairy lights were strung across the ceiling, casting a warm glow over the dark room. In the corner, our gigantic Christmas tree had been assembled, though they hadn't yet had time to decorate it. Boxes full of decorations sat around on the carpet, and to the left, they'd stacked a pile of Christmas gifts, wrapped so neatly with carefully tied bows that I knew Rafe had done the lot, whether they were from him or not.

"What is all this?" I asked on a gasp.

"Christmas," Rafe said simply, putting an arm around my shoulders. "Do you like it? I know none of us have been feeling very festive..."

I smiled up at him. "It's perfect." I eyed the gifts on the table and cringed. "Ugh. I didn't even go shopping. Worst girlfriend ever."

Rafe kissed the top of my head. "Not even close," while Colt said, "Yeah, you totally are."

Banjo threw a bauble at him. "Shut up."

"No, he's right." I ran my fingers over the spiky branches of the tree. "Completely lacking in tact, as always, but I hate that I didn't get you guys anything."

"It's fine, princess." Banjo stooped to kiss my cheek. "We have everything we need."

"Everything?" I side-eyed him. "Because there is one sort of gift I can give you guys, without actually going to the store."

Banjo cocked his head to one side. "Online porn subscription?"

This time I was the one who threw a bauble at him. He caught it easily, damn his stupid football skills. "That really what you want?"

He put his arms around my waist and hugged me tight. "Not even close."

"Good." I shrugged out of my robe, letting it drop to the floor. "Because while what I was thinking of is sexual, it's a little more personal."

Banjo groaned, watching me gather up my nightshirt. I did it slowly, deliberately taunting him, revealing first my thighs then my belly, before taking it all the way off to reveal my bare breasts.

"Lacey porn is better than any other porn ever," Banjo said, hand sliding to the bulge growing beneath his sweatpants.

I liked that I was already getting him hard, even though I'd really done nothing. He stepped in to touch me, but I batted his hands away. "This is about you guys."

He pouted. "So what? We don't get to touch?"

"Not yet."

Rafe groaned, but he moved in closer, too. I ran my fingers beneath the hem of his shirt, and he lifted his arms, letting me strip it off him. His drawstring was right there, tempting me to tug it, so I gave in to the urge. His sweatpants fell off his hips.

At the sight of Rafe's already growing erection, Banjo pulled off his own shirt. I shoved his sweatpants down over his hips before dropping to my knees in front of them. I took them both in my hands, stroking over their lengths, working them into full, hard, thick erections.

I glanced over at Colt, my gaze colliding with his only for the briefest of moments. But that was all he needed. He fisted the back of his shirt, yanking it over his head. His other hand snaked inside his sweats, and he jerked his cock a few times.

"Tease." My gaze trained on the bulge in his pants, wishing he'd lower them so I could watch him touch himself.

"Says the woman kneeling in nothing but tiny panties."

Well, he had a point. I let go of Banjo and Rafe and tucked my fingers into the cotton at my hips, sliding them over my thighs, then rocking back to get them over my knees. I fluttered my eyelashes at Colt and gave him the most innocent look I could muster. "Better?"

"Fuck yes," he growled. He shoved his pants down over his hips, and exposed his cock. "Want your mouth, Lacey."

He moved in, wrapping my ponytail around his fist. I opened for him, letting him slide deep inside my mouth. He and I both groaned in unison at the sensation. I found Banjo and Rafe with my hands, jerking them in the same rhythm that Colt thrust into my mouth. His grip on my hair was delicious, just tight enough to turn me on, but not enough to hurt. His hips worked slowly, pushing him to the back of my throat, until my clit ached with need.

I yearned to reach between my legs and stroke it, but this was their gift. All about them. And I was damn sure I was going to make it happen.

Colt pulled my head away, and to my surprise, guided it toward Rafe. I expected him to let go and allow Rafe to take over, but he didn't, and God if that didn't have me moaning. Rafe's cock filled my mouth, but now Colt was setting the pace. He jerked his own cock at the same time, guiding my movement between Rafe, and then eventually Banjo, before bringing it back to him. This time was faster, and every time his cock hit the back of my throat, I let out a moan of encouragement.

"I love how you love this," he murmured. "You're so fucking beautiful. I want you so bad."

"Merry Christmas," I whispered back.

He groaned, tugging me up from the floor and slamming his mouth against mine in a kiss that stole my breath. My nipples beaded, pressed to his chest, and when his fingers dug into my hips to pick me up, I didn't hesitate. I wrapped my legs around him and sank down on his cock.

"Oh!" I yelled, already so wet he met no resistance. The stretch of him sent tingles right through to my toes. I clenched around him, and he lifted me slightly, only to let me plunge down again. I rode him like that, sliding up and down on his shaft while he helped me with strong arms that rippled with muscle, his core contracting, abs popping to keep me on him.

I cried out as he slid from my body to lay me out on the carpet. The fairy lights sparkled above. "Can't come yet, baby. But you feel too good," he muttered.

He moved away, and Rafe took his spot between my legs, halting any argument I might have given.

"God, you're sexy," I said, looking over Rafe's perfect body with heated eyes. He really was, his body cut from steel from all the exercise he did. His eyes were bluer than ever in this light, and I got lost in them, barely even noticing when he raised my legs over his shoulders.

But fuck, I noticed his mouth landing between my thighs. I bucked, my ass coming off the floor, which he used to his advantage. He put his hands beneath my lower back, tilting my pelvis to give him access to everything I had to offer.

And I mean everything. His tongue slicked through my folds, then lower. I groaned at the sensation, not even caring that he had his tongue there. It was so insanely good there was no room for self-consciousness. His fingers joined the party, plunging inside my pussy and coating in my arousal, twisting until he hit my G-spot. I rode his fingers for a moment, forgetting all about how this was supposed to be *their* Christmas present. It was turning into mine, but I couldn't make him stop. I was so close to orgasm I was positive I'd self-combust if he didn't fuck me harder. His fingers trailed back to my ass and pressed inside, completely blowing my world to smithereens. I clenched around him, falling over into the abyss of pleasure, calling out his name in hoarse cries of ecstasy. His dick replaced his fingers, my ass clenching tight around him, and he drew out the orgasm until I was sure I'd go blind. He groaned, climaxing with me, slamming into my body while I screamed his name.

When he finally pulled out, he kissed my neck and whispered in my ear, "Most unholy Christmas morning ever. I love it."

I nipped at his bottom lip, but Banjo and Colt didn't give me time to respond. Colt took hold of my chin, twisting my head in his direction, while Banjo knelt to suck and squeeze my nipples. Colt slid his tongue into my mouth, devouring me, while I writhed beneath them. The beginnings of a second orgasm built, need pulsing between my thighs again. I put my hands on Banjo's shoulders, pushing him toward the spot I wanted him most. I was rewarded with his cock. He wasted no time in warming up, once he realized how wet and needy I was for him. I raked my fingernails down his back, scratching at his skin and urging him to fuck me faster. Our hips slammed together, and I arched my back, taking him deep. I grabbed at Colt's cock again, wanting to taste him, and lapped at the precum beading on his tip, his tang only making me want him more. I wrapped my lips around his cockhead and hummed with pleasure as he thrust into my mouth.

"Fuck, baby," Banjo cried.

His fingers found my clit, Colt worked my nipples, and then I was falling over the edge again, coming so hard I was sure the neighbors would hear my screams. Colt's dick kicked inside my mouth, his cum shooting down the back of my throat. Banjo's fingers gripped my thigh, and he rubbed my clit faster and harder, until he found his own release. I pulsed and clenched around him, taking everything he had, loving every second of the way they worshipped me.

When they both fell from my body, all four of us naked, sweaty, and sated, we lay on the carpet together, catching our breath, staring up at the fairy lights they'd strung across the ceiling.

"Can't say I've ever done that on Christmas morning," Banjo mused between rapid rises and falls of his chest. "Can that be the first Christmas tradition we make? The four of us as a family?"

Colt snorted. "You want our first tradition as a family to be a gang bang on Christmas morning?"

Banjo, Rafe, and I all threw punches and kicks in his direction.

"You're so crude. Can we stick with forgy?" I complained, but it was in good fun.

He rolled over and licked his way into my mouth. Despite the fact we'd just had sex and my body was aching in the very best way, I was still hungry for him. I kissed him back, loving him, even though he was a total jackass.

Eventually, Rafe stood, pulling me to my feet and wrapping my robe around me. He scooped up his clothes and kicked Banjo in the shins to get him moving, too. "Come on. Get up. We need to get showered and dressed and finish decorating this tree before everyone gets here."

"What?" I asked. "Who's everyone?"

He grinned at me. "You'll see."

That night, we sat around an imperfectly decorated living room, so full of Christmas food I could barely move. Banjo and Rafe sandwiched me in, Banjo's arm slung over my shoulders. Beside Rafe, his mom talked quietly to April about her new apartment and the job she'd accepted, working the front desk at a local dentist's office. George and Coach talked football from the doorway. Aria handed her mother a steaming mug of hot cocoa from a tray, then passed me one, too. Colt was minus his trademark smirk for once, and instead, he smiled at me from where he was sprawled on the carpet, only just done with complaining about his food coma. Selina was notably missing, and my heart hurt imagining how she was spending the day. But I hadn't forgotten her letter. I pulled my phone from my pocket and texted Meredith: *Merry Christmas. PS - You're going to be an aunty.*

My phone immediately started ringing, but I switched it to silent and put it away in my pocket with a smile. It was enough for her to know our friendship wasn't over, but today, I wanted to enjoy my family. All of them. They were an oddball bunch, and there were still a lot of bridges that needed mending, especially between April and me, but she'd come today, and we'd shared a meal. That was the beginning.

I eyed Colt, silently asking his permission, and then did the same to Rafe and Banjo. They all gave me small nods.

I cleared my throat. "We have something we need to tell you all."

All eyes in the room turned to me.

"We're having a baby."

There was a beat of silence, and then Aria's scream of excitement nearly split my eardrums. She launched herself at me, throwing her arms around my neck, and squeezing me tight.

"I'm gonna be an aunt!" Then she pulled back to look between Colt and me, and then to Banjo and Rafe in confusion. "Wait, am I? Who's the baby daddy?"

That was the million-dollar question.

But Colt stepped in, answering so I didn't have to. "Yes, you're going to be an aunty."

Rafe turned to his mom. "You're going to be a grandma, too. We don't care whose baby this is biologically. We all love Lacey, and we all love the baby. That's all that matters."

I held my breath, hoping this announcement wasn't going to ruin the nice day we'd had.

"You're all very young," Rose said quietly. "But I was young when I had Rafe, too. I'll never regret it. What about college?"

"We're still planning to go. All of us." I squeezed Banjo's thigh. "The baby is due over the summer. And we'll need help."

"Which you'll have," Willa said firmly. "From me."

"And me," Rose chimed in.

"And me, too, if you'll let me," April said tentatively.

I gave her a small nod. "I'd really like that."

"Best Christmas ever," Aria declared with a grin.

It could have so easily been the worst, but these people had made it something special. Something to be remembered. They made the good outweigh the bad. I rested my hand over my belly. "You're a lucky little baby," I whispered. "I can't wait to introduce you to your family."

EPILOGUE
LACEY

Sweat trickled from my temple, running down the side of my neck in a sticky, unpleasant river. I wiped it away with the back of my hand and huffed out an uncomfortable sigh. "Nobody should be this pregnant in the middle of summer. This is cruel and unwarranted torture."

Jagger slurped the last of her fruity drink, eyeing me over the top of the oversized glass. "Won't be for much longer."

As if insulted by my complaining, the baby kicked me, and my stretched-tight bump rippled.

Banjo glanced over from the sun lounger next to me and let his green eyes sweep over my body. "I hate that you're uncomfortable, but I for one am not hating that it's so hot. You're sexy as fuck in that bikini."

I glared at him. "You just like the fact my boobs are massive and this bikini does nothing to keep them in."

He grinned. "I never said my reasons were pure."

Colt swam to the edge of the pool with strong, sure strokes, and used his upper body strength to haul himself out of the water. Droplets fell from his bronze skin onto the sizzling-hot pavement surrounding the pool. He flicked his hair back, sending deliciously cool water droplets over me, and somehow managing to look like some sort of god in the process. Rafe sat on the edge of the pool beside him, shirt off, feet dangling in the water.

I groaned. "Damn you all for being so attractive while I'm a beached whale."

Colt leaned over and pressed a kiss to my lips. "You're not a whale."

I softened a little. It was nice when he was being sweet.

"A manatee perhaps. But not a whale." He winked at me then scuttled out of arm's reach before I could throw a punch at him.

"You know," Meredith said from the lounger on my other side. She raised her sunglasses so I could see her eyes. "This pregnancy book says that if you're near your due date, which we all know you are, because you haven't stopped bitching about it for days now—"

"You try being a week overdue in the middle of summer!"

Meredith ignored me. "The book says that sex can encourage labor. Apparently, there's some sort of magic juju in sperm that does something to your cervix?" She tossed the book at me and eyed the guys. "Sperm is one thing you aren't lacking in, Lacey."

I giggled at that and glanced at the guys hopefully. "Who's up for the task? Because at this point, I'm willing to try anything."

"Me," Banjo yelped, springing to his feet.

"Hell yes," Rafe agreed.

I eyed Colt. "Too manatee for you?"

He chuckled and smirked at me. "I happen to think manatees are really cute."

"So I'm cute now?"

He leaned down over me, his lips an inch from mine. "Come inside and I'll show you."

"And that's my cue to put headphones on," Meredith muttered.

Jagger held a hand out for one of Meredith's AirPods. "Share with me, sister."

I laughed at them and let Colt pull me to my feet. The moment I was completely vertical, though, liquid gushed down my legs, splashing onto the pavement.

I stared down in surprise as Meredith squealed and jumped backward off her chair. "Jesus fuck, Lacey! Did your cervix get loose at just the thought of having sex with them?"

Despite my shock, I burst into laughter, though it sounded slightly hysterical even to my own ears. "I think my water just broke."

"You don't say."

Banjo let out a hoot of excitement. "It's baby time!"

He ran inside like an overexcited puppy, while Colt and Rafe hovered around me like I'd suddenly grown an extra head.

"What do I do?" Rafe asked. "Are you in pain?"

I shrugged. "Not yet. But I'm guessing I will be soon. Shit."

Colt grabbed his phone from where he'd stashed it by the pool fence, well away from the water. "I'm calling my mom. I'll get her to meet us at the hospital."

I nodded and waddled toward the house. It was only when I got to the doorway that I realized there was amniotic fluid all over the pool area.

"Mer? Jag?" I asked with the most charming smile I could muster.

"Yeah, yeah. We're on cleanup duty. Just go have a baby, will you? And consider Meredith as a name. Meredith's a good girl. She cleans up when your baby makes a massive mess."

"What if it's a boy?" Rafe asked.

Meredith and Jagger both grinned at me. "It won't be," they said in unison.

In a quiet, private hospital room, the three men I loved crowded around a tiny pink bundle sleeping soundly in a hospital bassinette.

"How is she so small?" Colt asked. "Your belly was huge."

I rolled my eyes at him. "One could say the same about your head versus your brains."

He sniggered, but when he looked up at me, his gaze was filled with nothing but admiration. "You're a rock star, you know that?"

I knew. After an eight-hour labor, I felt like Superwoman. A really exhausted and slightly high on pain meds version of Superwoman, but it was a good feeling, nonetheless.

Banjo stroked a finger across our daughter's velvet cheek. "I can't stop staring at her."

"Me neither," Rafe whispered. "She's perfect. Just like her mommy."

My heart couldn't get any bigger. "Can you bring her here? I miss her already, even though I only just put her down."

Banjo picked the baby up and placed her in my arms, the three guys immediately crowding in around me.

Someone dropped a kiss to my hair, but I couldn't turn away from my daughter's face in order to determine who it was.

She blinked her murky-colored eyes open and stared up at me in quiet fascination. "Hey, baby girl," I whispered. "What are we going to call you?"

"I can't believe we went nine months without managing to agree on a name," Rafe commented, perching on the edge of the bed next to me.

"To be fair, it's hard to find a name four people agree on."

"Even harder when Colt refused to even consider the possibility she might be a girl."

Colt elbowed him.

Banjo cleared his throat. "Selina's name means moon. I googled it."

We all looked to him, and a lump rose in my throat. "You want to name her after Selina?"

He smiled. "She's your mom. And the closest thing I have to one as well."

"I love the idea, but I kind of think she deserves her own name."

"Agreed," Banjo said. "So I was thinking that maybe Luna might suit."

I sucked in a breath. "Luna. It's beautiful."

To my surprise, Colt and Rafe didn't say anything. They simply nodded.

My mouth dropped open. "Wait, are we all actually agreeing here?"

Colt kissed the top of her head. "It's beautiful. Just like she is."

I grinned down at our daughter. "Hey, Luna," I said quietly.

She made a gurgling sound that was so precious my

heart could barely stand it. "I love you, princess," I whispered, passing my own nickname onto her.

She'd wear that title with pride, just like I did. Because the three men who'd given me that name were no longer my princes but my kings. And I was their queen. Just as I'd vowed. Just as it was always meant to be.

THE END

A new Saint View series is here. Start Locked Up Liars (Saint View Prison #1) or keep reading for a sneak peek! A new murder to solve. Three hot new guys to fall for. Plus more of the characters you already love. Selina in jail. Colt in a dangerous new job. And so much more. http://mybook.to/LockedUpLiars

Want more Rafe and Banjo? Want to know who Luna's biological dad is? Want a glimpse into our favorite foursome's future? It's all in the bonus scenes! They're free to download onto your kindle from my website www.ellethorpe.com

LOCKED UP LIARS (SAINT VIEW PRISON, #1)

READ THE VIRAL TIK TOK SENSATION WITH OVER 2MILLION VIEWS.

Nothing prepares you for finding your sister's lifeless body covered in blood.

But when the police arrest her ex, a man I know is innocent, I can't sit by and do nothing.

Not when I've been secretly in love with him for years.

Heath may not want my help, but I won't take no for an answer.

To catch a killer, I'm forced to take a job at Saint View Prison. Maximum security. The place they send the worst of the worst.

But it's not just Heath who doesn't want me there.

Rowe, the sinfully sexy head guard has made it clear I don't belong. I'd tell him where to go with my middle finger up, if my skin didn't prickle with awareness every time he touches me.

And then there's Liam, hotshot lawyer and my old high school enemy. All that tension and chemistry is still there, burning between us like flames. I need his help, but I'll be damned if I beg for it.

With every lie we uncover, every secret we expose, the danger mounts.

Until there's only one thing we know for sure.

The killer is still out there.

And I'm his next target.

Locked Up Liars is an adult, #whychoose romance, meaning the main character has more than one love interest. This book contains enemies-to-lovers and romantic suspense /

dark themes that may trigger some readers. It is the first book in an ongoing trilogy.

Download or 1-click this hot new romance today.

Keep reading for a sneak peek!

LOCKED UP LIARS TEASER

MAE

I would have recognized the tattoo creeping up his neck anywhere.

For years, I'd been slightly obsessed with the way it swirled across his skin and into his hairline. I'd dreamed of tracing my fingertips along the swells and patterns, chasing them beneath his shirt collar, over his shoulders, and finding out how low the intricate design actually went.

I could have asked my sister, of course. She could have told me exactly how far it snaked down the side of his body. But I'd never asked. I couldn't.

Asking my sister about the tats on her boyfriend's skin?

Just no. That would have been awkward.

So I kept my inappropriate curiosity locked away, tucked deep inside, and never voiced it to anyone.

Then they'd broken up.

And I hadn't seen him since.

But one glimpse of that tattoo across a smoky bar was all it took for everything to come roaring back. The curiosity. The desire. The plain stupid, ridiculous fact that the man curled my toes even from this distance.

Inappropriate. Inappropriate. SO inappropriate.

Tori nudged me. "Who are you checking out?"

I jerked and turned to face her. "What? No one. It's nothing."

She gave me the sort of knowing grin only a best friend could. Then she peered through the crowd, past the waiters taking drinks and food to tables, over to the bar where he nursed a short glass full of an amber liquid with ice.

Her eyes widened. "Is that Heath?"

It was my automatic instinct to play dumb. "Heath? As in Jayela's Heath?"

I wasn't fooling anyone. Tori knew it just as well as I did.

Concern puckered her brow. "Please don't tell me you're still harboring that secret crush on him? It's been four years, Mae."

I knew exactly how long it had been. I'd thought I was done with the absurd crush. Who knew it was just simmering away under the surface, ready to explode back in full force at a single sighting? But sitting there, staring at his broad shoulders and the way they tapered down to his narrow waist, it felt like no time had passed at all. All those feelings I'd hidden from him, from my sister, from myself— they all swirled through my system, turning happy cartwheels because we were in his presence once more.

Traitorous frigging feelings. They needed to get their shit under control.

Tori let out a low whistle. "Don't even bother denying it. It's written all over your face."

I didn't want it to be. I tried to school my features into something that didn't look like the heart eye emoji.

Tori's concern morphed into something quizzical. "He's not your sister's man anymore, you know. He hasn't been for a long time. Jaye is over him. She's been over him for years. So, if you wanted to go there..."

A firm grip yanked the chair beside me out from beneath the table, scraping it along the floor. I jerked, the sound shuddering down my spine like nails on a chalkboard.

"Go where?" Jayela sat down heavily on the wooden chair and grinned at me and Tori.

Tori opened her mouth to answer, but I gave a shake of my head, praying she'd remember that I knew all her secrets as well. Even the one about what had happened with Todd Morsely at tenth grade church camp, which I'd never told anyone. So hopefully she'd keep my unhealthy little Heath obsession to herself, too.

She pressed her lips together, the deep crimson of her lipstick flattening into a line.

I breathed a sigh of relief. "Nowhere. It doesn't matter. Where have you been? We were supposed to meet an hour ago. Tori and I are already halfway to tipsy." We'd ordered two rounds of drinks, including some for Jayela, then polished off the lot while we waited for her. The alcohol was already pleasantly warming me from the inside out.

Jaye shrugged out of her leather jacket and draped it over the back of the bar chair. "I know, I know. But things at work went to shit. Boston and I had to debrief with the chief. He's pissed. We let him down."

Tori leaned forward, resting her elbows on the tabletop. "Ooh," she singsonged. She was definitely a little tipsy, too. "What happened? Tell us all the cop drama."

Jaye shrugged. "Same old shit as every other crappy day this month. We had another botched stakeout. And Boston is being a dick about it. He thinks it's a coincidence we've had three with the exact same useless outcomes this month."

Boston had been my sister's partner at work ever since she left the academy. Normally the two of them were peas in a pod. It was extremely unlike them to argue, but this wasn't the first time this month she'd seemed on edge after coming home from a day at work with him.

I made a slightly fuzzy mental note to prod her about it later and tried to keep my gaze from flickering in the direction of the bar. "If it's not a coincidence, then what? What's your theory?"

Jaye raised a hand to signal our waitress over, but the woman was busy. She gave a nod, though, indicating she'd noticed, and Jaye turned her attention back to me. "I think three is too many. Something else is going on. Someone is tipping them off." A muscle ticked at the corner of her eye. "I don't know why Boston can't see it. We kind of got into it tonight in front of the chief."

I bit my lip. Even without her explaining further, I knew that would be eating my sister alive, slowly tearing at her conscience from the inside out. There was nothing more important to my sister than her job. Not socializing. Not men. She hadn't really dated since Heath, putting her everything into being a cop.

I darted another glance over in his direction. I couldn't help it. He hadn't moved, though he'd drained his drink. I tore my gaze away. "I'm sure it happens all the time," I told Jaye, trying to sound reassuring. "Just because you and Boston don't normally disagree, doesn't mean that other partners are as in sync, right? Your chief is probably used to sorting out things like this."

The waitress came over, and Jaye ordered more cocktails for Tori and me, and a bourbon over ice for herself. The same drink Heath was probably having. Just another reason why the two of them should have been good together.

"I suppose you're right. It's just frustrating that Boston and I can't get on the same page." Jaye watched our waitress walk back to the bar with her drink order, her gaze sliding slightly to the left as the woman put down her empty tray.

I knew the exact moment she spotted Heath. Her entire body stiffened up, and she slunk down, trying to make herself smaller. "Is that Heath?" she hissed. "Fuck. I'm going to hide under the table."

Tori giggled. "It's him. He's been there since we got in. I don't think he's noticed us, though, if you want to make a run for it."

I laughed.

Jayela shot me an apologetic cringe. "Actually, I do."

I stopped laughing. "You aren't serious?"

"I'm dead serious. I can't deal with him tonight. I can't handle the puppy dog eyes, and the sad, 'You broke my heart' expression on his face."

I blinked, trying to figure out exactly how she'd come to the conclusion that Heath was still cut up about their breakup when the man hadn't even turned around. I parroted the lines that Tori had said to me earlier. "It's been four years. And the two of you only dated for a few months. I'm sure he's fine now."

Jaye just shook her head. "You weren't there when I broke up with him. It was horrific."

The waitress chose that moment to deliver our drinks, setting a tray down on the table and placing our glasses in front of us. I used the distraction to glance over at Heath again, my view blocked when Jayela pushed to her feet, after swallowing her drink in a couple of rapid gulps. I peered around her. Sure, the man was drinking alone at a bar, looking a *little* like a heartbroken loser with no friends. But that didn't mean he was sad still about their breakup. Maybe he'd been stood up? Maybe he just liked their nachos? Maybe his dog had farted so badly it drove him out of his apartment to seek refuge in a bar until it subsided? Point was, Heath drinking alone didn't mean he was still as broken as she seemed to think he was. Jaye was beautiful and smart and athletic. But she had flaws, just like everyone else. Did she really expect him to still be hung up on her after all this time?

It kind of bugged me.

Of course he's still hung up on her, the voice inside me that sounded just like my father, chanted in my ear.

Jaye threw a few dollar bills on the table, then pushed to her feet. "You coming?" She paused, waiting for me to answer her.

My cocktail was huge. I'd barely made a dent in it. And if I was being honest, I was still basking in the glow that being in Heath's presence seemed to cast over me. I wasn't ready for that to end. "No, I think I'll stay. I'm not in the mood to go home yet."

Jaye shrugged. "Suit yourself. I think I'll go back to work, anyway. I just can't let this thing go so easily. I want to go over some paperwork. I'll catch you at home later, okay? But don't wait up. I'll probably be late."

I nodded, picking up my drink again and taking a swallow.

Tori tilted her head, watching me for a second. Then she sprang to her feet. "Jaye? Can I get a ride?"

My mouth dropped open. "Wait. You're ditching me, too?"

Tori gave me a pointed stare, her gaze flickering toward where Heath sat. "Baby at home, remember? And a husband who is probably freaking out that I've been gone this long already."

"We've only been here an hour. What happened to girls' night?"

Tori ignored my feeble protests, seeing through them easily. "I think you'll be fine. Strong, independent woman and all that."

I would kill her later. I opened my mouth to answer, but Jaye beat me to it. "Heath is here. If you have any problems, just give him the signal. He's got that savior gene. He'd probably love to swoop in and rescue you." She rolled her eyes.

Tori giggled, but I didn't say anything. From where I'd been sitting, throughout their entire, disastrous relationship, Heath had been nothing but good to Jaye. They were just mismatched as a couple. Yeah, sure, he had a protector gene. But was there anything wrong with wanting to protect the ones you love? Was there anything wrong with wanting to keep your woman safe?

Sounded kind of romantic to me. And a hell of a lot better than my exes, who definitely seemed to be missing even the most basic of human decency genes.

But I did suspect it was this incompatibility that was the straw that broke the relationship camel's back, though my tight-lipped sister would have never admitted it. He had stifled her. She had that urge to protect, too. But hers had been syphoned into her career. She'd taken an oath to protect lives and property, to help people when they were at their most vulnerable.

Heath had nowhere for his to go but onto her.

"I don't need Heath to protect me." Which was one-hundred-percent true. On the outside, I might have been the sweet elementary school teacher, who wore flowery dresses and braided her long blonde hair into Elsa-style twists, just because the little girls I taught loved it. But that wasn't the only side of me. No, I didn't need a man's protection.

Though I probably wouldn't mind if Heath wanted to scoop me up in his muscled arms and whisk me away.

I wasn't going to tell my sister that, though. "I'll be fine. I just want to have a drink and unwind a little bit. I had a hectic week. End of the school year and all."

I don't know if Jaye didn't hear me or if she just was too preoccupied glancing over at Heath again, but she let out a low groan instead of answering. "Yeah, okay. He's seen me. Time to leave. Tori, if you want a lift, I'm going now. See you later, Mae."

Tori gave me a final pointed look, and I knew exactly what she was saying with her eyes.

You've had a crush on that man for four years. You're single. You're both alone in a bar. Make something happen.

The two of them weaved around the crowd at the bar and exited out the main doors. Through the glass windows, I watched them walk across the darkened parking lot with their arms linked, Tori laughing about something Jaye said, and then the two of them disappeared into her car.

A shadow fell across me.

"Hey, Mae."

My heart rate went haywire at the sound of my name on his lips.

I swallowed hard. "Hi, Heath."

1-click or download in Kindle Unlimited here. http://mybook.to/LockedUpLiars

ALSO BY ELLE THORPE

Saint View High series (Reverse Harem, Bully Romance. Complete)

*Devious Little Liars (Saint View High, #1)

*Dangerous Little Secrets (Saint View High, #2)

*Twisted Little Truths (Saint View High, #3)

Saint View Prison series (Reverse harem, romantic suspense. Complete.)

*Locked Up Liars (Saint View Prison, #1)

*Solitary Sinners (Saint View Prison, #2)

*Fatal Felons (Saint View Prison, #3)

Saint View Psychos series (Reverse harem, romantic suspense. Complete.)

*Start a War (Saint View Psychos, #1)

*Half the Battle (Saint View Psychos, #2)

*It Ends With Violence (Saint View Psychos, #3)

Saint View Rebels (Reverse harem, romantic suspense. Releasing in 2023)

*Rebel Revenge (Saint View Rebels, #1)

*Rebel Obsession (Saint View Rebels, #2)

*Rebel Heart (Saint View Rebels, #3)

Saint View Strip (Male/Female, romantic suspense standalones. Ongoing.)

*Evil Enemy (Saint View Strip, #1)

*Unholy Sins (Saint View Strip, #2)

*Untitled (Saint View Strip, #3)

Dirty Cowboy series (complete)

*Talk Dirty, Cowboy (Dirty Cowboy, #1)

*Ride Dirty, Cowboy (Dirty Cowboy, #2)

*Sexy Dirty Cowboy (Dirty Cowboy, #3)

*Dirty Cowboy boxset (books 1-3)

*25 Reasons to Hate Christmas and Cowboys (a Dirty Cowboy bonus novella, set before Talk Dirty, Cowboy but can be read as a standalone, holiday romance)

Buck Cowboys series (Spin off from the Dirty Cowboy series. Ongoing.)

*Buck Cowboys (Buck Cowboys, #1)

*Buck You! (Buck Cowboys, #2)

*Can't Bucking Wait (Buck Cowboys, #3)

*Mother Bucker (Buck Cowboys, $#4)

The Only You series (Contemporary romance. Complete)

*Only the Positive (Only You, #1) - Reese and Low.

*Only the Perfect (Only You, #2) - Jamison.

*Only the Truth - (Only You, bonus novella) - Bree.

*Only the Negatives (Only You, #3) - Gemma.

*Only the Beginning (Only You, #4) - Bianca and Riley.

*Only You boxset

Add your email address here to be the first to know when new books are available!

www.ellethorpe.com/newsletter

Join Elle Thorpe's readers group on Facebook!

www.facebook.com/groups/ellethorpesdramallamas

ACKNOWLEDGMENTS

Wow. What a ride this trilogy has been. By far the most complicated story I've ever written, but also the one I fell for the hardest. I love my Saint View boys and the way they love their girl. I can't wait to write more stories like this, so make sure you've joined my newsletter and my readers group so you know when they're releasing! There's more Saint View coming in 2021, but which part of Saint View? I'm going to leave you wondering on that one.

A big thank you to my Drama Llamas readers group for always having my back, and keeping me entertained on a daily basis. You guys are the bomb. I hope you caught the little shout out I hid in this book for you.

Thank you to Jolie Vines, Zoe Ashwood, Emmy Ellis and Karen Hrdlicka who make up my stellar editing team. And an extra thanks to Jo and Zoe for being my author besties too! Thank you to Sara Massery for the chats, sprints, and graphic design advice. Thank you to Shellie, Karen, Dana, Melissa, Samantha, and Louise for your early feedback. A massive thank you to my promo and review team for really jumping on board with this series. Really hoping I didn't forget anyone!

And as always, a huge thank you to my family. To Jira, Thomas, Flick, and Heidi. You four are the loves of my life and I couldn't do any of this without you.

Love, Elle x

ABOUT THE AUTHOR

Elle Thorpe lives on the sunny east coast of Australia. When she's not writing stories full of kissing, she's a wife and mummy to three tiny humans. She's also official ball thrower to one slobbery dog named Rollo. Yes, she named a female dog after a dirty hot character on Vikings. Don't judge her. Elle is a complete and utter fangirl at heart, obsessing over The Walking Dead and Outlander to an unhealthy degree. But she wouldn't change a thing.

You can find her on Facebook or Instagram(@ellethorpebooks or hit the links below!) or at her website www.ellethorpe.com. If you love Elle's work, please consider joining her Facebook fan group, Elle Thorpe's Drama Llamas or joining her newsletter here. www.ellethorpe.com/newsletter

facebook.com/ellethorpebooks

instagram.com/ellethorpebooks

goodreads.com/ellethorpe

pinterest.com/ellethorpebooks

www.ingramcontent.com/pod-product-compliance
Lightning Source LLC
Chambersburg PA
CBHW050132120726

47903CB00002B/321